THE LAST GETAWAY

CLAY SAVAGE

Ocean Park Press

This is a work of fiction. Names, characters, places, and incidents are products of the author's imagination or are used fictitiously and are not to be construed as real. Any resemblance to actual events, locales, organizations, or persons, living or dead, is entirely coincidental.

The Last Getaway. Copyright © 2019 by Clay Savage

www.theclaysavage.com

All rights reserved. No part of this book may be used or reproduced in any manner whatsoever without written permission except in the case of brief quotations embodied in critical articles and reviews.

Published by Ocean Park Press, Los Angeles, California

ISBN 978-1-7338806-0-2 (paperback)
ISBN 978-1-7338806-1-9 (ebook)

For my parents. And for my kids.

ACKNOWLEDGMENTS

It was my good fortune to have met Jennifer Silva Redmond at the Southern California Writers' Conference. She has been an invaluable editor and guide. If the book works, its path to success runs through her. I am also thankful for the keen eyes of Mary Vensel White and Katherine Flitsch—any remaining errors are mine alone. And I am forever grateful to Dannie Festa, who long ago believed in the story and in me.

To all my early readers, your critiques and encouragement have been invaluable.

CHAPTER ONE

RICHIE PULLED THE black-on-black '68 Camaro to the curb, its rebuilt 425-horsepower engine grumbling. With a glance in the rearview, he adjusted the Dodgers cap holding his blonde wig in place, then turned to the four other men in the car. "Have a good day at work," he said.

Gavin pointed a .38 revolver at his newest recruit. "Don't get nervous and do something stupid."

Richie returned the glassy-eyed stare. "You mean like rob a bank?"

Gonzo, the big Mexican in the back seat, laughed as he pulled down his ski mask and opened the rear door, his massive shoulders turning toward daylight. The two other assholes Gavin had brought remained silent as they followed Gonzo, hustling across the sidewalk toward the front door of American Federal.

Gavin kept his gun on Richie a moment longer, intent on making his point, and then he, too, left the car, moving a bit slower than the situation called for.

The bank occupied the corner of a two-story cement and faux-wood building built sometime in the mid-seventies, judging by its uninspired architecture. It was drab in every way, though it still might have won a beauty contest on this particular stretch of Sherman Way in Reseda, a working class neighborhood surrounded by other working class neighborhoods in the San Fernando Valley. The wide street had two lanes in each direction with a median in between. On one side of the street was a Miss Mystic Psychic Reader and a second-hand appliance showroom, on the other a tire repair garage and a marijuana dispensary. Telephone wires hung like spider webs above the sidewalks, and the only greenery was mostly brown.

Richie's foot absently revved the Camaro's engine, startling him. He glanced anxiously at the timer counting backward on the iPhone resting in his lap. Four minutes. That was the amount of time Gavin had insisted they'd need, even though he'd never robbed a bank. Liquor stores, sure, too many to count, probably. A bar here and there, perhaps, in his earlier days. But never a bank. Of course, robbing American Federal hadn't even been his idea, but what difference did that make now? Gavin was the one running the show and he'd picked four minutes, probably because he'd heard someone say it in a movie.

Still, as far as Richie was concerned, four minutes sounded about right. Certainly better than five. The less time it took for the four idiots to intimidate whoever was unlucky enough to be there on a Saturday morning into doing as instructed without getting shot, the better. Then he could get the hell out of Dodge and never again have to see Gavin Hendricks' ghostly pale face or smell his rotted breath.

The sidewalk in front of the bank was empty, but cars whipped past the Camaro with alarming frequency. Richie wondered how much attention he would draw if he opened the door and threw up in the street. It was hot, the air stagnant in the smoggy way Los Angeles can get in June, and the lingering scent of the joint

Gavin smoked on the ride over made it difficult to draw a breath without it catching in Richie's throat.

What the hell would the legendary Michael Glass think of his only child now? Whatever reserve of hope for his wayward son's redemption had been held by the old man—before his heart exploded three years ago on the eighth tee at the Riviera Country Club over in Pacific Palisades—would have certainly been depleted by this latest predicament. Drinker, gambler, anti-authoritarian, smart-ass—all of these intolerable traits were easily recognizable in his son. But goddamn getaway driver for a bunch of shit-for-brains bank robbers? Michael Glass died ahead of the curve and didn't even know it.

Richie, however, fully realized how far he'd fallen. Hell, he was still falling so rapidly he could feel the wind whipping past as the ground rose up to greet him. Only now, nobody was left to secure the safety net he'd so blithely relied upon for all his twenty-eight years. He gripped the steering wheel with his gloved hands, steeling his twitching nerves.

If only.

Those two words haunted him. If only his mother, the ballast to his mercurial whims, hadn't died. If only his father, that standard-bearer of stolid decorum he could not abide, had left him more money. If only he'd drawn different cards, if only he'd pulled a few of those bets back, if only he'd left town when he'd had the chance.

He'd stayed in LA because eight days prior to his morning appointment at American Federal, he'd convinced himself that his luck had finally turned. Sure, with every run of bad luck he *always* convinced himself the tide was about to turn, that the next card would be the ace or the next roll of the dice would come up sevens, but this time felt different. This time was kismet and, as every gambler knows, kismet should never be ignored. His last-chance ticket to renewed sustainability arrived at the Packard Club on Sunset Boulevard, when he ran into an old girlfriend named Dina Gordon. He and Dina had been together for five months a couple years before, their blissful relationship (so he thought) deepening by the day. But it turned out he was the only one falling in love, a state of affairs he painfully discovered when she blindsided him with the news of her engagement to a development executive at Paramount Studios. Once engaged, Dina left both him and the club scene altogether. And now here she was, ringless in Hollywood, a vision in short black dress and red nails, partying as though she'd never left. Only now, instead of hanging on Richie's arm, she was hanging onto a reed-thin Silver Lake hipster she introduced as "my boy, Amir-Ali."

"You can call me Al," the hipster said as they shook.

It had to be eighty degrees in the place and Al's clammy hand was cold.

"That's a song, you know," Richie said, casually wiping his palm on his thigh.

"Yeah, my parents were big fans of Paul Simon and they thought it was hilarious."

"My mom was into him, too," Richie said.

"Who's Paul Simon?" Dina asked.

Richie remembered why he'd gotten over her so quickly.

Al raised a coke bullet to his nose and inhaled sharply. "He's some old folk singer."

"So, what happened with the Paramount guy?" Richie asked Dina over the pounding music, leaning close to her perfect, shell-shaped ear.

"Some stupid movie about time travel flopped and he lost

his job." Dina took a sip of apple martini. "He's an agent at CAA now. But he said he couldn't sign me, so whatever."

"So you dumped him?"

"What?" She was almost shouting.

Richie waved off the question. "You look good," he said.

"Thanks. You too. New haircut?"

"No."

"Dina mentioned you used to play in Kendall Kelly's poker game," Al said, leaning forward in his seat, his bloodshot eyes practically vibrating in the low wattage light of the VIP section.

"Not for a while," Richie said.

"You should come with me next week," Al said. "I've been playing the past few months. Those guys are cool."

Richie nodded, relieved that neither of them seemed to have any idea that he'd been blackballed for failing to pay off his losses. "You must have some serious coin to be invited up to Kendall's," he said, raising his glass to Al.

"Well, I'm not broke." Al grinned.

Richie nodded again, trying to ignore the sting of Al's boast. As he finished off his Whiskey Sour, Al explained that his family had moved from Tehran to America when he was nine, making their fortune in real estate. "Mostly in apartment buildings, but also a bunch of office space in Dallas. Oil money and all that shit." He spoke with a swagger that suggested he had something to do with it. "My dad's expecting me to take it over someday, but I'm not into it." He took another hit of coke.

"What are you into?" Richie asked. "No, wait, let me guess."

Al waved him off. "No way you're gonna get it, dude."

Richie sized him up, the little shit, then pointed emphatically and said, "Music producer. Pop-rap fusion or some bullshit like that. You're gonna be huge in Japan."

Al laughed. "I'm goin' international, yo!"

"You should totally do that!" Dina shouted, pushing her shoulder into Al's.

"Yeah, I could do that, for real," Al said. "But that ain't my jam. No, my shit is all about the ponies."

"You wanna be a professional gambler?" Richie asked. "Trust me, you might want to reconsider."

"It's not gambling. What I'm talking about is ownership. That's where the real money is." Al's face perspired as he relayed his coked-up fever dream. "You get a horse winning the Kentucky Derby and it's worth millions. And I'm not talking about the purses. I'm talking about stud fees at, like, a couple hundred Gs a pop. And you don't even have to win the Derby or Preakness or whatever, to make serious bank. That's why all the sheikhs are into it. You know who Mohammed bin Jennat Khah Doust is?"

"Is he a terrorist?" Dina asked, laughing.

"Ha ha," Al said. "He's a billionaire, a hundred times over. Owns, like, a hundred stables or something. All over the world, the Middle East, Europe, the US, everywhere. And I'll tell you what, my dad's got a couple horses right now that look like they can do it, too. Get this shit seriously started, I mean. He only does it as a side deal, but *that's* the business I'm gonna take over. He's got this one filly, Miss Laurie Lee—named for one of his fucking secretaries—that's running at Santa Anita this Sunday. She's gonna kill it, guaranteed."

Richie stared at the sweaty hipster from Tehran, the universe laying out the red carpet for him to stroll right onto newfound solvency, and smiled. "Guaranteed, huh?"

"I can give you five thousand for both."

Richie stared at the saleswoman as she set his father's blue

Omega Sea Master watch next to the one his dad had given him on his twenty-first birthday.

"That's ridiculous," he said. "He paid more than that for just one of them."

"Yes, I'm sure that's the case," she said with an understanding smile. She calmly tucked her satiny black hair behind her ear. "But for the resale market, that's the best I can do. I'm afraid the engravings reduce their value even more."

You and I, together.

His father's words echoed in Richie's memory as he stared down at the matching watches. Other than his car, which he kept in case he needed a place to sleep once the bank finally foreclosed on his house, the watches were the only things he had that were worth anything. He picked up the birthday watch and ran his thumb along its stainless steel edge.

Our time together is short, Richie.

The memory ached in his chest.

"Can you go five-five?" he asked the saleswoman.

Three days later, Richie kept the additional five hundred in his pocket and put the five grand on Miss Laurie Lee to win the second race at Santa Anita. The math was clear. He had a hundred and seventeen grand in outstanding gambling debts and the minimum payment due to avoid a visit from a lead pipe was twenty-five. While Kendall Kelly was just another rich kid in Beverly Hills who fashioned himself a player, Gavin Hendricks wasn't the type to merely boot you from the game when you came up short. Gavin was the type to put a bullet in your stomach and drop you off at the emergency room. Richie figured the three-to-one odds on Miss Laurie Lee were better than the odds he could outlast Gavin's patience.

It wasn't until they were standing at the betting window that Richie discovered Al was—at least partially—full of shit. His father did own a horse named Miss Laurie Lee, but Al had no standing within the family to take part in the race day festivities. Turned out that Al had three older brothers who didn't have a coke habit and who hadn't been put on a spending allowance that if exceeded by so much as a penny, would be cut off for good. Richie had envisioned sitting in the premium suites, enjoying bottle service with the Jahandar family as Miss Laurie Lee ran her way directly into his bank account. Instead they watched the race from the grandstand rail with all the other schlubs, hiding from Al's father.

"I'm gonna own all those bitches someday," Al said, eyeing the horses being loaded into the starting gate. Surreptitiously, he shoved his coke bullet into his left nostril and sharply inhaled.

As the track announcer rattled on to the thirty thousand or so attendees, Richie's sweaty palms held tight to the rail. With so much riding on an event he had no control over, the crush of bodies and mingling voices around him were nearly too much to withstand. He lowered his head and closed his eyes as Al kept on narrating his plans for world domination.

"…bring hip-hop to the racetrack," he was saying when a shrill bell rang.

"And they're off!" The announcer's voice boomed and the crowd roared, finally drowning out Al's incessant chatter.

Please God. Jesus. Mary. Allah. All of you, let this horse win.

There are eight furlongs in a mile. A thoroughbred can cover that distance in about a minute-forty. It took Richie slightly less than fifty seconds to realize he was totally screwed. As the nine horses came down the stretch he even didn't bother trying to find Miss Laurie Lee as she struggled at the back of the pack, her name called out by the track announcer only as a pathetic footnote to the main event taking place a full twelve lengths ahead. The frenetic wave of cheers and screams built and built and built, louder and louder, until it crested as the thundering horses crossed the finish line, and then, like a rapidly receding wave, the voices dropped to a background hum. Richie's body was limp, his muscles spent. His head hung low on his neck, his nose pointed at his shoes, his eyes shut. He had no fight left.

At least until Al laughed.

"What the hell you laughing about?" Richie challenged him.

"She sucked!" Al said, riding his cocaine high. "That was so funny! Damn, my dad's gonna be pissed!"

Richie stared at him, the little prick with his groomed stubble on his narrow cheeks, his stupid porkpie hat and bullshit skinny jeans, his face shining with sweat beneath his aviator sunglasses. "You're a dipshit," Richie told him.

"What's your problem? It was one stupid race."

"It was five thousand dollars, asshole," Richie said, shoving him away. "Maybe if you kept your finger up your nose instead of that shit you use, none of this would've happened."

A heavy brick of a hand landed on Richie's shoulder, spinning him around. His first thought was that security was there to calm him down but instead, he found himself staring up into the thickly bearded face of Gonzo.

"You two maricóns having a problem?" Gonzo asked.

"What're you doing here?" Richie asked, trying to break free from the grip Gonzo had on the back of his shirt.

"I've been following your ass ever since this Indian dude picked you up this morning."

"I'm not fucking *Indian*," Al said.

Gonzo ignored him. He kept his hardened stare on Richie. "Gavin ain't happy, esé."

"Is he here, too?" Richie asked, a sheen of perspiration turning his forehead shiny.

"Why? You miss him or something? Cause you ain't been around lately."

Richie finally broke free from Gonzo's hold. "I was getting ready to call you guys, I swear."

"Yeah?" Gonzo nodded his big block head at Al. "It looks to me like instead of taking care of business, you're wasting all our money hangin' with this Mumbai-lookin' motherfucker."

Al widened his arms as if inviting the challenge. "What's your problem, dude?"

Gonzo finally turned the majority of his attention to the skinny transplant from Tehran.

"Leave it alone, Al," Richie warned before Gonzo had the chance to demonstrate why he should. Of all the problems he was responsible for, Richie didn't need Al's health to be added to the list. "Seriously, get the hell out of here. It's all good."

"Actually, it's not all good," Al insisted, a cocktail of misplaced pride and cocaine spurring him on. "This guy's an asshole."

"Oh, crap," Richie sighed.

With an impressive economy of motion for a man his size, Gonzo swung his arm, his open hand landing with a sharp crack across Al's face, sending both his glasses and his hat flying. Al stumbled backward, his nose bleeding. The people around them, who had been streaming in all directions, were suddenly frozen in place.

"You broke my glasses, man!" Al screamed.

A man behind Gonzo called out for them to knock it off, and when Gonzo turned, Richie bolted. He cut wildly through the crowd, pushing his way into the open concourse beneath the grandstand. He had made it to the entrance of the park before he realized Al was running behind him.

"Who was that guy?" Al asked, without breaking stride. His upper lip was smeared with blood.

"Don't follow me," Richie said, breaking to his left, past the turnstiles, through the front gate and toward the expansive parking lot jammed full of empty cars.

"What does he want with you?" Al asked, keeping pace.

"Al, dude. Get the fuck out of here, all right? Actually, wait. You drove. You remember where we parked?"

A Chevy sedan skidded to a stop beside them and Richie was suddenly standing a mere two feet from the face of Gavin Hendricks. Gavin stared at him from behind the wheel, his bony, white elbow resting on the door as if he were out for a casual Sunday drive. His eyes were bloodshot, his hollow cheeks tight above his angular jawbone. He said nothing. He just stared.

"I'm sorry, man," Richie said.

Gavin remained silent.

And Richie took off.

He made it fifty yards away before he realized that this time, Al wasn't following.

Ducking behind a parked car, Richie turned back to see Al standing motionless, his arms held out at his side, staring down the barrel of the gun Gavin had trained on him from the window of his Chevy. A moment later, Gonzo caught up to the scene and laid Al out with a flying forearm to the side of his head.

"Shit," Richie sighed.

And then, with no place left to run, he began the slow walk back to Gavin's car.

The tiny boat gently rocked as the cinderblock dropped into the water, the chain attached to it rattling as it unspooled. Al let loose a sharp scream through his gag, his wide eyes pleading as

Gonzo pushed him over the edge, his ankles tied to the other end of the metal chain. His body made a sickening splash into the oily, black water of the marina, and then the only sound in the moonlit night came from the quiet chiming of halyards slapping gently against their masts.

Richie stared down at the chained cinderblock between his feet.

"It's up to you," Gavin said, after a long moment. "You join us, or you join the Indian."

Richie slowly looked up, shook his head. "He wasn't Indian."

And so Richie eventually found himself sitting in the stolen '68 Camaro in front of American Federal in Reseda on a Saturday morning, haunted by the words, *if only.*

At least it can't get any worse.

But Richie Glass, inheritor of every advantage a twenty-eight-year-old white boy from Beverly Hills could ask for, was—yet again—wrong.

A rust-brown Toyota Corolla pulled to the curb at the corner behind him, and four men, faces obscured by opaque face-masks, Tec-9 semi-automatics held tightly to their chests, poured out and ran into the lobby of American Federal.

Richie couldn't fathom who they were or what the hell they were doing there.

But he would find out soon enough.

CHAPTER TWO

CALVIN SPOTTED THE gel-haired douche talking on his cellphone as he walked up Melrose Avenue. Approaching the black SAAB parked at the curb, the man said loudly into his phone, "He's way out of his league. Until this year he wasn't even making two commas. Have you seen that shithole sandbox he's using as an office?" He fished keys from a pocket of his dark blue suit and held out his arm to unlock the car, but instead of the locks clicking open, the engine turned over.

Calvin raised his head back up from under the dash and nodded casually at the confused man, whose thumb was still on the key fob, arm still extended. "W'sup, cuz," he said. "You can catch the number five bus couple blocks that way."

He then popped the SAAB into gear and peeled out.

Calvin Russell was a pro.

He was no doubt already pulling the SAAB into Delvon's warehouse in Compton before its owner finished giving the police his statement. Even though all the guy he'd jacked could say was that he was some black guy in his early thirties, Calvin was irritated for having cut it so close. He knew better than that. Hell, he normally wouldn't have gone for the SAAB in such a public setting, but he owed Sollo one more and Sollo was growing impatient. So the risk was taken. After all, it was even riskier to disappoint Sollo.

Delvon held up one hand while using the other to push the front half of a chili dog into his mouth, and Calvin pulled the car to a stop. "Damn boy," he said, climbing from behind the wheel. "Ain't you ever heard of Jenny Craig? You should have some respect for your body."

"I do," Delvon said, running his hand down the belly that supplied a good portion of his three hundred pounds. "It wanted a chili dog and I respected its wishes."

"Whatever you say, Professor Klump. Where's Sollo's ride?"

Delvon nodded to the newly refurbished, cobalt blue BMW facing the rear exit of the warehouse.

"Oh, hell yeah," Calvin said.

Reese, Delvon's little brother—who, at twenty-one, was fifteen years younger and a hundred and fifty pounds lighter—tossed Calvin the keys. "Tell Sollo I got her up to one twenty-seven before I ran out of real estate," he said. "But she's good for more."

"You boys do not disappoint," Calvin said, walking around the Beamer.

"Yeah, this one's nice," Reese said, rubbing out a smudge with a rag. "When he's done with it, I'm gonna ask if I can give it to my lady. She liked it. Asked for it to be pink, though."

"She does know this car is stolen, right?"

"So's her engagement ring."

Calvin smiled. "You're quite the catch, Reese."

"Shit, I ain't been caught yet," Delvon's skinny little brother said, sliding behind the wheel of the SAAB and pulling it into the one available spot in the warehouse, which was full of cars in varying degrees of drivability.

The warehouse's business was about seventy-percent legit, more than enough to create a paper trail in case the police came knocking. The other thirty was reserved for stripping stolen rides, metal scrapping, and taking care of local bangers willing to pay cash when they needed a new windshield or side panel free of bullet holes.

With a glance at his watch, Calvin climbed behind the wheel of the BMW.

"You best get over to see Sollo real quick," Delvon said, leaning down to the window. "He's already called twice to see where you was, and he ain't happy 'bout it ."

"If he calls again," Calvin said, recoiling from the acrid scent of chili dog and onion, "tell him I had to take care of something first."

"It's your funeral," Delvon said, straightening up and pushing the last of the chili-dog into his mouth.

"Seriously," Calvin said, putting the car in gear. "You best get to a spin class or it's gonna be your funeral."

Then he drove off as Delvon slowly chewed.

For over a year, ever since Martin was enrolled at Mount Olive pre-school up in Ladera Heights, the wealthy, predominantly African-American enclave a few miles north of Inglewood, Calvin hadn't missed a day picking up his little boy. And now, despite each passing minute undoubtedly adding another stone to the avalanche of invectives Sollo was sure to deliver, he had made the drive in Sollo's new BMW all the way up from Delvon's shop in Compton, even though he'd then have to turn around and go right back after dropping Martin off at home.

When his wife first broached the subject of Mount Olive, Calvin insisted there were good enough schools closer to their home in South Inglewood, but Tracey wasn't having it. She argued that Mount Olive was close enough to West Los Angeles College (where she was studying to be a nurse) that she could drop him on the way to class and Calvin could pick him up those days she was either stuck in school or at work down at the Target off Crenshaw Boulevard.

"Besides," Tracey had pointed out, "Martin makes friends with some of them rich kids, and their parents can help get him into one of their private schools when the time comes. Half those kids up there end up going to Marlborough or Archer and places like that."

"His new friend's parents gonna pay for all this, too?" Calvin asked.

"Stop with the negative attitude. They have all sorts of scholarships at those places."

"People gonna think we tryin' to be bougie," Calvin said.

"Let them think what they want," Tracey said. "It's a good school and Loretta said she's gonna see if she can get Marcus in there, too."

"Yeah, that's 'cause Loretta's tryin' to be bougie."

Calvin leaned against the Beamer as kids streamed through the gate in front of Mount Olive. The phone in his pocket vibrated and he saw it was his cousin Garrison, no doubt calling to tell him how pissed Sollo was to be kept waiting. He ignored the call, wondering if he shouldn't have let his pick-up streak end. That would have no doubt been the safer play, especially with everything Sollo was waiting to discuss. But then he'd have had to lie to Tracey about why he couldn't pick up their son and that would only create a whole other set of problems; Tracey had an unsettling ability to sense when she was being lied to. Besides, having Martin jump into his arms was worth the verbal ass-whipping from Sollo.

"You have a good day, little man?" he asked as Martin climbed into the back seat of the BMW.

"It was boring," Martin said. "We didn't get to do art because Warren spilled all the paint on purpose."

"Warren's a little troublemaker, huh?" Calvin reached down and snapped Martin's seatbelt.

"He's weird," Martin said, straining forward to get a better look at the dashboard.

Calvin used a gentle hand to guide him back into the seat. "All right, we gotta go."

Martin's brow furrowed. "How many cars do you have, daddy?" he asked.

An hour later, Calvin was still ignoring his phone. His mother-in-law had said she'd be available to take care of her grandson, but when Calvin and Martin arrived home they were met with a note explaining that she'd forgotten about the meeting down at the Baptist church, and that she had to be there to take notes in her official capacity as parish secretary.

His phone dinged with a text from Garrison: *You best b dead or something or Sollo gonna kill you for real.*

"Yo, little man," Calvin said, leaning on the closed bathroom door, typing his reply that he'd be there in twenty. "You almost finished in there?"

"Almost," Martin said, his voice straining with effort. "But I don't wanna wipe. It's gross."

"Come on now, you gotta take care of your business. If your mom don't get home in the next few minutes, I'm gonna have to drop you at Marcus's house until she does, all right?"

"I don't wanna go to Marcus's," Martin whined.

"Why not?"

"I'm tired."

"Yeah, you sound like you gettin' some exercise in there."

Martin was still in the bathroom ten minutes later when Tracey finally arrived.

"Baby, where you been?" Calvin said, impatiently greeting her on the front porch.

"I decided to get the two-hour massage, where the hell do you think I've been?" she said, her irritation on full display as she blew past him. Dropping her backpack on the floor, she made a beeline for the bathroom.

"Martin's in there," Calvin said, following her.

"Hi, Mommy!" Martin called out from behind the door.

"Hey, sweetie," she answered with a much more forgiving tone than the one she used with Calvin.

"I'm going poop."

"Okay, but Mommy's gotta use the bathroom, too."

"I'll hurry."

"He's been saying that for the last half-hour," Calvin said. "So, I gotta go."

Tracey's shoulder's sagged. "No, you don't."

"I'm sorry," Calvin tried. To get her home he'd had to tell her he needed to make a delivery to Sollo. "I didn't mean for you to miss your study group, but ain't nobody there gonna kick your ass if you do, you get what I'm sayin?"

She put her finger to her lips and walked him into the living room.

"It's not about missing my study group," she said when they were out of Martin's earshot.

Calvin considered glancing at his watch to indicate the severity of his predicament. But if there was one person who could effectively kick his ass besides Sollo, it was his wife. "I understand," he said instead.

She raised her eyebrow. "No, you don't. If you did, you wouldn't still be working for an asshole like Sollo Gibson, jumping to attention every time he calls."

"You notice it's not as often as it used to be."

"Yeah, I noticed. But when you get arrested again for stealing cars, the judge ain't gonna say, 'Well, if you promise to only do it every so often, then you're free to go.' And then where's that gonna leave us? I'm not playin', Calvin. We can't have this life no more. It's gonna eat you up like it does everyone else. And when they finish with you, they gonna come get Martin."

"I ain't gonna let that happen."

"How're you gonna stop it if you're in prison?"

Calvin said nothing. Truth was, the odds said that's where he'd end up. Another black man from the neighborhood going to prison didn't exactly raise eyebrows.

"I'm standing right here with you," Tracey went on, her stare holding his eyes steady. "I'm tired of it though. I'm tired of you doing things you keep telling me you're gonna stop doing, I'm tired of lying to Martin about where his daddy's going when he leaves in the middle of the night, and I'm tired of still living in the house I grew up in, holding my damn pee because we only got one bathroom between four people, five when my mom brings home Singletary." She went to her dropped backpack and pulled out a handful of real estate flyers. "Every time I'm sitting in some class and I'm barely hanging on because I'm so goddamn tired, I look at these." She handed them to Calvin. "Because those are why I'm doing it. Those are why I go to study groups after school and put up with all those damn idiots down at Target who yell at *me* because *they* can't find what they're looking for. I do all of it so you and Martin and I can have something of our own."

As Tracey spoke, Calvin scanned the flyers. Two-story houses. Four bedrooms. Three bathrooms. Family rooms. Dining rooms. Pools. Fences that weren't chain link. Basketball hoops over garages with nets that weren't shredded. All of it pissed him off. He couldn't picture the people that lived there, but he was damn sure they were nothing like him and wanted nothing to do with people that were.

"These are in Arizona," he said, defiant.

"So?"

"So there ain't no black people in Arizona. It's too damn hot."

"Too hot? We're from Africa, Calvin. It's like three hundred degrees in Africa."

"Girl," he said, cocking his head to one side, "we from Inglewood."

Tracey stared hard at him and he returned the same. This is the way it was too often, the same old shit kept coming between them, and they both kept digging in. Calvin wanted to apologize for the attitude, for the problems he brought to her life, to reach out and give her a hug, tell her she was doing the right thing and he was the one screwing it all up. But he didn't do any of that. He dropped the flyers on the coffee table.

"Can somebody wipe me?" Martin called out.

The corner of Tracey's eyebrow went back up. "You go on and get to Sollo, deliver that damn car I saw parked out front," she said. "I gotta stay here and take care of our son."

Calvin pulled the BMW up the driveway of Sollo's sorry-looking place off West 153rd in Compton. It was not the house that Sollo lived in, of course, with its peeling beige paint and patchy brown lawn, but it was the house where he did business. His Uncle Floyd lived in the house, had for over forty years, but everyone in the neighborhood still called it Sollo's place.

And there was no reason for it to look as it did, either, since Sollo could certainly afford to put some money into it—a fresh coat of paint, resod the lawn, put on a new roof. Hell, he could even take the bars off the windows, make it look real nice; nobody with bad intentions would so much as consider breaking in, not with Sollo's reputation. He probably didn't even need to put locks on the damn doors. Even the local Latino gang, the Compton Varrio 155, which had taken a dominant position in the turf wars as the demographics of the neighborhood changed, respected Sollo's sovereignty.

Sollo had gained his status by showing respect—the most transactional of all commodities—and by staying in his lane, leaving the drug trade to the local gang bangers. Not that he was above shooting a motherfucker when the situation called for it. So the mutual respect left him to do as he pleased, which didn't extend to fixing up the house. It continued to look like it did, no matter how much money Sollo made, and Uncle Floyd never complained about it, so there it was.

Despite being worrisomely late, Calvin parked up close to the garage at the end of the cement driveway and then sat in the car for another five minutes before going inside.

You ain't like the rest of us.

Calvin thought of what Garrison had said when he told him he'd accepted Sollo's offer to drive. Though only five years older, Garrison had always acted like the dad Calvin could barely remember, and was always looking out for him.

Not even when we was kids and you was always tryin' to front like you was tough, so you could hang with me and my crew. What

Sollo's talkin' about is some serious shit, man. It's federal, you know what I'm saying? You sure you good being a part of this?

I'm sure, Calvin had told his cousin, even though he wasn't. But if it goes right, there's the down payment Tracey dreams about.

Unless she finds out how you got it. Man, you still frontin' like you did as a kid. Your dad would kick my ass for letting you do this.

Yeah, well he's dead and here I am, Calvin had answered.

That's why you gotta follow through and get the hell out once you get paid. So Martin never has to say the same thing.

Garrison was right about that. Martin was getting older now and pretty soon he'd figure out what was what with his father. His boy was smart, good hearted, and Calvin sure as hell didn't want to screw things up by exposing him to the life. Sitting there, in the car he originally had stolen a month ago, before it was repainted and tricked out, he tried to imagine himself taking the computer class at West LA College, the one Tracey told him about, but he couldn't hold onto the thought. Okay, fuck computers. And Arizona. But maybe they had something else in the school catalogue he could look into. There had to be something he could do, HVAC technician or something. He started to text Tracey, typed out a few ideas, but he put the phone back in his pocket without hitting send, and went inside the house.

Stepping through the back door he heard Garrison, Andre, Stitch and Uncle Floyd playing cards around the kitchen table.

"Yo, Rain Man, what's the matter with you?" Andre said in his customary rasp of irritation. "Didn't you hear him ask for threes just ten seconds ago?"

"I thought he was bluffing," Stitch answered.

"There ain't no bluffing in this game, dumbshit, it's for ten-year-olds. Damn, Floyd, why can't we play poker?"

"Cause none of you has the folding money to keep up with

me," Floyd answered, his sixty-year-old gravelly voice a counterpoint to all the youthful energy surrounding him. "Now shut the hell up and give me your damn ace."

Calvin rounded into the tiny kitchen and Garrison jumped up from the table. "What's up with you?" he said, getting into Calvin's face. "Where the hell you been?"

Stitch shook his head. "Damn, when you two get married?"

"Shut up, fool," Garrison snapped.

He pushed Calvin into the living room, away from the others.

"Man, get off me," Calvin said, knocking his cousin's hands away.

Garrison leaned into him and whispered, "You keep your mouth shut and let me handle this, all right?"

Calvin had no time to agree to his cousin's terms before Sollo walked in, looking like a man ready to inflict some serious damage. He moved with the fluid momentum of an athlete, which he had been twenty years earlier—a starting fullback for two glorious seasons at Ohio State University—before he tore the ACL in his left knee and got hooked on pain killers trying to get back on a team that had moved on without him.

"You gonna walk in here like you out for a Sunday stroll, motherfucker?" he said. "Delvon said you left his place over an hour ago."

Calvin set his shoulders back, determined not to cower, despite his fear. "It couldn't be helped, I had some business to take care of."

"*This* is your fucking business."

Sollo kept moving forward and Calvin readied himself, but Garrison stepped between them. He wasn't as strong as Sollo, but he had played some football in his day, too, so he could certainly throw a good block.

"Yo, Sollo," he said, one hand pressed to Sollo's chest, the other making sure Calvin stayed back far enough to avoid a quick left hook. "Let's not lose focus, man. That's what you always say, right?"

Sollo stared at Calvin over Garrison's shoulder. It was apparent he wasn't truly interested in putting a beating on, or he would have kept right on charging. "You best be in this all the way," he warned.

"I'm here, ain't I?" Calvin said.

"I don't know, punk. You tell me."

"He's good, man," Garrison said, not yet lowering his hand. "He had to take care of his boy, that's all." He looked to Calvin. "Ain't that right?"

Calvin hadn't told his cousin why he was late, but he was glad Garrison had said it. It made him feel good, prideful, that he had that one thing on Sollo. Rumor was Sollo had six or seven kids, but he never talked about them and they certainly were never around to be counted. "That's right," he said. "But like I said, I'm here now and I'm all in."

The exchange didn't register on Sollo's face and Calvin figured the big man didn't give a rat's ass about the reason for his absence as he processed whether or not to cut him loose right then and there. A needling hope rose up in Calvin that he would.

"Do we have a problem here?" another man's voice came from behind Sollo.

Uncle Floyd, Andre, and Stitch came into the living room from the kitchen as the man who had brought them all together rolled into the room from the hallway. All eyes moved from the white man sitting in the wheelchair, back to Sollo. It was a question only he had the authority to answer. He kept his eyes on Calvin, and then said, "No, we ain't got no problems."

"That's good," Connor Weeks said.

From the waist up Connor was as thick and muscular as any of the men standing before him, and despite being five years north of fifty, with thinning hair that had gone gray and legs that hadn't moved for over two decades, he retained the aura of a hard son-of-a-bitch who might have once been the toughest of all of them.

"Because what I have in mind, I clearly can't do alone," he said. "But for this to go down as planned, gentlemen, we have to work as a team." His eyes shifted to Calvin. "And trust me, *timing* is everything."

Three days later, Calvin was sitting inside the rust-brown Toyota watching Sollo, Garrison, Andre, and Stitch run into American Federal.

As the world slowed down and time became an enemy, he thought of Tracey and Martin and realized he'd made a terrible mistake.

CHAPTER THREE

GARRISON WAS THE last to enter the bank. He stopped at the door and looked back to Calvin still sitting in the car. It was only a brief turn, an impulse he couldn't resist. Yesterday, his younger cousin was a just a car thief; today he was a bank robber. And it was Garrison's own damn fault for allowing it to happen.

In that split second of hesitation, he heard Sollo inside, yelling for everyone to get on the floor. But there was no response—none of the panicked screams he'd been prepared to expect from those few, unlucky people caught in the trap, no echoing voices from Andre or Stitch yelling for them to stay calm and do what they were told. Only that odd, unsettling silence.

Garrison stepped into the lobby, raising the TEC-9 pistol Sollo had supplied, and was greeted by a handgun held a few inches from his left temple by some big dude wearing a ski mask.

"Take it easy, ese," the Mexican said.

Garrison breathed heavily behind his opaque plastic mask, a trickle of sweat falling down his cheek.

From his vantage point he could see several people face down on the marble floor. A middle-aged security guard with a beer belly and a red face was on his knees on the carpeted section of the lobby, where there were a few desks with a handful of bank workers sitting silently, their hands raised. Another ski-masked man stood a few feet away from Garrison, his sawed-off shotgun pointed at Andre, who, in turn, was pointing his own gun at yet another man wearing a ski mask, positioned in the opposite corner.

There was a fourth ski-masked man at the teller windows, his gun pointing at Sollo, who stood motionless in the center of the lobby, not bothering to raise his gun at all. Garrison could see that Stitch had already moved behind the teller window, his TEC-9 trained on the man who was currently staring at Sollo.

"We're gonna do our thing and then you can have what's left behind," the man said.

"That ain't gonna happen," Sollo calmly answered.

"Then I guess we have a problem."

At the man's feet, a redheaded woman in her forties, wearing a baggy sweatshirt and yoga pants, began to cry. The man kicked her in the shoulder, the first sign he was not nearly as composed as Sollo. "Shut up," he yelled at the now whimpering woman. "This is what you get for not using the ATM." He then swung his pistol away from Sollo and aimed it at the teller, who held a duffle bag in front of him, frozen in fear. "Keep filling the fucking bag!" the man yelled.

The nervous teller did as she was told.

"This is bullshit, man," the big Mexican next to Garrison said, "We're taking too long. We gotta get the hell outta here."

The leader of his crew continued to lose whatever cool he once possessed. "We're not leaving until we get what we came for!" he screamed.

"You should listen to your friend there," Sollo said. "And try again another day."

"No! He's not making the decisions, I am!" The man moved along the counter with the teller, who was obediently filling the bag with money at each register.

"Then it's your choice to die or not," Sollo said, finally raising his gun.

The man laughed and trained his gun on Sollo. "Yeah? Well I'm ready, how 'bout you?"

The masked man standing by the kneeling security guard, moved slightly forward. "Screw that," he said. "I'm not ready."

His crew-leader lost another hinge and was barely holding on. "What'd you say?" he asked.

"I said I'm not ready to die for this," the man said, his voice shaking, sounding painfully youthful. "It's all messed up, Gavin. Let's just go."

The air thinned as the man now known as Gavin to every damn person in the bank, took two small steps away from the teller windows. "You fucking idiot," he said, his voice barely loud enough to travel across the lobby.

"What?" the young man in the ski mask said, clearly not paying attention to the finer details of robbing a bank.

"You really disappoint me, kid," Gavin said.

And then he shot him in the chest.

"What the hell!" the big Mexican yelled, taking a half step forward.

With sharp yelps of panic darting across the room, Gavin returned his gun to Sollo. "I guess it's your move now," he said.

Garrison had no idea how Sollo would respond, but he silently agreed with the kid on the floor slowly dying from a gunshot wound: none of this was worth dying over. The gun pointed at his head moved slightly off, as the Mexican shuffled slightly to get a look at his fallen compatriot, and Garrison jerked away.

With that spark of action, a gunshot went off somewhere to Garrison's right, and Armageddon was unleashed inside American Federal. Bullets flew back and forth as tellers and customers scrambled for cover. From the corner of his eye, Garrison saw Andre get shot in the head and drop to the ground. The big Mexican beside him was firing off shots toward Sollo when he, too, was cut down, a hail of bullets ripping through him from chest to legs.

Swinging his gun wildly, unsure where he needed to aim to protect himself, Garrison's stomach went hot, as though an ember had been lit a few inches above his navel. He fell to the ground, the gun dropping from his hand, and stared up at the ceiling. He blinked twice as the enormity of what was happening landed in his loosened mind, and turned his head to see Sollo, the most invincible man in the world, get half his face blown off.

Richie heard the shots, but they sounded distant, muted, more like children playing with firecrackers than anything. And now there was only a heavy silence. Blood beat in his ears as cars continued to whip past unaware and tiny birds continued to sit passively on telephone wires overhead. He glanced at the phone counting down in his lap. Two and half minutes had passed. That was it. Whatever had gone so horribly wrong inside the bank had taken no time at all, despite the eternity it had felt like sitting there, waiting.

An Asian man and woman walking down the sidewalk had stopped to stare at the doors of the bank, as if they could not be sure what they'd heard, trying to reconcile the disconnect between the lazy Saturday morning outside the bank and the notion of a gun battle raging inside.

Richie revved the engine, unsure what to do. He ducked lower in his seat, making sure his wig and ball cap were still in place. Every second was a torture of horrific expectations.

The door to the bank swung open and one of the ski-masked men came out carrying no gun and no money. He held his empty hands to his stomach, blood seeping through his fingers. A second bullet had evidently found his leg. He half-ran, half-limped along the sidewalk toward the Toyota parked on the street perpendicular to Sherman Way.

The Asian couple who'd stopped to investigate retreated quickly back up the sidewalk, the woman holding a cellphone to her ear as they ducked behind a parked car.

Richie popped the car into gear, ready to leave before the cops showed up, when Gavin came out of the bank behind the bleeding man, a full duffle bag in one hand, his gun still clutched in the other. He, too, was bleeding badly, his wound in the upper chest.

Gavin stood there on the sidewalk as though he was some damn tourist looking for directions. Then, he turned toward the ski-masked man making his way to the Toyota, raised his gun, and shot him in the back. The man fell to the ground and moved no more.

"Oh, shit!" Richie screamed, unable to keep silent. He stared at the dead man as Gavin stumbled to the Camaro, yanked the front passenger side door open, and collapsed inside.

"Drive," was all he said.

"What about the others?" Richie asked, his hands shaking so badly it was difficult to grip the steering wheel.

Gavin raised the .38 to Richie's forehead, his hand steady,

despite being covered with his own blood. With the bank alarm's piercing blare now announcing the mayhem to the entire neighborhood, Richie's foot found the gas pedal.

"This is one fucked-up carpool," he said, as the car's wheels found traction.

Behind them, Calvin had been stunned into inaction as he starred at Garrison's lifeless body lying on the sidewalk. His cousin was no more than twenty feet away from him, but it might as well have been a mile.

Get up. Come on, man. Get up and let's go.

The bank alarm kept ringing and people started to flow out of the bank.

Calvin's mouth hung open, tears dropped down his face.

Come on, Garrison. Please. Get up.

A crowd gathered, unaware of the idling Toyota around the corner or the man inside it. But then the Asian man raised his arm and pointed directly at him. A few in the growing crowd turned his way.

Calvin quickly pulled a U-turn and was gone.

Only one block away, the sound of the wailing bank alarm receded into a faint buzz, and Calvin's instinct to flee was subsumed by another primal urge. He turned left and went south, cruising up the street parallel to Sherman Way. If he kept going, he'd eventually hit the Van Nuys airport. Did they have a plane gassed up, ready to fly them to freedom? Or maybe they were making their way to the 405 freeway. No. Only a goddamn moron would risk getting caught in congestion on the 405.

He sped up, his heart pulsing in his ears.

The image of Garrison motionless on the sidewalk pushed its way back in and Calvin blinked away tears. Rational thought returned and he eased off the gas pedal, careful not to draw attention.

They have to ditch their ride somewhere close by.

He made another turn at the next intersection and headed for Lake Balboa Park, the spot Sollo had picked for their car exchange. That's all he could do. He would ditch his ride and hope for a miracle. The City of Goddamn Angels. Why the hell not?

Garrison is dead. Garrison is dead.

That was the reality. This bullshit search for the men who had killed him was not. The impulse to chase them down had come on like a fever that was now, all at once, broken. Tears were salty on his lips. He slammed his fists on the steering wheel until his hands ached. His stomach tightened around the truth. He was lost in every way.

And then the Angels of Los Angeles descended.

He heard a horn and spotted the Camaro as he drove through an intersection, turned at the next corner and came back around. He had time. The Camaro sure as hell wasn't going anywhere.

He pulled to the curb a few houses from where the Camaro had come to a sudden, violent rest, horn still blaring. A few people had already descended on the scene, gawking at the wreckage of the car horrifically slammed into the telephone pole. An older woman wearing a bathrobe was shuffling down her driveway, helplessly waving her hands as her bath-robed husband leaned on his walker halfway up the driveway, yelling at her to stay back.

Calvin climbed from the Toyota and stayed a few feet behind the others as he surveyed the damage. The Camaro's passenger was on the hood, covered in blood. White smoke billowed from the crumpled hood and rose up smelling like burning, damp leaves. Of course, only Calvin knew that a good portion of the man's blood was due to a couple of bullet holes, not from the short trip through the windshield. The driver's seat was empty, the door pushed open.

"He's alive!" the elderly woman in the robe yelled. "His hand moved!"

Two men in the crowd told the dying man that help was on the way.

"Put those damn cameras away," Calvin snapped. "Show some respect!"

Two of the people filming the scene sheepishly put their phones down, though a third, a young man wearing glasses and a polo shirt one size too small, kept filming. Calvin stepped behind him, his breath hot on the back of the man's neck. "How 'bout I shove that phone up your white ass?" he said, pitching his voice as deep as he could. And that was that. With the last camera gone, Calvin went to the Camaro and bent down to the man who had shot his cousin dead.

"W'sup, asshole?" he said into his ear.

"Is he breathing?" another of the gawking men asked.

"Stay back," Calvin called, needing to raise his voice over the blaring horn. "Looks like this shit's about to blow."

The onlookers stepped away and Calvin got close to the dying man's ear. "Who the fuck are you?"

The man looked up at Calvin, making a wet rasp from somewhere deep within his throat. "Glass," he said, blood coming up along with the word.

"Yeah, there's a shitload of glass," Calvin said. "Your ass just went through it."

With his last ounce of energy, the man laughed, his hooded eyes barely opening enough to see. "Richie," he said.

"That's your name?"

The man shuddered, spit and blood flowed from his mouth, a string of saliva stretching from his lower lip to the hood of the car. Another rasp came up his throat. He was silent for a moment and then he weakly managed two words. "Richie...Glass."

They were the last two words of Gavin Hendricks.

CHAPTER FOUR

FBI AGENT GRACE Luelle stood over the body stretched out on the sidewalk outside American Federal as a CSI team continued to process the scene. She turned to look at the front door of the bank; slowly, her eyes traced the sidewalk back to the body. "Almost made it," she said under her breath.

"Excuse me, ma'am?" asked the CSI crouched down, getting fingerprints from the dead man.

"I'm sorry?"

"Were you talking to me?"

Agent Luelle shook her head, thought a moment more, and said, "He was sure trying to get to someone, wasn't he?"

"Yes, ma'am. Seems that way."

"You guys find any good tire prints?"

"That's not my detail," the CSI said. "But I can ask."

"No, no. That's fine. We'll get to it. Just thinking out loud."

Agent Luelle had grown up in Thousand Oaks, a sprawling suburb of Los Angeles half an hour from the front door of American Federal. She was the daughter of a CHP officer and followed his lead, with a degree in Criminal Justice from Cal State Northridge and a law degree from UCLA. But her intended path of convicting criminals—rather than catching them—was detoured during her second year of law school, when her father's killer walked free, due in part to what the final report called "investigator malfeasance." Turned out, when they tracked down the man who shot her father as he climbed from his unit, the lead investigator on the case planted evidence as an insurance policy to make sure the murder charge stuck. Seeing her father's killer walk from the courtroom, smiling, twenty-three-year-old Grace became obsessed with the idea of hunting him down. That specific quest never came to be. The man, a junkie named Colin Abbott, disappeared for nine years until his wasted body was found in the living room of an abandoned house near downtown LA. But in those intervening nine years, Grace Luelle, Esquire, had become Grace Luelle, Assistant Special Agent in Charge. And now, having edged past forty, Agent Luelle had a reputation for doing everything by the book, taking no shortcuts, and making sure those around her did the same.

She glanced at the throng of media jockeying to get a shot from behind the yellow tape stretched corner to corner across Sherman Way. "Be sure to have your family and friends watch the news tonight," she said to the CSI kneeling beside her. "Looks like you're gonna be all over it."

"They'll be watching the Lakers," the CSI said, not looking up as he rolled the dead man's left index finger across an ink pad. "Game one of the finals."

Agent Luelle cocked her head, her dirty-blonde ponytail swishing on the back of her nylon FBI jacket as she studied the inert face of the dead man on his stomach, eyes still open, eternally staring at the grey section of cement a few inches beyond his nose. "Wonder if he was planning to watch too," she said.

Leaving the CSI to his duties, she headed inside the bank.

The air inside was cool, cold even. The six bodies remained on the floor where they had fallen. Blood splatters had been measured and photographed; bullet casings were still being identified and marked. LAPD officers stood watch as detectives and FBI Agents conferred. The nine employees and seven patrons who had witnessed the robbery were huddled together at the far end sipping cups of coffee.

Agent Luelle flashed her ID for the LAPD officer at the door and waded into the controlled chaos of it all.

"I was wondering when you were going to show up," Lead Detective Kevin Sutherland said as she approached.

"Busy day."

"Welcome to one hell of a cluster fuck."

"It is quite the mess."

"You'll be proud to hear that your people have completely ignored all the evidence we've already collected and are starting from scratch."

"Don't take it personally."

Detective Sutherland received a file folder from a passing officer but didn't immediately open it. "You guys have any idea who these morons are?" he asked.

"Give us a couple hours," Agent Luelle said. "We've got one of the getaway cars about fifteen blocks away, decorating a telephone pole with one of these masked shitheads."

"The driver?"

"Nope."

Detective Sutherland exhaled sharply through his nose. At sixty, he had been on the job for thirty-six years and Agent Luelle figured nothing surprised him anymore. But she could tell by his expression as he flipped through the file in his hands that this one came close. "You wanna run this down for me?" she asked.

"Two crews robbing the same bank on the same day at the same time? You go first."

She shook her head. "Can't be a coincidence, right? Despite the make-up of the involved parties, whatever went down here, it isn't gonna turn out to be simply black and white."

"Ha-ha."

Agent Luelle nodded at the absurdity of it all. "You wanna show me the back?"

In the vault, two CSI techs were busy dusting a wall of safety deposit boxes with aluminum powder, hoping to grab some fingerprints that weren't supposed to be there. On the table behind them lay an open box, empty.

"Any idea what they took?" Agent Luelle asked.

Detective Sutherland patted his slightly rounded belly. "Nope."

"You've been a huge help so far."

"I can only tell you that two of them came in here when the shooting started. This box was the only one pulled."

"Who's it belong to?" Agent Luelle asked.

"A company called Midas, Inc."

"And what does Midas, Inc. do?"

"Once again, no idea."

"At least you're consistent."

"It was set up 6 months ago, but the guy who opened the account—using a fake name no doubt—hasn't been back since." He held up the file. "All indications are that it's a dummy corporation, set up solely to store whatever was in that box."

"Which one of the crews came back here for it?"

"We're still not sure."

"Well, were they black or white?" asked Agent Luelle.

"They were wearing masks."

"Yes, ski or opaque? And please don't tell me one of each."

"Wish I could, but these guys were intent on creating as much confusion as possible."

"At least that part went according to plan." She looked at him sideways. "I'm assuming you'd agree these guys didn't go to all this trouble to rob their own box?"

"Agreed."

"Yet, looking at the evidence over there, it appears they had a key?"

"Had a key, but the bank has a dual control system. They needed a bank rep to open the box along with them."

Her eyebrows went up. "And who might that bank rep be?"

David Perlstein was trying his best to catch his breath, but the adrenaline flushing his face bright red was also keeping him from drawing enough air into his lungs to sustain his composure. He sat in his office, his right heel bouncing up and down like it was trying to tap out a mayday message in Morse code.

"Have another sip of water, Mr. Perlstein," Agent Luelle suggested.

Perlstein used both shaking hands to bring the cup to his lips. He took a sip and then another. And then he broke down into tears.

"Not this again," Detective Sutherland said under his breath.

Keeping her eyes on the bank manager, Agent Luelle swept her hand across the detective's chest, pushing him back a few paces.

"I'm sorry," Perlstein cried. "It was just so intense."

"I understand that," Agent Luelle said, kindly. "But we need to figure out exactly what happened as quickly as possible, so if you could try to walk us through it."

"But I've already done this with the officers when they first arrived," he said through his tears. He pointed at Detective Sutherland. "I explained it all to you, didn't I?"

"Yes, but I'd like to hear it from you firsthand," Agent Luelle said.

Perlstein set down the cup of water and turned to the FBI laptop already uploaded with the bank surveillance footage.

"Like I said before, the ski-masked men came in first," he said, pointing at the screen. "See, that one there, the one that shot his partner for using his name—Gavin, I think it was?"

"Yes," Agent Luelle nodded, her eyes still on Perlstein, rather than the screen. "We're already running the name."

"Well, this Gavin guy was out of his goddamn mind. He was yelling at Brenda—that's her at the teller window—to fill the duffle bag."

"Did he say anything to Brenda or anyone else about going into the vault?"

"No. When the other gang came in, everybody started yelling at each other. Nobody knew what was going on. And then the shooting started, but I couldn't see anything. I was face down on the floor and then there were hands on my back, pulling me up."

On the video, chaos ensued, bullets flying, bodies dropping. Only one camera angle caught the two other men—one in a ski mask, the other opaque—pulling Perlstein from the floor and into his office, where he retrieved the deposit box key.

"What did they say to you when they pulled you up?" Agent Luelle asked.

"That they would shoot me in the face if I didn't do as they instructed," Perlstein said, the recollection bringing up more tears and more shaking.

"Oh, boy," Detective Sutherland sighed.

Agent Luelle shot the detective a look and he turned an imaginary key on his lips.

"What did they sound like?" she asked. "Did they have accents?"

"No, they sounded normal. Not normal, I didn't mean it like that. I mean they sounded like regular English-speaking guys, you know, like the others."

"Which others? Did they sound like black guys or white guys?"

"Okay, I get it. I suppose they sounded white, but I'm really not in tune to that sort of thing."

Agent Luelle pressed a key on the computer, freezing the image on the screen. "Where were they before all this? Only eight guys in total came into the bank. I don't see these other two anywhere on the video before they popped up here."

"I don't know," Perlstein said.

Her brow furrowed. "Hmmm," she said, staring at the bank manager.

"What?"

"That's strange."

Perlstein sighed. "This whole thing is strange, if you ask me."

Agent Luelle smiled, but this time it wasn't a kind smile. "I *am* asking you," she said.

"Look, I'm as confused as you are!" He pointed at Detective Sutherland. "As he is! Hell, as everyone is. I don't know what to tell you. They snuck in, maybe out of camera view?"

"Maybe," nodded Agent Luelle. "Or could they have already been in the bank when it opened?"

Perlstein's face reddened even more, and he used both hands to wipe the moisture from his cheeks. "No," he said, asserting his authority on the subject.

"Why not?"

"Because I was the one who opened this morning. The alarm was on. I would have seen them. Patterson, Eric Patterson, came in right after me, maybe five minutes later. He would have seen them, too."

"The security guard," Detective Sutherland said to Agent Luelle. "He said there was definitely no one else here when he arrived."

Agent Luelle stared at the bank manager another moment, studying him. And then, with a stroke on the computer she brought up the video from inside the vault as the box was pulled and opened, a gun pressed to the bank manager's head the entire time. The two masked men then removed a rectangular wooden box and left, leaving Perlstein behind, crying. They were in the vault thirty seconds, tops. Long enough, though, for the carnage in the lobby to finish. As the footage played, she kept her eyes on Perlstein, before casually asking, "And then?"

"What do you mean? That was it. By the time they left the vault, their partners were either dead or gone. See? Right there," Perlstein said, needlessly pointing at the screen. "People started running from the bank and they went out the exit on the west side of the building, on Kirkwood, not Sherman Way."

"I guess they had no choice," Detective Sutherland said. "Their rides were gone."

"Okay, Mr. Perlstein," Agent Luelle said, shutting the laptop. "I appreciate how difficult this is for you. Take a few minutes, and I'll have one of my agents come get you. You're gonna have to go over all of this again with him."

The bank manager's expression contorted as if he'd swallowed something sour. "Are you serious?" he cried.

Luke Stanton couldn't sit. He stared at the television, holding the remote by his thigh like a six-shooter. Every so often he would raise it as though he were a gunfighter drawing a bead on an opponent and change the channel to another local station covering the bank robbery. They were all saying the same thing: they had no idea what had transpired inside American Federal, beyond the ratings-boosting basics of the shootout, which they were happy to repeat ad nauseam.

Luke had no idea what had happened inside the bank, but he couldn't help but worry it had something to do with the deal he'd made five days before. *What are the fucking odds?*

His doorbell rang and he shut off the television. He stood silently, like a deer hearing a twig break. A moment later, his cell phone rang, startling him. "Hello?" he said.

"Answer the fucking door if you're home," the familiar voice with the thick accent said.

"Okay, yeah, I was going to do that as soon as—"

The line went dead. He tucked the phone back into his pocket and let out a long breath before opening the door.

"What happened?" the dark-haired man on his doorstep said.

"I have no idea. I mean, the bank was hit, if that's what you mean."

The man brushed past him. "Yes, that's what I mean." Two others, both dressed in similar dark button-down shirts and pressed slacks, also walked into Luke's living room as if they owned the place.

"Okay, yeah," Luke said, closing the door as the men spread out into the room. They were all in their mid-thirties, with lean, athletic builds and thick dark hair that looked to have been styled by the same barber. "I've been watching the news since the story broke."

The three men glanced around the room, but said nothing.

The home was spacious, four thousand square feet, with lots

of places to hide things. Luke had reached the top of his considerable income bracket by keeping his nose to the grindstone for the past twenty years and had moved his family to the big house in Santa Clarita, a mostly Republican city an hour north of Los Angeles, after the birth of his second daughter. But even after hitting his stride in all ways, he still wasn't content. That's why he'd pursued the business opportunity with the man now standing in his living room holding a .30 caliber Carbine pistol.

"Have you heard from anyone?" the man in charge asked him.

"No. I mean, only you guys right now. Do you know what's going on?"

The man smiled. "We have a pretty good idea."

"Really?" Luke's eyes darted to the other men then back to the one who was now pointing the gun at him.

"This was a bad idea you had," the man said.

"Hold on," Luke nearly shouted, stumbling back against the leather ottoman his wife had bought at Pottery Barn. "None of this was my idea. I had nothing to do with any of this."

The man shrugged. "Yes, okay. So it's all a coincidence. Two days after we put the coins in the bank, two days before the sale would go through—two days you insisted on needing to raise the rest of the cash—the bank is hit?"

Luke's forehead was dotted with perspiration. "I didn't say it was a coincidence. I said I had nothing to do with it. I can show you my bank account, man. I was still gathering the last of the money, I swear. As far as I knew, the sale was going through."

The dark-haired man knitted his brows. "You are very nervous."

"You're pointing a gun at me."

"Yes, I am. So you shouldn't be lying."

"Man, I'm not lying. I didn't do this. I was going to pay you the full price we agreed on, no problem."

"But now we do have a problem. Who else did you tell about the deal?"

"Nobody, I swear. I didn't even tell my wife. This whole thing was going to be a surprise."

"The score of a lifetime for a man like yourself."

"Exactly," Luke said. "That's why I can't believe that today, of all days, the bank was robbed."

The dark-haired man considered him. "I don't believe in coincidences and I don't believe in you. I will give you one more chance to tell me why you thought it was a good idea to steal from us."

"I swear to God I wasn't behind this," Luke said, his voice trembling. "Hell, maybe the coins weren't even taken, right? I mean, nobody's saying on the news, so—"

The rest of what he meant stayed in his mouth. It was difficult to speak once the bullet ripped into his stomach. Luke Stanton, the middle aged CPA who met a gangster in a bar and thought he could jump ahead by going into business with him, fell to the floor and moaned. The last thought he had as he lay there, bleeding all over the Calistoga area rug, was how scared his wife would be when she got home with the kids.

CHAPTER FIVE

IT TOOK RICHIE a little over two hours to get from Reseda to Hollywood. Deciding to ignore the second car Gavin left near the park, he had walked to the Metro Station, ditching the wig in a storm drain and the Dodger's cap in a homeless man's shopping cart. The gloves were dropped in separate garbage bins, one behind a liquor store and the other at a construction site. There was nothing he could do about the duffle bag full of cash except wear it around his neck and under his shirt.

Nobody paid him much attention on the train. He was on the Metro after all, and nobody in their right mind purposely makes eye contact while using public transportation, especially with someone who is sweating profusely and bleeding from the forehead, as Richie was.

He hadn't intended to ram the Camaro into the telephone pole; that had been a happy accident. Hell, even if he had thought of it, he wouldn't have had the nerve to go from forty to zero in half a second. But Gavin had pressed the gun to Richie's temple as a request for him to speed up, and the cold steel against his skin sent a twitch down both arms to the nervous hands that were otherwise occupied with steering. The Camaro swerved,

Richie overcompensated, and Gavin learned the hard way how important it is to wear a seatbelt.

Other than the cut on his forehead from hitting the windshield and two very sore knees from being jammed into the crumpled dash, Richie was no worse for wear. He had managed to climb from the car and grab the duffle bag from under Gavin's body before the first person came onto the scene. A few concerned voices trailed after him as he shuffled away from the carnage, but it seemed as though they weren't sure if he was a witness to the accident or a participant.

As he walked east along Hollywood Boulevard, he blended in nicely with the oddball inhabitants of the famed thoroughfare. While throngs of tourists came to spot celebrities—or at least their stars embedded in the sidewalk—the reality of the street was a swarming mix of homeless beggars, street hustlers and badly cast doppelgängers of superheroes and dead movie stars working tips in exchange for a picture taken in front of grungy storefronts selling novelty tees, tourbus rides, and falafels.

"Son of a bitch," Sam O'Dell said, when Richie walked into his souvenir shop. "You lying prick."

"Don't waste all that charm on me, Sam. I just saw a tour bus pull up out front." He picked up a plastic Mr. T doll, Clubber Lang from Rocky III. "The folks back home are gonna be so jealous."

"You said one week," Sam said, his left eye twitching as usual. "That was a month ago."

The store was long and narrow, a rectangle stuffed with cheap crap. Selling every bit of it wouldn't keep a dog fed, so luckily for Sam he had another income stream. Richie made his way to the back counter where he sat with an oscillating fan blowing stale air directly into his face. Sam was tall and lanky, with the anxious disposition of a recovering addict. He had a tendency to sweat no matter the temperature and was clearly suffering in the heat.

"I'm touched that you missed me," Richie said.

"Shut up. Where's my damn money?"

Richie placed the duffle bag on the counter and took out a stack of bills. "I told you I was good for it."

"If your word was worth a damn you wouldn't have to come to a shit hole like this to find someone dumb enough to take your action. And why do you look like you got run over?"

"Cut myself shaving," Richie said, counting out the bills on the counter.

Sam looked him over. "Somebody lit you up for not paying, huh? Same thing I should have done a month ago."

"Beyond the exercise, it wouldn't have done you any good. But as you can see, the situation's changed. That's two thousand."

Sam shook his head. "Try twenty-five hundred. Interest."

Richie looked at him. "How 'bout we make it an even three? All you gotta do—if it ever comes up—is say I was here with you this morning."

Sam's eyes moved from Richie, to the bag, then back. "Where the hell you get all that money?"

"Does it matter?"

"Not for *four* grand, it doesn't."

Richie smiled. "Deal."

"Just like that, huh?"

"Just like that." Richie counted out the extra bills. "And for what it's worth, I would have gone to five."

"You prick," Sam said as he picked up the cash to recount it.

"I came in here this morning," Richie said, making sure he was getting everything he paid for. "I brought you a sausage

McMuffin and we talked about the Lakers. I left around ten-thirty. Got it?"

Sam finished counting the bills, his suspicious eye continuing to twitch. "Who's gonna be in here asking all the questions? The cops?"

"A lot of people might be. Maybe the FBI even. Either way, we have a deal, right?"

Sam looked past Richie, even though they were alone in the store, and then asked, "What'd you do, kid?"

"Just remember the sausage McMuffin, okay? It's a nice touch."

Sam stared at him, as if calculating all the angles of their agreement. Once he had decided he came out ahead on the deal, he scooped up the money from the counter and shrugged. What the hell. After all, if he had one professional ethos, it was keeping his mouth shut. As he bent down to deposit the money into the safe tucked under the counter, Richie pulled a sheet of paper from a note pad beside the register and scribbled a note, which he then stuck inside the duffle.

"Seeing as how we're all up to date and you're looking pretty flush," Sam said. "What do you say we go ahead and have that conversation about the Lakers? I can give you some good action."

Richie patted the duffle bag and slung it over his shoulder. "Sorry, Sammy. My losing streak is finally over. No sense in starting a new one."

"Suit yourself."

Richie started for the door, but got only five paces before he turned back. "What's the spread?" he asked.

CHAPTER SIX

CALVIN SAT ON the couch in his living room, his eyes glued to the television as a reporter droned on, the camera zeroing in on the yellow tarp covering Garrison's body on the sidewalk. A chyron in the upper corner said it had been recorded earlier. The footage of his dead cousin's body would probably be played on a loop until everyone got bored gawking at it.

"Seven of the robbers died in the shootout and an eighth died in a car crash only blocks from the bank. There are still four suspects at large, two of whom are the getaway drivers who weren't inside the bank at the time of the shootout, and two others who ran away on foot. Now, police aren't giving any specifics as to what happened inside American Federal, but some are calling it a miracle that no bystanders were hurt in the hail of gunshots. Witness are still being questioned as—"

"Are you okay, daddy?" Martin asked, taking a seat next his father, his eyes moving cautiously from the television to his father.

Calvin turned off the TV and ran his palms down his wet cheeks. "I'm sad," he said.

"What happened?"

Calvin looked over to Tracey, sitting with her mother,

Vanessa, at the dining table tucked into the corner off the kitchen. Vanessa had her daughter's hand in hers as she softly prayed to Jesus. While her mother's eyes remained closed, Tracey looked at Calvin and he took in the anger and the pain in her eyes like an injection of hot liquid right to the chest. The heat spread out, filling him up, souring his stomach.

He still hadn't said anything specific to her about the robbery or Garrison's death or the role he played, but then, he didn't have to. She had been home when he returned, still in her pajamas, not even dressed yet for her Saturday afternoon shift down at Target. But he could tell she knew the minute he came into the house. Her eyes were bloodshot from crying and she looked like she was on the verge of throwing up. The players were all from the neighborhood and the information had traveled from house to house before the KTLA news team started beaming it across the southland. Before he could speak, she slapped him across the face, walked into the bedroom they shared, and closed the door between them.

She had come back out only when her mother arrived home. "I ain't gonna ask you nothin' about it," was all his mother-in-law had said to Calvin when she came in. "I don't need to know nothing anyway."

And now they were all there, avoiding him as though he were a danger to the life they had built.

"Uncle Garrison got hurt, little man," he said to Martin, pressing his son to his chest so he wouldn't have to look into those innocent brown eyes. "He got hurt really bad."

"How did he get hurt?"

The emotions Calvin was working so hard to tamp down started to seep through the cracks. "He was shot."

Martin tensed in his arms. "Is he going to die?"

Calvin drew in a breath. "Yes, he is."

Martin fell quiet, his body tucking tightly into him, and Calvin couldn't tell if he was crying or not.

"DeSean's daddy got shot too," he said after a moment. "Remember?"

Calvin locked eyes with Tracey. "I remember, little man," he said. "I remember."

Tracey caught up to him as he stepped off the porch that evening, heading for the bus stop. Better if his car wasn't seen where he was going.

"You ain't gonna talk to me?" she said, stepping from the house.

He stopped, but didn't turn to face her. "There's something I gotta take care of," he said.

"Yeah, there is," Tracey said, her voice drained of energy. "He's sitting in his bedroom right now, wondering where his daddy's off to."

Calvin finally turned toward her. "I wasn't inside that bank," he said.

"All right."

"That's the God's honest truth. But there's more truth you gotta understand."

She nodded as if to say she already understood.

"I wasn't anywhere near that bank at all. I was at Delvon's place helping him rebuild the engine on a '96 Chevy. Anyone asks, he'll tell them the same thing."

"I understand," she said.

The emotions of the day had ebbed. He was no longer in danger of crying unexpectedly or shaking uncontrollably when he pictured Garrison dead on that sidewalk. That part of him had been hollowed out, the space now filled with a firm resolve.

"I'm sorry, Tracey," he said. "I swear to God, I am."

She crossed her arms. "Exactly what're you sorry for?"

"For not being the man you want me to be."

"Don't try to play me, Calvin. You're never gonna be the man I want you to be, if you can't even be the man *you* want to be."

A car passed by, headlights glowing in the dusk, blaring some classic Tupac wondering if heaven's got a ghetto. Calvin watched it go, the hand in the pocket of his jacket touching the gun Delvon had given him. "You gonna be here when I get back?"

"Of course," Tracey said. "I don't have anywhere else to go."

By the time he looked back to the porch, she was already walking inside, another door closing between them.

Richie looked for anything else he could fit into the one suitcase that still had room. He didn't have any idea how long he'd be gone or where he was going, so it was difficult to determine what he might need when he got there. His plan was to start driving and keep on driving until he ran out of gas. Then he would fill up the tank and repeat the process three or four times before he made any concrete decisions.

He glanced out his bedroom window for the fiftieth time since arriving back home. The house was set back from the road on a sloping hillside. Go a few blocks south and you'd hit the noise and congestion of Hollywood Boulevard, near where he had made his deal with Sam, but here it was calm, residential, close to Runyon Canyon Park, where a person could walk amongst actual nature. He looked quickly up and down the street. It was dark and quiet, which bothered him. Everything bothered him. Every car horn was a SWAT team getting into position, every barking dog a K-9 unit about to break down his front door.

He closed both suitcases, turned off the lights and headed for the front door. It struck him as he did so that anything could happen once he left. He could be arrested, sure, but he pushed that possibility as far away as possible. He chose to consider the fantasy of finding a new life somewhere else. He had his passport and some fresh cash, so the world was his oyster. It was much better to imagine himself as a vagabond rather than a fugitive hiding from the law.

The house had been his mother's originally, a place she could call her own once the problems with her husband became too much to bear. The house in Beverly Hills was more his father's style and she had always hated it, with all its columns and chandeliers. The little house near the big park was perfect for her. And then the lump in her right breast turned into something evil and she died before the separation could turn into a divorce. "Sorry, Mom," Richie said to her lingering spirit as he took one last look around the place.

And then he opened the door to the business end of a nine millimeter pistol.

"W'sup, punk?" Calvin asked.

"Shit!" Richie stumbled backward. "Take it easy, man. I don't want any problems."

"Little late for that, Richie Rich," Calvin said, reaching behind him to shut the door. "You alone up in here?"

"Yes. I mean no."

Calvin pressed the gun to his forehead.

"Okay, yes. Please don't shoot me."

Calvin eyed the suitcases. "Goin' somewhere?"

"How do you know who I am?"

"Me and your boy had a little conversation on the hood of your car. Ain't nobody anonymous anymore. Not if you got a name, twenty-nine ninety-five, and an internet connection."

Richie was slowly able to process more than his own fear. "Holy shit, you were one of those other guys today—"

"What the hell's a rich boy like you doin' robbing a bank?"

"I didn't rob anything, I was just the driver. I'm having a major cash flow problem and I was in deep with them, so I didn't have a choice."

Calvin's face scrunched up in an irritated grimace. "Why you tryin' to bullshit me?"

Richie's hands shook, his fingers cold as ice as he continued to hold them up. "I'm not, I swear."

"Livin' in a place like this, and you trying to sell me on cash flow issues? You want a bullet in your fucking head?"

Richie's words increased in both volume and speed. "No! Listen, no! I've borrowed so much against the equity in this place to pay off gambling debts, I'm as broke as anybody you know. I have nothing left. Nothing. It's only a matter of time before the bank kicks me out of here. Can you *please* stop pointing that gun at me?"

Calvin left the gun where it was. "Where's the money from the bank?"

"I don't have it anymore."

"Try again, Prince Dumbshit."

"Okay, okay, listen…I kept a couple grand, that's it. The dude I was with, the one from the hood of the car, he had a partner. I left the rest of the money on his doorstep with a note saying that my debt's been paid and I've moved to Sweden."

Calvin stared hard at him. "Where?" he said.

"Sweden. It's a country in Europe."

"I know what Sweden is, you fucking moron. I mean where's this guy live?"

"Why?"

"What difference does it make?"

"Look, I don't have any idea what happened today. I was only there to drive. If I didn't, they would've killed me. They already killed this other guy I was betting with because he was in the wrong place at the wrong time. And he was kind of a dick. So they tied a cement block to his feet and drowned him. That's the way these guys are. Whatever the hell went down today, it wasn't anything personal."

"It's personal now."

"Yes, I got that. But I had nothing to do with any of it."

Calvin looked unsure of himself for the first time. "Where's this guy you were working for live?" he asked for the second time.

Richie shook his head. "Come on man, you don't understand. You don't want anything to do with them, all right? They're psychotic. They shoot people like they're living in a Sony PlayStation."

Calvin's hand twitched. "Well, it's either them or me, take your pick."

An impulse came to Richie as Calvin's expression slackened ever so slightly. It was the same impulse that he'd so often relied on back in the days of reading other players during poker games at Kendall Kelly's house in Beverly Hills. At first he tried to ignore it, the safer bet being to keep trying to talk his way out, but he couldn't think of anything else to say. He scanned the face behind the gun and worked up the courage to follow his instinct, even though it was his instincts which had led him to the current situation. He swallowed what little moisture remained in his mouth and said, "Okay. I pick you."

Calvin's eyes narrowed. He raised the gun a few inches and tipped the barrel toward Richie. "You really wanna die like this, punk?"

"I don't wanna die at all," Richie said. "But if that's what you came here for, go ahead and shoot me."

Calvin bit down on his molars, muscles rippled up and down his jaw line. "Don't push me, asshole."

Richie's body shook. His hands were numb from having them up so long. The seconds ticked away as he stood his ground, saying nothing more.

Calvin stared at him, his eyes getting wider and wider, the gun twitching in his hand. "Mother fucker!" He hissed in frustration, lowering the gun like it weighed five-hundred pounds.

Richie let out a burst of air. He bent over, hands on his knees, and took in a series of deep breaths to keep from losing consciousness. "I can't believe it," he said. Sweat tickled his forehead and he wiped it away. "Holy shit, that's some gambling right there." He looked up, an unintended smile creeping in. "I totally read you."

"Yeah, you did," Calvin said. "But you must have skipped a chapter."

"What's that mean?"

Calvin cracked him on the side of the head with the gun, dropping him like a marionette doll who had his strings cut.

Richie wasn't sure how long he'd been out. He rolled onto his back and stared up at the ceiling. His ears were ringing and he had a hell of a headache. He checked his jaw, opening it wide and then moving it back and forth. Everything was evidently in working order. Rolling onto his side, he pushed himself up to his knees and then spotted Calvin, sitting on the floor, his back against the front door. He raised the gun again, pointing it at him.

"Oh, please," Richie groaned. "Seriously?"

"They killed my cousin," Calvin said.

Richie wasn't sure, but it looked as if the badass black dude with the gun had been crying. "Yeah, well," he said, climbing unsteadily to his feet. "Your cousin was a bank robber. It happens."

Calvin lowered the gun and stared up at Richie. "And now I only got two people left in the world to care about. That's why I need that money. So unless you're lookin' for me to break every goddamn bone in your face, you're gonna take me to it."

Richie stretched his back and nodded. He knew this time, it wasn't a bluff.

CHAPTER SEVEN

CALVIN STOOD IN the driveway as Richie backed his faded blue 2007 Subaru hatchback out of the garage. "What the hell is this?" he asked, when the car stopped for him.

"I told you I was broke," Richie said.

"You don't have to fucking advertise it," Calvin said, climbing in.

They drove in uncomfortable silence for a few blocks until Richie couldn't take it anymore and turned the radio on. Eminem blasted from the speakers and he nodded at Calvin, as if to confirm his choice of tunes.

"We ain't making a goddamn video," Calvin said. "Turn that shit off."

Richie did and the silence continued.

It was a slow drive from Hollywood down to the 10 freeway. Lots of idling at red lights. Lots of creeping through jammed intersections. The silence took on a painful awkwardness. By the time they reached the freeway and started heading west toward Venice, Richie was about to climb out of his skin. "I never got your name," he said.

Calvin looked out the side window as if he hadn't heard him.

"I'm just trying to make conversation."

Calvin kept his eyes out the window. "Garrison," he said.

"Garrison," Richie repeated, surprised and pleased he got that much. "All right. You from LA, Garrison?"

But the conversation went no further.

By the time they reached Venice, Richie had had enough. His knees still ached from the accident that morning, his back threatened to spasm with each shift of his body, and the headache from Calvin's beatdown was expanding at such a rate that its pressure felt like it could reopen the cut on his forehead.

"Look," he said. "I've been trying to imagine how this could possibly end well and I've come up empty. I mean, I understand you're upset about your cousin, but seriously, catching a bullet with my face would be upsetting to me, so once I show you the place, you're on your own."

Calvin checked the gun in his lap. "No."

"No? That's all you're gonna say? No?"

"You don't have to go in with me, but you're gonna have to wait until I'm done. I ain't gonna be calling no Uber."

"C'mon, man," Richie continued to press, his frustration boiling over. "This was pretty much the worse day of my life and whatever you have planned isn't gonna make it any better. Seriously, Garrison. Let's give this some thought. You couldn't even shoot me, but you're gonna walk in there acting all tough and intimidate them?"

"That's *exactly* what Garrison would do," Calvin snapped.

Richie looked sideways at him. "I'm sorry, is that something you do to hype yourself up?" he asked. "The whole referring to yourself in the third person thing?"

Calvin was perspiring and no matter his effort to appear

in control, it was obvious he wasn't. "Don't worry about it," he said. "I got this."

"I don't think you do, but it's your life, man," Richie said, pulling the car to the curb. "So, like I said, this is as far as I go."

The street was quiet and in desperate need of a streetlamp. The houses were all well kept, a combination of mid-century and craftsman, with a fair number of the two-bedroom beach bungalows surviving the influx of tech money over the past decade, and a few newer homes that hadn't.

"The place you're looking for is at the end of the block on the right," Richie said, pointing through the windshield. "Little craftsman with a wheelchair ramp in front."

Calvin jolted as though he'd been hit with a Taser. His eyes were big, unblinking. "Hold up, the guy you owed the money to is in a wheelchair?"

"Yeah, so what? You afraid he's gonna run you over?"

Calvin lowered the gun to his lap and his shoulders dropped, all the air leaving his body with a sigh.

"What's the problem?" Richie asked.

Calvin stared through the windshield, his gaze lost in the grey night. "Things just got a lot more complicated."

"So we were set up," Richie said, trailing a few paces behind Calvin as they walked down the sidewalk. "So what? Haven't you ever had a bad date before?"

Calvin wheeled around and grabbed a fistful of Richie's shirt, shaking him like a doll. "Typical rich-ass attitude. You got what you needed, so screw everyone else, right?"

"What exactly are you hoping I'm gonna bring to this party? 'Cause where I come from we sue people, we don't shoot them."

Calvin let go of Richie's shirt and tucked the gun into his

belt. "We're not gonna shoot nobody, all right? I ain't no banger, but I am one hell of a thief. So we gonna go up there and see what's up and then we're gonna figure out a way to break in and take back what's ours."

Richie's eyebrows knitted together. "By *ours* you mean the bank's?"

"Yeah, that's right, Richie Rich. Just like that two grand you pocketed. You gonna give that back to the bank or are you gonna shut the fuck up?"

Richie readjusted the shirt around his shoulders. "I've established that I'm not rich anymore, so can you please stop calling me that?"

Calvin glanced anxiously up and down the street. "All you gotta do is stand lookout and then drive us out of here. You think you can handle that?"

"No."

Calvin grabbed his shirt again and dragged him down the sidewalk.

They approached the small craftsman with the wheelchair ramp slowly, purposefully, though it was clear neither had much idea what to do once they got there. The house was lit only by a single porch light, the front windows dark. The house to the left was even darker, and the one to the right had a single window that glowed and flickered from a television inside.

"I'm gonna go around that side," Calvin whispered, pointing to the left. "I can get over that fence and then I'll see what's up. You got a cell phone?"

"Why?"

"Give it up," Calvin said.

Richie reluctantly handed him his cell. "What're you gonna do? Google how to break into a house?"

Calvin sent himself a text from Richie's phone and then handed it back. "Turn the sound off," he instructed. "I'm gonna text you once I see what's up. But if you see anyone coming, hit me up and I'll jump out the back fence."

"This should go just fine," Richie said, turning the phone's ringer off and tucking it back into his pants pocket. "It worked out so well for everyone this morning."

"You got that on vibrate?"

"No."

"Then how the hell you gonna know when I text you if you got it in your pocket?"

"I would have thought of that," Richie said, pulling the phone back out. "But you probably gave me a concussion when you knocked me out, so I'm a little hazy at the moment."

"All right, now stay on this side of the street, maybe up there near that tree, and don't bring any attention to yourself. And if you see anyone come up to the house—"

"Text you, yeah, I got it. You just told me that."

"Hey, would you relax? Damn."

"Don't tell me to relax, you're the one acting all jumpy and shit."

"Shut up, I'm fine," Calvin said, glancing behind him. "Now get over there and wait."

Richie retreated to the tree as Calvin darted across the street and disappeared into the darkness between the craftsman and the house beside it. Even though there wasn't another soul on the street, Richie pretended to look at his phone, pantomiming a search for an address he wasn't sure about. He had the sudden impulse to make a run for it, to dash back to his Subaru and take off before any shit went down. He took a few steps in that direction, trying to do the math on whether he could get back to his place, grab his bags and hit the road before his new friend could call some of his buddies and have them there to put the bullet in him that he couldn't. He considered the traffic, the odds of making every light. Twenty minutes? Thirty? Fuck it. He'd take the risk. He was reaching into his pocket for his keys when his phone vibrated.

But it was a call, not a text.

Crap. Garrison had probably been watching him the whole time. He answered the phone and whispered as casually as he could, "What's going on?"

"You bored out there all by yourself?" a man's voice asked.

The voice was deep, unfamiliar. And it scared Richie shitless.

"I'm fine," he said, stupidly.

"Why don't you come inside where it's warm," the man on the other end suggested.

"I'm okay out here."

"But your friend Calvin is not so okay in here."

Richie's mind raced. "Who's Calvin?" he asked.

The man laughed. "Are you turning on him already?"

He looked toward the house. "Who is this?"

"I'm the guy pointing a gun at your idiot partner's head. Come have a look."

The door to the craftsman opened and light streaked out onto the porch. Richie ducked behind a tree. "Put Garrison on the phone," he said.

There was a rustling sound on the end of the line and then the man returned, still laughing. "There's no reception in the morgue, so Garrison can't talk right now."

Richie's chest constricted. "You killed him?"

The man couldn't stop giggling. "Hold on," he said.

A second later Calvin's weary voice filled Richie's ear. "Sorry, man," he said.

"Garrison?"

"No, that was my cousin."

Richie's temples throbbed and another sharp pain spread across his forehead. "Your cousin? What the hell are you talking about? Jesus, did you set me up?"

"It ain't like that."

"No? What's it like?"

"They got me."

"I thought you said you were a good thief? You suck!"

Calvin screamed into the phone. "Go, man! Get the hell outta—"

Richie made a startled move for the sidewalk as a red light flashed across his eyes. He took two more steps before realizing the light was still there, only now it was making tight circles on his shirt, over his chest. He froze as the man's voice returned. "Not a good idea to run," he said. "I like a moving target."

Richie's eyes followed the red beam from his chest, all the way across the street, to the figure standing on the porch, pointing a laser-scoped rifle at him.

CHAPTER EIGHT

"GENTLEMEN, LET ME explain something to you," Connor Weeks said, rolling his wheelchair in front of Calvin and Richie. "When you get away with something, you should *stay* away."

The three henchmen on either side of them in the wood-accented living room laughed.

"And what exactly did we get away with?" Calvin asked, his anger barely contained.

"Your lives, for one thing," Connor said.

"Why'd you set us up?"

"Because ten years' worth of taking bets from losers like your new friend here wouldn't be worth a quarter of what I took from that pathetic little bank. And thanks to the sublime performance in the lobby, the police will be barking up all the wrong trees trying to figure out which of the bodies dead on the floor is responsible." He smiled at his men. "So will Sotereanos. By the time he works out who stole from him—if he ever does—I'll be living the good life on an isolated beach somewhere in the South Pacific."

"Won't your wheels get stuck in the sand?" Calvin said.

"Would you please shut up," Richie snapped at him. "Connor, listen, c'mon, we aren't gonna say anything and you know it."

"Yes, I do." He looked to one of his men. "Let's do this. I'm done with these two."

The man beside Calvin crossed to the hallway.

"Hold on," Richie said, "we can work something out."

Connor laughed. "So young and full of piss."

"Better than being old and full of shit," Calvin said.

"Seriously! Shut up!" Richie yelled at him.

The henchman returned with a badly perspiring man in a wrinkled suit. The man's face was pinched, rat-like. He twitched like a rat, too, his pink eyes nervously darting from face to face as if trying to find an ally. Both Richie and Calvin recognized him, though neither could immediately place from where.

"There he is!" Connor said with a flourish. "The man of the hour. Gentlemen, meet your partner in crime, without whom none of us would be here today."

Something clicked in Calvin's mind and he realized where he'd seen him before—being interviewed on the channel four news. "You work at the bank," he said.

David Perlstein ignored the two newcomers. "Connor, I have to get going."

"Oh, what's your rush?" Connor said. He snapped his fingers twice and put out his hand. Perlstein handed him a wooden box. "Boys, do you realize the risk this man has taken? You look at him and perhaps you don't suspect it, but it's the God's honest truth, he's the bravest of us all. The absolute bravest." He shook a finger at Perlstein. "Though, that FBI Agent sure did have your number! Be honest, when she suggested that my men were already in the bank when you arrived this morning, you must have shit yourself."

"It was an uncomfortable moment, yes," Perlstein said.

"But handled well, I have no doubt. No doubt at all."

"Thank you, Connor," Perlstein said, clearly straining to make his smile appear genuine. "But Sotereanos is expecting me. I'm already late to meet him."

"He must be so pissed!" Connor laughed and his henchmen followed along.

"That's putting it mildly," Perlstein said, wiping the sweat from his palms on his pant leg. "It's causing him to act irrationally."

"For Sotereanos, that's saying something," Connor said, eliciting more chuckles from his men.

"I've tried to impress upon him that it's not a good idea for me to see him tonight, but he's insisting."

"Well, if he's *insisting*," Connor said, as if not taking any of this seriously.

"If I don't show up, he's going to start suspecting me of something. I can put the blame on that idiot buyer they had, Stanton, but if I don't play this exactly right, he won't believe a word I say. I have to go, now."

"Yes, yes. I agree that you do. But I asked you here to thank you in person first, for everything you've done."

The bank manager practically genuflected. "I would do anything for you, Connor."

Connor looked warmly at him. "Yes, I truly believe you would."

He then pulled a .38 from under the blanket covering his legs and shot him in the chest. Perlstein let out a quick puff of air, his rat-face widening in shock. His pink eyes watered, but then softened, as though he had, all at once, found relief. Knees buckling, he fell to the floor. Calvin and Richie stared in stunned disbelief as Connor looked at the dead man for a long moment, a passing shadow of sadness crossing his expression.

"As you can see, gentlemen," he said, his face hardening again. "There is no negotiating to be done here. Despite your assurances of silence, I can't have any loose ends." He retrained his .38 on Calvin. "You really should have stayed away. Until you showed up uninvited, I was considering allowing you two to live."

Calvin closed his eyes, there was nothing to be done. Death was coming for him, he could feel it pulling him down. Only one thought animated his mind. "I'm sorry, Martin," he whispered.

Richie looked on in horror as Connor extended the gun, its barrel only a foot from Calvin's chest. And BLAM.

Connor's head snapped back, the gun falling from his out-stretched hand as his forehead exploded, brain tissue and blood flying out like confetti. Everyone dropped to the floor—though the henchman to Calvin's right was a hair too slow. A bullet sliced through his neck, leaving him gurgling up blood as the room was torn apart. It was as if they were all in a blender whirring at top speed, glass flying everywhere, bullets fired from an automatic weapon destroying everything in their path. Lamps shattered, furniture shredded, the walls pockmarked with holes.

Richie pressed his chest to the floor, covering his head and waiting for the carnage to abate. It seemed like it never would. "This way!" he called to Calvin, who was already pulling the wooden box from Connor's lap. He crawled on his stomach toward the hallway, Calvin crawling behind him. They disappeared up the hall as the shredded front door, its hinges blown to hell, was kicked open. The last of Connor's men capable of mounting a defense sprang to his feet and fired wildly before he was struck dead, his gun falling as silent as he now was. As quiet as the whole damn house was.

The three men entered with the same brazen confidence as they had at Luke Stanton's house in Santa Clarita.

As two spread out to check the house, the leader of the pack stood over David Perlstein's body. With a flash of anger he kicked him in the stomach. It was like kicking a bag half-filled with sand, and the lifeless body rolled only slightly before falling back into place.

The man turned to the last henchman breathing, who was bleeding from seven or eight different places. "Where is it?" he asked.

"They took it," he sputtered.

"Who?"

"Kiss my ass," he managed to say before taking his last, labored breath.

"Stavos," one of the men called out.

Stavos turned to his best friend, Christos, holding up the duffle bag from the bank. "Is it in there?" he asked.

"No," Christos said, re-zipping the bag. "Only money."

"Listen," the other man said. He held up his hand for quiet and then pointed toward the ceiling. Scuffling sounds traveled above them from right to left. Stavos moved quickly back down the hallway, stopping at the hall closet door, which was ajar. He stepped inside and looked up to where the attic's trapdoor had been removed.

Richie and Calvin duck-walked to the end of the low-ceilinged attic and pushed open the window looking out over the backyard.

"In case I forget to mention it later," Richie said as he climbed onto the ledge of the window, "thank you so much for bringing me along."

And then he jumped.

His knees, already bruised from the car accident, buckled badly when he landed on the grass below, pain shooting up into his hips like an electrical current. It took a moment for him to collect himself as he stood, raising his hands for Calvin to toss down the box he'd pulled from Connor's lap. Calvin crouched over the window frame, one leg dangling free, the other still planted on the attic floor, when there was a clatter of noise behind him. He turned to see the assassin pop up through the attic hatch and swing his gun toward him. Before he could fully react, the gun fired, knocking him backwards, through the open window.

Stavos and his men tore into the backyard as distant sirens grew louder.

"We have to go!" Christos warned.

Stavos seethed, running to the back porch before spinning back around. "I know I hit him!"

But the two men, one black, the other white, were nowhere to be found.

CHAPTER NINE

DETECTIVE SUTHERLAND SQUATTED next to the body of David Perlstein, using a pen to move the collar of his shirt to get a better look at the bullet hole in his chest. "Son of a bitch didn't have so much as a parking ticket," he said.

"Be that as it may," said his partner, Detective Hector Lopez, shaking his head at the four other bodies scattered around the torn-up living room, "someone was very angry with him."

The room smelled of fresh gunpowder and stale sweat. Sutherland stood and nodded to the forensic photographer, who resumed taking overlapping pics of the dead bodies in relation to each other. As the other CSI gathered evidence and the seven or eight LAPD officers catalogued the scene, Lopez said, "Gotta be connected to the bank job, right?"

"That, or he had the unluckiest day in history."

"Lakers gave him a run for it tonight, though," Lopez said.

"Yeah, that last shot was brutal," Sutherland agreed. "Guy was behind mid-court, for Christ's sake."

"Detectives?" an officer called out. "We got something."

Sutherland and Lopez followed the officer into the kitchen.

"Well, that answers that," Detective Lopez said.

On a shelf above the microwave were two masks—one a ski mask, the other opaque.

"So," Sutherland said, rubbing the stubble on his cheek. "Double-cross, maybe. Perlstein helps rob the bank, his partners then eliminate him and the other members of the crew."

Lopez nodded. "Okay, let's do the math. Five guys survived the bank this morning. One of them goes through a windshield, leaving the two who were in the vault and the two drivers. I'm gonna go out on a limb here and suggest that forensics matches two of those bodies out there to the masks in here."

"Possible," Sutherland agreed. "We'll see."

"If that's right, that leaves two people still at large."

"The drivers."

"The drivers, yeah."

Sutherland drew in a breath. "It's time we call our friends at the Bureau."

Lopez took out his phone. "They better hurry," he said. "If this shit keeps up, there's not gonna be anyone left to arrest."

The McDonald's on La Brea was open until two-thirty in the morning, so Calvin and Richie had an hour left to sit there and try to figure out what the hell to do next. The place was empty, except for a dude who'd pulled the short straw in life sitting at a table drinking coffee, having a mumbled conversation with a companion only he could see. Calvin watched him as Richie continued to stare in amazement into the wooden box and occasionally reach for another French fry.

"You look at that crazy, brokedown dude right there," Calvin said, "and it's easy not to believe in God. But, man, it is a true-ass miracle that I'm sittin' here, still alive."

"It wasn't a miracle," Richie said, washing down another fry with a sip of Diet Coke. "But it was lucky as hell, I'll give you that."

Calvin reached across the table and slammed the box closed. He pointed at the bullet hole in the lid. "That's a fucking miracle," he said. "A few inches higher and I'm a dead man. And what about them showing up right when we was about to get shot by Connor? I mean, at the *exact second* we needed it, they start shooting up the place? How do you explain that?"

"Did you not hear me the first time?" Richie said. "You're reading too much into it. It was luck—which I *am* a firm believer in. We had it, Connor didn't. I mean, what about him and those other assholes? If it wasn't luck, that means God *chose* them to die instead of us?"

"Maybe he did."

"Yeah, right. If God exists, he doesn't play favorites."

"How the hell do you know?"

"Because if he did," Richie said, "why would he choose guys like you?"

"What do you mean, guys like *me*?"

"Don't get all butt-hurt, I'm only saying you should recognize the choices you've made in life that put you in that situation to begin with."

"You were in the same damn *situation*, boy. You think you different than me?"

Richie chewed another fry. "I don't even know you, Garri—. I mean, *Calvin*. But I know your type."

"Oh, it's like that?"

Richie leaned across the table and whispered, "You're a car-jacker who chose to rob a bank. That's a definite type."

"First off, shit-for-brains, I'm not a carjacker. I'm a car *thief*.

There's a difference. And second of all, you robbed a goddamn bank yourself."

Richie shrugged. "Not by choice."

Calvin sat back and studied him, unsure whether to punch him or school him. "You and I are the same damn type, fool," he said.

Richie grimaced. "Please."

"See that? You so wrapped up in your white privilege, you can't even recognize it."

"Oh, here it comes," Richie said, rolling his eyes.

"Man, it ain't coming or going, it's always here. See, it was your *choices* that led you to that bank, same as mine did. But just because they were *different* choices, don't mean the person *making* them is any different. It's only that you had better options than becoming a car thief because you white and you had money. So you took all that white boy capital from your daddy and became a gambling addict instead of a criminal. Hell, brothers in the hood don't have all them high-class ways to screw up their lives, like they do in Beverly Hills. That's the only difference between you and me, Richie Rich. Powder cocaine versus crack cocaine. *Options*."

Richie leaned back into the red, molded-plastic seat and sucked Diet Coke up through his straw. He placed the cup back down and said, "You got it all figured out, huh?"

Calvin shook his head. "I ain't got nothing figured out."

"Well, we better come up with something before neither of us have any more options."

Calvin nodded at the wooden box. "I don't even know what those things are."

Richie took out one of the gold coins, ran his thumb along the irregular, ragged edge. "This one has some dude in a chariot," he said.

"Put that away, fool," Calvin said, glancing at the homeless guy who was paying them no mind, then over his shoulder at the two Latino women working behind the counter.

"Relax," Richie said, dropping the coin back in the box and picking out another, this one silver. "I don't think those Russian guys are gonna be coming in for a Big Mac any time soon."

"Russian? They weren't Russian. They were Italian or something."

"Italian? You better guess again. That wasn't an Italian accent."

"What the hell does it matter?"

"If it doesn't matter, then let's say they were Russian."

Calvin grabbed the coin from him, dropped it back into the box and slammed it closed. "We can say they were the goddam Jamaican bobsled team, if it'll get you to shut up about it."

Richie ate his last French fry. "They definitely weren't Jamaican."

Calvin leaned back and ran his hands down his face. "You're fucking exhausting."

Richie finished off the Diet Coke, then wiped his mouth with a napkin. "Look," he said, his tone turning serious. "I have an idea what we can do with these."

Calvin shook his head. "There ain't no *we* in this equation."

"Oh, come on. Like it or not, we're in this thing together now. We're like Black Cassidy and the Sundance Kid."

"This ain't a game," Calvin said, leveling his weary eyes on Richie. "You don't seem to get that. So from here on, I'm gonna take care of things myself."

"Yeah, right, what're you gonna do with these? Make a necklace out of them so you can look like you're livin' large with the bling-bling?"

"That's cold."

Richie grew more resolute. "If it weren't for me leading the way back there, you'd still be lying on Connor's floor getting ready to party with some big Italian-Russian-Jamaican dude."

Calvin stared hard at him, then said, "Say what you got to say."

Richie leaned forward and took on a more conspiratorial tone. "All right, since there's obviously a lot of heat on these coins, we need someone who can handle this quietly and fast, before the Psycho Posse catches up to us again."

"True that," Calvin nodded.

"Now, my dad used to do business with this guy that's connected to some very heavy hitters with lots of money and few ethics."

Calvin pointed a finger at him. "Options," he said.

"Point taken," Richie said. "So, we connect with him and he gets one of his clients to take these coins off our hands for some serious cake, so I can take Connor's place in Fiji and you can open up a Pizza Hut franchise or something."

Calvin stared at him across the table. "That's it? That's all you got?"

"What more do you need?"

"More than what you're giving me. I thought you had some names, son. But all that bullshit you spewed boils down to you knowing a guy who *might* know some other guys."

Richie waved him off. "Fine," he said. "Then I'll take my cut of that box right now, so you can go with plan B and walk your half into Eddie's Liquor Mart and ask some dude who barely speaks the language to give you change. I know how to play this, Calvin. So let me get it done. You gotta trust me on this."

Calvin considered, then said, "All right, we do your thing, see if your dad's boy can get us a buyer. But I don't trust you worth a damn, so until we cash out, I ain't letting that box out of my sight."

"Then we have a problem, don't we?" Richie shrugged. "'Cause I'm sure as hell not gonna let you walk out of here with it. So what's it gonna be?"

Tracey sat in her pajamas and robe at the table off the kitchen, her eyes not leaving Richie sitting opposite her. The exhaustion of the longest day she'd ever lived through showed on her face. Her makeup had been scrubbed off hours before, revealing the darker patches of skin on her forehead, and her hair was tightly wrapped up with bobby-pins under a yellow silk scarf. Under normal circumstances, she would not have been comfortable being laid so bare, but at the moment, she truly didn't give a shit.

"Baby," Calvin said, his voice low to ensure he didn't wake Martin. "He wasn't gonna leave me with the box and I wasn't gonna go to his place. If I didn't come home tonight to show you what was up, you'd think something was wrong."

Tracey's eyes finally came off Richie and shifted to her husband. "It's three o'clock in the morning and I got a white frat boy with a box of stolen coins sitting in my kitchen. What part of that you think isn't wrong?"

"Well, for starters," Richie said, enjoying Calvin's discomfort under the glare of his pissed-off wife. "I was never in a fraternity. I didn't even go to college. Did go to some crazy sorority parties though."

Tracey sat motionless. It was clear that if she addressed the fool sitting next to her husband talking nonsense, there would be no chance Martin would stay asleep.

"It's only until we sell them," Calvin said.

"And I know a guy who knows a guy," Richie added.

Tracey's eyes shifted back to Richie, then she slowly stood, tightened the belt on her robe, and walked from the room.

"Don't worry," Richie said. "I think she likes me."

CHAPTER TEN

MARTIN WAS USUALLY the first one up. First to sleep, first to rise, that's the way things went in the house he shared with his parents, his grandmother and, on occasion, his grandmother's boyfriend, Singletary, whom he called G-Dad. But this morning, Martin awoke to find his mother in his bed, her warm brown eyes already open and looking at him.

"Why're you in here?" he asked.

"I missed you," Tracey said. She watched as he stretched his arms upward.

"You missed me while I was asleep?" he asked.

"Yes. I missed you so much I tried to jump right into your dreams."

He chuckled and rolled away from her on the narrow twin mattress, but she grabbed him and pulled him into her chest before he could get away. He was getting so strong. If only the room was big enough for a queen mattress, she could continue to sneak in and sleep with him comfortably. Pretty soon, she realized, he was going to outgrow both the bed and her playful grasp.

"Did Daddy come home?" he asked.

Tracey wished she could keep on hugging him forever, keep

him an innocent, giggling little boy, and she silently cursed Calvin for chipping away at his childhood. "Yeah, Daddy came home," she said, stroking his back with her fingers. "Just like I told you he would." Despite her efforts, he squirmed free and jumped from the bed. "Hold on, Martin, he's still asleep," she called after him. "Besides, I need to talk to you before you see him."

Martin stopped at the door, looked surprised by a yawn that crept up on him. "About what?"

"He brought a friend home with him last night."

"A friend?" Martin asked, as though the word tasted strange on his tongue.

"That's right," she said. "A white friend."

Martin's eyes widened in disbelief. "That's weird," he said.

Tracey nodded, unsure which part her son thought was weird.

Calvin stumbled from his bedroom a half hour later to find Martin tentatively poking Richie with a plastic baseball bat as he snored on the couch.

"What're you doing, little man?" he asked.

"Poking him with this bat," Martin said. "Mommy said it was okay."

Calvin wiped some sleep from the corner of his eye and said, "Do it harder."

"Really?"

"Really."

Martin obeyed his father and Richie's left eye popped open. "Who're you?" he said.

"Martin."

"You know how to make a Bloody Mary, Martin?"

Martin took a step back, the bat still raised in his hand, and then ran to hide behind his mother, who sat at the table off the kitchen drinking coffee with his Grandma V.

"Get your ass off my couch," Calvin said. "This ain't no Holiday Inn."

Richie pulled off the thin blanket and swung his legs to the floor. He looked over at the two women, their coffee cups hovering halfway to their pinched mouths. They were already dressed, wearing their church clothes.

"Morning," Richie said, a shiver of cold running through his body.

"It's Sunday," Vanessa said, putting down her cup.

"Yes, ma'am," Richie said.

"You believe in Jesus?"

"I'm not sure how to answer that, ma'am."

She shook her head. "That's your problem, right there."

He reached down for one of his shoes. "You can add it to the list."

"Don't get smart with me, boy. This is my house, you understand that?"

"I do," Richie said, slipping the shoe on and reaching for the other.

"Good. 'Cause I don't need you bringing your troubles in here. We got enough of those on our own."

Richie sighed as he pulled on the other shoe. "Believe me, there's some overlap in that area at the moment."

"I said, don't get smart with me," she snapped. "I'll knock that right out your mouth. What I'm saying is that I can't lay all this at Jesus's feet and ask him to help carry it. There ain't none of this that's right, and he don't play around when it comes to this sort of sin. So whatever it is you have to do, I don't wanna know nothing about it, but I do want you doing it quick, you got me?"

"We're in total agreement, ma'am," Richie said.

Vanessa looked at her daughter. "White boy keeps calling me ma'am. I can't tell if he's trying to be respectful or if he's a smart-ass."

Tracey finished her coffee and snapped her fingers at Martin, who was under the table. "Get out from under there, Martin," she said. "Go put your shoes on, we gonna be late for church."

A heavy bass line, pounding out of custom speakers inside an approaching car, drew Calvin to the window. He pulled the curtain back slightly and stared out at the '75, metallic blue Ford Thunderbird pulling to the curb, blocking the driveway with its long body. "Shit, we don't need this right now," he said under his breath.

"Who is it, daddy?" asked Martin.

He snapped his fingers at his son. "Go get your shoes on like your momma said."

"I'm guessing it's not the ice cream truck," Richie said, stepping next to him.

"Shut up," Calvin answered. "Get away from the window."

Calvin let the curtain drop and crossed to the front door. Before opening it, he stared hard at Richie until he obediently backed away.

Tracey stood up from the table. "Who is it?"

"Randall," Calvin said.

"Damn," she sighed.

"Can I see?" Martin asked.

"You stay in here with Mom and Grandma V, little man," Calvin said, opening the front door and pushing open the screen.

By the time Calvin stepped onto the porch, Randall Washington was halfway up the patchy front lawn. Delvon's little brother, Reese, walked beside him, looking nervous as hell. The driver, a notoriously silent dude named Big Mike, stayed behind the wheel of the Thunderbird, eyes hidden behind a pair of black Ray-Ban sunglasses.

"'Sup, Calvin," Randall said, stopping on the lawn in front of the raised porch. "Been a while."

Calvin nodded casually. He could smell the weed coming off Randall like he wore it as cologne. No doubt he'd been making up for the blunts he couldn't smoke during his stay in Corcoran State Prison. "I heard you got out," he said.

"Last week. Twenty months. Good behavior, you know what I'm sayin?"

"You look like you been hittin' them weights."

Randall gave a side-mouth grin, clearly pleased. He was wearing a black wife-beater that made it impossible not to notice the added bulk. He'd always been solidly built, but he looked like he had put twenty pounds of muscle onto his lean frame. His afro had grown too, but he had it pulled straight back, away from his face, making it easier to see the knife scar half an inch above his left temple. "Sorry about your cousin," he said. "Garrison was for real."

Calvin nodded. "We all pretty shook up by it."

"Can't believe they got Sollo and Floyd, too, man. That shit's crazy. So what the fuck happened?"

Calvin glanced at Reese, then back to Randall. "Whatever you heard, I guess."

"Nigger, please, don't even try to play it like that." Randall nodded at Reese, who kept his hands deep in the pockets of his low-slung pants, his belt flopping below his waist like a tired tongue. "Homeboy already told me he set Sollo up with a G-ride you delivered to him right before this shit went down. I know you was with his set, so why don't you stop with the bullshit and say what happened up in that bank yesterday?"

Calvin shrugged as casually as he could manage. "I can't help you, man. I mean, Garrison didn't even tell me what was up. So Reese must be confused about my involvement, because I was with his brother in the shop yesterday morning, then here once I found out about my cousin."

Randall sized him up, then said, "You better be for real, 'cause Sollo and I had some unfinished business and I wanna get what's mine. People be saying somebody got some serious coin from that bank."

"People talk some crazy shit."

Randall spit on a patch of dirt at his feet. "I'm gonna give you one more chance to say what's up."

Calvin hoped Randall couldn't see the heartbeat pulsing in his neck like a jackhammer. "Like I told you, I got nothin' to say about it."

Randall pulled a .9 mm out from where it was tucked in his belt behind his back. He held it down at his thigh, all casual like. "You sure about that?"

Big Mike slid every inch of his six-foot-six frame out of the Thunderbird and rested his thick forearm on the car door.

"Damn," Calvin said, "Sollo's only been dead for twenty-four hours and you already trying to take his place."

Randall pointed the 9 millimeter at him. "Long live the king, right?"

The screen door behind Calvin squeaked open and closed. Without even looking, he knew it was Tracey. He moved to the side to block her from the line of fire, but she pushed her way up to stand beside him. "W'sup, Randall," she said. "It's been a minute."

Though Calvin hated seeing her there, there was no doubt her presence dramatically lowered the odds of a bullet leaving the chamber.

"Damn, girl," Randall said, lowering his gun. "You still looking fine."

She had grown up with Randall, had even kissed him in the seventh grade, and she was one of only a handful of locals who could remember when he was a sweet little boy instead of a total fucking menace. "Looks like you takin' care of yourself, too," she said.

"You know how it is," Randall said. "Yard time is hard time if you don't hit them weights."

She nodded. "No doubt you survived just fine. In fact, your mom was talking about it last week in church, said she was real happy to have you home, hopes it lasts a while longer this time. We're gonna see her in church today, so we'll be sure to tell her you stopped by."

Randall's smile turned into a laugh. "You crazy-ass bitch."

Her gaze hardened. "For real," she said.

He tucked the gun back into his belt and Big Mike climbed back behind the wheel.

"We still got business, Calvin," he said. "I'm gonna find out what's up."

"If Garrison didn't tell me, he didn't tell nobody. Sollo made sure his crew kept it tight."

"Yeah, well, Sollo's a dead man now," Randall said. "So things about to change."

"No doubt," Calvin said.

"That's right. Ain't no doubt at all." Another smirk brightened his face. "I'll be seein' you around." He winked at Tracey. "Be seein' you too, girl."

Tracey kept quiet and Randall and Reese headed back to the Thunderbird.

"Yo, Reese?" Calvin called after them. "You best stop spreading rumors, understand?"

"Yeah, man," Reese said, hanging his head like a wounded animal.

Randall kicked him in the ass. "Shut up, punk. Get the fuck in the car."

As the Thunderbird pulled away, the bass line pounding so deep he felt it in his chest, Calvin said to Tracey, "Start packing."

CHAPTER ELEVEN

THIS WAS NOT how Agent Grace Luelle had planned to spend her Sunday. She had intended to make the two-hour drive up to Oxnard for her best friend's baby shower, but instead of eating spongy white cake and playing stupid games like The Baby Bucket List, she stood at a white board on the eighth floor of the Federal building on Wilshire Boulevard in Westwood, studying the faces of eight dead men. She held a pen between her thumb and index finger, tapping her thigh like a metronome set to three hundred beats per minute.

"The money was not recovered at the Venice house," she said, pen still beating away. She pointed with her other hand at Gavin's picture on the board. "But the money left the bank with Gavin Weeks and was missing when the Camaro was recovered. Nobody saw the driver, but according to eye witnesses, an unidentified black man was on the scene immediately after the accident. He talked to Mr. Weeks and then left without the duffle. Which means—"

"The driver took it," said Agent Frank Daniels, fresh from the Academy and eager to please.

Agent Luelle turned away from the board and tossed the

pen onto her desk. "Yes, okay. It's the most logical assumption, so I'll buy that for now. And we assume the black man spotted at the scene—who made sure he wasn't recorded as he talked to Gavin Weeks—was the same person who left the Toyota from the bank job at the curb."

"Strange behavior if it wasn't the driver for the black crew," Agent Eddie Hicks said. Hicks had a long face that looked like a partly deflated balloon—the top half still held its shape, more or less, but his cheeks sagged inward and his jaw tapered quickly to the rounded tip of his weak chin. He'd been on the job twenty-two years and despite looking like a cartoon dog who'd been doused with a hose, he was probably the sharpest agent in any room. "And by the way," he said. "We need to get some better names than the *black crew* and the *white crew*."

"Steve's working on a couple names for the press," Agent Luelle said, waving him off. "What's bugging me is *why* the Toyota driver was there at all. Why risk being seen like that?"

Agent Hicks used his thumb to crack the knuckle of each finger on his left hand as he said, "Maybe he was supposed to meet up with the Camaro. Maybe that was the spot they'd predetermined to do some sort of exchange and the Camaro screwed it up by hitting the telephone pole. Maybe everyone was supposed to meet there, along with the two guys from the vault, get in their car, which nobody has identified, and be on their way?"

Agent Luelle turned back to the board and the four blank columns titled: GETAWAY DRIVER #1, GETAWAY DRIVER #2, VAULT MAN #1, and VAULT MAN #2.

"Makes sense that it was the four of them that planned the double-cross." Agent Hicks continued, "The getaway drivers stay safe outside and the vault guys go in, fire off the shot that starts all the chaos, rob the safe deposit box, and then blow out of there."

"But if Getaway Driver One and Getaway Driver Two knew ahead of time it was going to be a double-cross, why would both of them wait?" Agent Luelle said, working through the logic. "You'd only need one car at that point, right?"

"They had to wait in case there were any survivors. They'd get them out of there and then kill them later, exactly like they did David Perlstein and the other members of their crew."

"Only one problem with that," Agent Don Pierce said, stepping up with a file in his hands. He was a timid sort, with thinning hair and nostrils that flared when he got excited. "David Perlstein didn't actually exist."

Agent Luelle held out her hand and Pierce handed her the file.

"Then who had the bullet hole in his Weeks'?" asked Agent Daniels.

Pierce smiled and his nostrils practically exploded. "His brother."

As Pierce spoke, Agent Luelle studied the pictures of two young men in their early twenties paper clipped to the front flap of the file.

"David Perlstein's real name was David Weeks. He and Connor had quite the early career as petty thieves. That is until Connor fell from a fire escape on one of their jobs up in San Francisco and broke his neck. His very nervous little brother left him behind in the alley where he landed and he'd spend the next seven years in prison and the rest of his life in a wheelchair."

Agent Luelle studied the crime scene photo of David's body. "I guess it took Connor thirty years to figure out how to pay him back."

"After Connor's accident," Pierce went on, "David changed his name to cover his past, got a college degree in accounting, and became a CPA. Before working for American Federal, he worked for an import company in Boston that went out of business six years ago."

"What did they import?" Hicks asked.

"Handmade rugs from Europe," Agent Luelle said, her eyes scanning the file.

Pierce shrugged. "All legit."

Agent Luelle looked up. "I don't see a ballistics report."

"It's in there."

"No, Don, it's not."

"I'll go see what happened to it."

"Just tell me what it said," she said, flashing annoyance for the first time.

"Oh, sure. Perlstein was the only one of the vics killed by Connor Weeks's gun."

"Interesting," Agent Luelle said, her eyes narrowing.

Hicks said, "Then we can deduce that Connor comes up with a plan to rob a bank and calls on his little brother for help. And when the job is done, he kills him."

"So much for brothers in arms," Agent Luelle said, picking up the pen from the desk. Turning to the board, she wrote "Weeks" under Perlstein's name and then the pen went back to work against her thigh. "And if that's the case," she said, "then who the hell shot Connor and his men?"

The Sotereanos house sat on three acres at the end of Preston Lane, in upper Bel Air. The house was eleven thousand square feet, a mid-century masterpiece with polished concrete floors, silk rugs larger than a two-car garage, hand-painted wallpaper, and views that overlooked the Bel Air reservoir and stretched all the way to downtown LA. At night, standing by the huge, pristine pool, the city lights far below could easily seduce you into believing you were a demi-god, looking down on the mortals who could only look up and dream of the space you called home.

Mikos Sotereanos had started out in manufacturing—his first company made high-end alabaster chess sets. With his next few million he founded Dýnami AE, a marble mining company that grew to be the second largest in Greece. His financial empire grew rapidly from there; at one point, he owned three shopping malls, two in Athens and one in Maroussi. Always looking for another place to spend his money, in the mid-nineties he started Kínisi, an export business that dealt mainly with olive oil and wine but eventually expanded to include metalworks, pottery, and rugs. While Kínisi had started out legitimate, it soon drifted—as did Mikos. A favor for a connected friend led to another favor and pretty soon Mikos had the reputation in certain circles as the man to speak to if you needed to move something without alerting customs officials. All of this expansion had the same effect on Mikos himself. As his wealth grew, so did his capacity for anger and paranoia—which were not in limited supply to begin with.

So it came as no surprise when Mikos slapped his meaty palm across Stavos's face when his son delivered news of the messy killings of Luke Stanton, David Perlstein, and Connor Weeks—all without the benefit of recovering the coins. The blood smeared across Stavos's cheek from his bloodied nose had no emotional effect on Mikos. He slapped him again.

"I'm doing what I can," Stavos said, refusing to wipe away the blood.

Mikos picked up the duffle bag from the glass dining room table and threw it at Stavos, the bills flying into the air. "You call this doing what you can!" He stared at Stavos and took several deep breaths, before nodding once, pleased with his son's silence, which he undoubtedly took as an admission of disgrace and failure. He pulled a handkerchief from his pocket and handed it to him. As Stavos wiped the blood from his face, his father put his arm around his shoulders, turning him to the giant oil painting of his dead mother hanging over the credenza.

"When I married your mother," he began, his gravelly voice suddenly calm. "I could not afford to buy her a ring. So I cut a tiny strand from my father's fishing net and tied it around her finger. It was seven years before I could buy her a proper ring. The diamond I finally gave to her was so small it would catch almost no light at all. Worthless. A poor fisherman who needed to feed his family saw this worthless diamond and he took it from her." His arm tightened around Stavos's neck. "One at a time I took his fingers from him. With each one he begged for mercy. He could not fish without his fingers." He gazed upon the painting of his wife looking down on them both. "Find these men and bring back what's mine." Mikos let go of his son and walked off, waving with disgust at the fallen money littering the floor. "And clean this up."

Stavos continued to stare at the passive face of his mother as he finished wiping the blood from his face. Behind him, his men bent down to pick up the loose bills.

"Stavos?" Christos said as he gathered up a note mixed in with the money.

Stavos dropped the handkerchief onto the credenza and took the slip of paper Christos handed him. The handwritten note explained that a man named Gavin was dead and the money was being returned as a sign of good faith that some debt had been paid. *You won't see me again*, the note ended. It was signed by someone named Richie and printed across the top was a store name: Sammy's Hollywood Souvenirs.

CHAPTER TWELVE

MARTIN DID NOT let go of his mother's hand as she led him into Richie's house.

"How long are we gonna stay here?" he asked.

Tracey looked to Calvin, the corner of her eyebrow raised.

"Couple of days maybe," Calvin said.

Richie turned on the lights and tossed his keys on the entry-hall table. "I wasn't sure if I was ever coming back, so there's not much food or anything. But I do have the essentials, like a PlayStation 4."

Martin let go of his mother's hand. "Really?" he said. "A boy in my school says he has one of those."

"You've never played?"

Martin shook his head.

Richie smirked at Calvin. "No Grand Theft Auto for him, huh?"

"Don't get smart," Tracey warned.

"Okay, okay. How about Fortnite?" Richie asked Martin.

"What's that?"

"What's that?" Richie pretended to stagger. "Are you kidding me?"

child trying to process what he'd heard. "I'm sorry, baby," she said, crossing to sweep him up into her arms. "Everything's all right. I didn't mean to yell like that."

She took Martin back into the living room, leaving Calvin behind.

"Sorry," Richie said with a shrug. "It's not that big of a house."

Calvin remained silent, staring after his family.

"So, ah, I'm sorry to be in the middle of this," Richie said. "But, what do you want to do? I mean, are we going to—"

"Let's go," Calvin said.

"Cool. Okay. I'll get changed and we can hit it."

"Make it quick."

Richie hesitated. "Are you going to—"

"Am I gonna what?" Calvin interrupted, finally looking at him.

Richie pointed at Calvin's black Dickie pants and plain white t-shirt. "We're meeting my contact at the Isis Lounge, so—"

"So what?"

Richie again hesitated, before offering a tight smile. "Nothing. You're good like that."

"Yeah," Calvin nodded. "I know."

Richie parked his Subaru in a twenty-dollar lot south of Hollywood Boulevard, far away from the judgmental eyes in front of the Isis Lounge.

"I really wasn't eavesdropping on your conversation with Tracey," Richie said as he and Calvin walked back up Vine, stepping on the grimy, inlaid stars of mostly forgotten Hollywood royalty. "But I guess you guys are having a bit of a disagreement about all this?"

"Don't worry about it."

"I'm not worried. I'm curious. I heard you say you might be leaving LA when you cash out?"

"For someone who wasn't eavesdropping, you sure did pick up a lot."

"Her voice carries."

"Yeah, no shit."

"Well, for what it's worth, I'm guessing she might change her opinion about us doing business if my dad's lawyer hooks us up with a buyer."

"Tracey's opinions don't change that easily."

"She seems to have warmed up to me a little, though. She even asked me a question earlier—it was how I turned into such a loser with all the advantages I had, but at least she's talking to me." Calvin smiled, which pleased Richie. "Though I am a little hurt you called me *that white boy* when you were arguing with her," he said. "I was hoping with everything we've been through, we were past all that."

Calvin gave him the side-eye. "Past all what?"

"You know, the racial tension."

"I ain't fuckin' tense. Why are you tense? Maybe ask yourself that."

They walked in silence for another half a block before Richie said, "You make me nervous."

Calvin's smile returned with a shake of his head.

Richie said, "Oh, you're enjoying my discomfort, huh?"

"No, man, it's funny to me because growing up I was always the uncomfortable one in my crew. Always afraid of doing something wrong, not looking cool, you know? My mom was always telling me it was good I was like that, hugging me all the damn time, saying she hoped I never changed. She didn't do me no favors, though. In Inglewood, you show that side and you get the shit kicked out of you."

"Your mom still live in Inglewood?"

Calvin took a few silent steps. "She had a stroke. Died when I was twelve."

They walked over Cary Grant and Clark Gable. "My mom had cancer," Richie said, finally. "Made it till I was twenty, though."

"Guess you won that round too, huh?"

"Didn't realize it was a competition."

"Everything's a competition."

They walked in silence for a bit then Richie asked, "What about your dad?"

Calvin kept his eyes on the street up ahead. "He died in prison."

They reached Henry Fonda and Jimmy Durante and Calvin hadn't elaborated on the details of his father's demise, so Richie let the subject go.

They crossed the corner at Vine and Hollywood Boulevard and the Isis Lounge came into view half a block away. The Lounge took up both floors of the old Kingdom Theatre, which once hosted plays put up by a Catholic group, The Knights Of Decorum, extolling the virtues of living a religious life, replete with chastity, teetotalism, piety, and grace. So it was particularly ironic that the club, now named for an Egyptian goddess, attracted a strictly hedonistic crowd who advocated the Knight's virtues only as ironic slug lines printed on designer t-shirts.

Calvin and Richie waded into the thick and desperate crowd out front. Most of the chattering and preening throng standing in line were young women in short dresses, trying to pretend they weren't freezing in the night air. The male of the species was predominantly represented by well-dressed specimens in their mid-twenties, evidently all paid-up members of both Gold's Gym and the Gel Club For Men. There were high-end cars in a long valet line and seven or eight paparazzi holding clunky cameras, smoking cigarettes and chatting amongst themselves, waiting for someone worth chasing down to arrive. It was early, not yet ten, and the heavy hitters wouldn't be arriving for at least another hour.

"You sure you got this?" Calvin asked, as Richie led him to the front of the line.

"He said we'd be on the list," Richie said, not sounding particularly confident.

There were two doormen, one a six-foot-three black man in a black polo-shirt stretched tightly across his barrel chest, the other a lanky white guy with perfectly mussed blonde highlights in an identical polo shirt, holding a clipboard.

"Excuse me," Richie said to the one with the clipboard, but he was ignored.

"What up?" the tall black guy said to Calvin.

Calvin nodded and they dapped knuckles. "How you doin', man?" Calvin said.

"Oh, you guys know each other?" Richie asked, and the doorman looked at him like he was a complete idiot.

"Just do your thing," Calvin said, shaking his head.

"We're meeting someone here," Richie said to the doorman with the clipboard.

"We're at capacity," the doorman said with a dismissive glance. "You're gonna have to get in line and wait for it to clear out a little."

Richie had stood in that line enough times to understand what that meant. "It never clears out," he said.

"No, it really doesn't," the doorman agreed. "But for now we have to keep this area clear, so I need you to step aside."

"I was told we're on the VIP list," Richie said.

The doorman looked at the clipboard. "What are the names?"

"Richie Glass and Calvin—what's your last name?"

"Russell," Calvin said.

They showed their IDs as the doorman flipped a page on the clipboard and then casually stepped aside without apologizing for the attitude. "Have a good time," he said. The tall black doorman leaned to open the door for them, nodding again at Calvin as they went inside.

The Isis Lounge was cavernous, with two elevated stages on either end of the first floor, one set up for a live band, the other currently occupied by a skinny Asian DJ wearing a black hoodie and blaring a Diplo remix. The valley between the two stages was filled with a scrum of dancers. A glass bar that reflected light like a prism ran along the entirety of one wall, with tables and couches hugging the other three walls. In each corner of the first floor hung seven-foot steel cages with go-go dancers writhing to the beat in short white dresses and neon-colored wigs.

"So where's your boy?" Calvin asked, raising his voice over the music.

"VIP section, upstairs," Richie said. "But what do you say we get a couple of drinks before we do this?"

"This ain't a party, this is about business. Keep your focus."

"Don't worry, I'm all about—hey, what's up?"

A passing blonde in a tight red dress gave him a playfully challenging pose. "What's up with you?" she asked, arching a finely plucked brow.

Calvin stepped between them. "He's got chlamydia, that's what up. Have a good night."

The blonde continued on, looking pissed that she had wasted her attention on someone so unworthy.

"I get that you're married, so you're used to not having sex," Richie complained to Calvin over the pounding music. "But my penis still works, so maybe you can cut me some slack."

Calvin glanced up at the long balcony jutting off the second floor. "I feel you, but let's get this done. And then you can put as much stank on your hang-down as you need."

"That's nasty!" Richie laughed. "I'm gonna put that on Twitter, dude."

There was another round of "I can't let you in here" with yet another set of bouncers before they gained access to the rarified air of the second floor VIP section. The music was quieter upstairs, the light diffused into a soft mist, the crowd more sedate. The further into the rear of the club they went, the more evident it became that the people here weren't monitored too closely.

To a certain segment of Hollywood club goers, upstairs at the Isis Lounge was simply referred to as *the second floor*—as though it were a separate club all of its own. Which in many ways, it was. Reserving a table on the second floor ran a couple grand, with bottle service three times that. Celebrities were A-list only (reality TV stars never made the cut) and bouncers looked the other way when rules were broken. Here, music producers in their sixties snorted coke with rock stars in their twenties, and Russian mobsters entertained high-end hookers who looked like Victoria's Secret models.

"That's him," Richie said, nudging Calvin with his elbow. "I think that's him, at least."

"What's that supposed to mean? You know this guy or not?"

"It's been a few years and I only ever saw him on the golf course when I played with my dad."

"Damn, can you sound whiter?"

"Golf isn't only a white thing anymore, or have you forgotten about Tiger Woods?"

"Name another," Calvin challenged him.

Richie thought a moment, then said, "Okay, maybe not professionally, but lots of black people play golf."

"I'm not having this conversation with you."

"Michael Jordan plays golf. And Samuel L. Jackson."

Calvin pointed at Chad. "Is that your boy or not?"

Richie looked past Calvin, narrowed his eyes. "Yeah," he said. "That's him."

Chad Richards sat in the center of a royal blue, semi-circle couch, between two girls in matching mini-skirts who looked like they should be home studying for a geometry test. He wore what could be described as cashmere pajamas that hung loosely on his bloated frame. He was sixty-seven, but his mop of dyed black hair covered his forehead like a young Ringo Starr.

"You sure this guy is hooked up?" Calvin asked out of the corner of his mouth.

"He may look like his only hook up is to the mother ship," Richie assured him. "But he's the real deal."

"This shit better not be a waste of time," Calvin said as they approached the couch, drawing curious stares from the two young women.

"Look who's here!" Chad said. "It's Lenny and Squiggy."

"Hey, Mr. Richards," Richie said.

"You're a big boy now, son," he said, sipping his vodka. "Call me Chad."

"Old habits," Richie shrugged.

"But new opportunities," Chad smiled. "You're looking good, Richie. Your father would be proud."

"Let's not get ahead of ourselves," Richie said.

Chad chuckled. "I was sorry to hear about his passing. He was both a good man and good for business."

"Yours and mine both," Richie agreed.

Chad casually rested his hand on the thigh of the brown-haired girl to his left. "You mentioned on the phone you've been having some cash-flow issues."

"Maybe we can do this without your nieces?" Calvin suggested.

Chad took another sip, set down his glass, and grinned at the two girls. "Why don't you ladies go get yourselves another drink?"

The two girls stood to sidle past Calvin, who didn't move to give them more room. "Don't forget your fake IDs," he said to them as they passed.

Richie took one of the seats vacated by the girls, but Calvin remained standing.

"You're not going to join us?" Chad asked him.

"I'm fine where I am."

"He's not a real *people* person," Richie said.

Calvin said, "This is business for me, not a party."

Chad nodded, his eyes sparkling with amusement. "No reason the two can't coexist. But I suppose more formal introductions are in order. Where exactly did the two of you meet? Let's start there."

Richie looked over to Calvin, then back to Chad. "Through mutual friends," he said.

Chad shook his head. "I find it difficult to believe the two of you have any mutual friends. Unless I'm reading you incorrectly, Calvin?"

"You ain't," Calvin said.

"Does it really matter how we met?" Richie asked.

Chad turned his head on his sweaty neck and looked seriously at him. "If we're to do business, I'm going to need the specifics on how you two came into each other's orbits. One can never be too careful."

"I'm not a cop, if that's what you're thinking," Calvin offered.

"I'm thinking a lot of things. That being one of them, yes."

"He's not a cop," Richie said. "I wouldn't screw you like that."

"No?" Chad winked at him. "Is there another way you'd screw me?"

Richie laughed uncomfortably.

"Yo, pimp, that's not what's happening here," Calvin said.

"I'm sorry?" Chad said. "Which part?"

"You keep acting like a whack job and it's gonna be every damn part."

"I'm not crazy," Chad said, waving him off. "I'm eccentric. Like Vincent Van Gogh. He cut off his ear, yet still managed to paint great works of art. Think of me that way, as an *artist*. The art of the deal and all that. Now tell me how it is that two young men from such different worlds get slammed together and decide to go into business together?"

Calvin shrugged. "Opportunity knocks, you gotta answer."

Chad leaned forward slightly and clasped his hands together. "I'll ask you one more time," he said. "What door were you standing behind, when you heard the knocking?"

When Calvin remained silent, Richie leaned close to Chad and said, "The door to the vault at American Federal Bank in Reseda."

Chad's mouth opened, but no words came out as he worked through the implications of Richie's admission.

"What the hell's wrong with you?" Calvin snapped.

"He's legit," Richie said. "I don't want this whole thing going away because neither of you is willing to back the hell down. He's not gonna talk, I promise. So you gotta trust me that he's cool."

"I don't trust you any more than I trust this Jabba the Hut lookin' fool!"

Chad let loose a disbelieving sort of laugh. "What have you two gotten yourself involved with?"

"We weren't involved in nothin'," Calvin insisted.

"But we know people who were," Richie added.

Chad nodded in continued amazement. "Yes, I believe I saw some of them on the news. It's my understanding they're all dead."

"Not all of them," Calvin said.

"Ahhh," Chad said, putting it all together. "Which means there are others besides me who are interested in what you have. Police included, I assume."

"Yes," Richie said. "So we'd like to finish our business arrangement as quickly and quietly as possible."

Chad clapped Richie's thigh. "Richie, Richie, what would your father say if I were to help you with this…opportunity? I'm not sure he would approve."

"Let's not get overly sentimental," Richie said, squirming under the heavy warmth of Chad's hand. "He certainly helped you with a few of your own *opportunities* over the years."

Chad left his hand on Richie's thigh, giving it two quick squeezes. "You do have a point. I assume you brought something I could look at?"

"Yes," Richie said. "But you're gonna have to move your hand first."

"Why?"

"Because it's blocking my pocket."

Chad's hand came off Richie's leg. "Okay, let's see what you have. That's truly all I'm interested in, anyway."

Richie gave a cursory glance around the room, then pulled out one of the coins and handed it to over.

"Well, I'll be," Chad said, turning the coin with his finely manicured, chubby fingers. "Looks like you two are for real after all."

"That's right, Jabba," Calvin said. "And you better be for real, too."

Chad considered them a moment, then asked, "How many of these do you have?"

Calvin said, "I'd guess about—"

"Eight hundred and seventy-five," Richie said.

"When the hell you count them?" Calvin asked.

"Couldn't sleep last night."

"Last night? Man, don't be messin' with them when I'm not around."

"I wasn't *messing* with them."

Chad put the dime-sized coin in his mouth, then stuck it out on the tip of his tongue.

"Make that eight hundred and seventy-*four*," Richie said. "You can keep that one."

Chad dropped the coin into his palm. "Gentlemen, as the song says," he smiled, breaking into an off-key version of Herman's Hermits. "*Something tells me we're into something good—*"

Calvin stared at him. "What fucking song is that?"

Richie sat forward on the couch. "So we're in business?"

Chad nodded. "If the others are like this, then we're definitely in business."

"Quick business," Calvin said.

Chad's odd laugh returned. "Burning your greedy little fingers, are they?"

"Looks like they burnin' yours right about now, too."

"Indeed, indeed. And as it happens, once I got Richie's phone call, I contacted a client, a connoisseur of antiquities who is very interested in the collection. As soon as you give me the rest of the coins, I'll make the transaction and you two can continue your journey down the yellow brick road."

"Fuckin' A," Richie said.

"Screw that," Calvin said.

"Oh God," Richie sighed. "Come on."

"Is there a problem?" Chad asked.

Calvin stared at him, didn't answer.

Richie shook his head. "Why's there always gotta be a problem with you?"

Calvin finally said, "I wanna be there when you make the deal."

"I'm afraid that's not possible," Chad answered. "My client prefers to remain anonymous."

"And I prefer not to trust complete strangers who never learned to say nope to dope and ugh to drugs."

"I assure you I'm a business man, not a thief."

Calvin leaned closer. "There ain't no fucking difference."

"Touché," Chad said, leaning to the side to hold up a finger for the two girls waiting impatiently at another table for the party to continue.

"There's gotta be a way we can make this work," Richie said.

Chad pulled a business card from his shirt pocket. "I will have to check with my client to see if he's amenable to your demands," he said. "If he is not, I'll give you boys a call and we go our separate ways, no harm, no foul." He held the card out for Calvin. "If, on the other hand, you don't hear from me, then be at that address tomorrow at eleven a.m." As Calvin reached for the card, Chad shifted it towards Richie. "Or should I be giving this to him?"

Calvin again set his eyes hard on him. "You best not be wasting my time."

"Life's much too short for that," Chad said, returning the card to him. "So how about you have a seat and join me in a little magic carpet ride?"

Richie settled into the couch and smiled at the suggestion, but Calvin did not. "C'mon, man," Richie said.

Without another word, Calvin turned and headed back down the stairs.

CHAPTER THIRTEEN

SAM SAT BEHIND the counter wondering if it was worth it to keep the store open any later. It was close to eleven and the crowds of tourists out front had thinned dramatically. While a few of those who had gone to the movies over on Highland would soon stream out onto Hollywood Boulevard and might possibly find their way inside to buy a California prop license plate or an Avengers poster, the odds were long. And Sam always went with the odds.

The front door opened with a ding and Stavos entered with Christos and another man.

"You've got about five minutes before I close," Sam said.

"Very nice shop you have here," Stavos said, his accent making him seem like just another tourist looking for a keepsake to take back home and eventually stuff into the back of a closet. "Are you Sammy?" he asked.

"It's Sam. Sammy sounded better for the sign. What can I do for you?"

Stavos stepped to the counter. "We're looking for something very rare."

"Take a look around, pal. You've come to the wrong place."

Stavos's smiled faded. "Is Richie here? Maybe he could help us."

Sam's attention was instantly sharpened to a point. "No, Richie's not here."

"No? Where is he?"

"I have no idea."

"Does he work here?"

Sam shook his head. "Richie doesn't work anywhere. He's kind of a bum that way. Why are you looking for him? You guys cops or something?"

Stavos smoothed his shirt. "Do we look like cops?"

Sam swallowed a knot of saliva and glanced at the two men still standing by the front door. "Yeah, you look like the tourist police. Out to save the world from overpriced t-shirts."

Stavos looked to Christos, then back to Sam. "We aren't the police, so you have nothing to worry about. We only want to talk with Richie. Maybe you have a phone number for him?"

"Afraid not."

"No? Hmm. When was the last time you saw him?"

"He comes in here every once in a while. In fact he spent a few hours in here morning before last. Brought me an Egg McMuffin."

"Really? Those are very good. Lots of salt, but very good."

Sam chuckled. "Anyway, like I said, I'm about to close up, so if you'd like to leave me your number I'd be happy to pass it on to Richie next time I see him."

Stavos looked as though he was considering the offer, but then shook his head. "No, I'm not going to leave you my number."

Sam's hand rested on the gun kept atop the safe under the counter. "Well, is there anything else I can do for you?" he said.

"Yes. You can stop lying."

Sam noticed the sign hanging in the door had been turned to CLOSED. He shifted his weight on his seat to get a better angle on things as his hand tightened around the gun, his finger finding the trigger. As he drew it back to clear the shelf, Stavos head butted him, blood bursting from his broken nose like a popped water balloon. The gun fell from his hand into the small trash can at his feet.

He was yanked by the shirt over the counter and thrown into a curio display case, which broke apart as he crumpled to the floor. He heard the front doorbell ding, followed by the rattle of the metal security gate being pulled down outside the storefront, sealing off the outside world. And then his mind went blank from the pain vibrating through his skull.

"Where are my coins?" came Stavos's voice from above him.

Blood from Sam's shattered nose dripped into his mouth and was salty on his tongue. "I don't know what you're talking about," he said, spitting onto the floor.

A polished black shoe landed on his back, sending an icepick of shock down the length of his spine. He spit more blood and rolled onto his side.

"Yes, you do," Stavos said, his foot now hovering over Sam's head. "So give me what I need. I don't want blood on my shoes, you understand?" He pressed his foot to Sam's cheek.

His jaw aching from the pressure, Sam said, "Richie paid me a couple grand to tell whoever asked that he was in here. He had a bag full of money, that's it. No coins."

Christos, who had moved behind the counter, said something in Greek and Stavos flipped open a switchblade. "What's in the safe?" he asked.

"Cash and a betting ledger," Sam said. "That's it."

Stavos bent down beside him. "I don't believe you," he said.

"Please," Sam begged. "It's the truth."

"No, it's not." He grabbed Sam's hand and cut off his ring finger.

Sam screamed, his face paling. Stavos then nodded at Christos, who yanked Sam to his feet and dragged him back behind the counter. "Open it," he said.

Sam knelt at the safe, crying. Pain pulsed in his swollen hand so he was barely able to function. His hands shook from the shock to his system, and sweat stung his eyes. Stavos was suddenly over him again, retaking his hand, the switchblade now pressed to his index finger. "God, please!" Sam begged. "Don't! Don't."

"That's right, beg. Beg me!"

He cut off the index finger and Sam screamed.

Stavos said, "Open the safe before you have no fingers left to turn the dial."

Sam breathed through the terror blurring his eyes, the taste of mucus and blood making him gag, as he worked the combination. When the safe was opened he was kicked away, knocking over the trash can and spilling out the gun. He rolled on top of it and reached his good hand under his stomach to grab hold.

Stavos pulled out the ledger and hurled it away in frustration. "Damn it!" he yelled. He kicked Sam in the back, sending another tremor down his spine. "Tell me where he is!"

With the little strength he had left, Sam rolled over, the gun now pointing up. He fired, but his hand shook so much that he couldn't hold his aim. The bullet only grazed Stavos's upper thigh as it passed by and shattered the cabinet door behind him.

Before Sam could squeeze off another round, the back of his head was blown clean off.

Stavos drew in a breath and looked over to Christos, who lowered his gun and gave a shrug of his shoulders as if to say, "Now what?"

Tracey's cell phone rang at eight-twenty the next morning, waking her.

"Trace, it's me," Vanessa said, sounding way too stressed for that hour.

"Momma, what's up? You okay?" she asked, rolling onto her back and placing her hand on Calvin's stomach as he slept.

"The police were here."

Tracey sat up in bed, her hand now pounding Calvin awake. "What'd they say?"

"What's going on?" Calvin asked, barely able to keep his eyes open in the morning light pouring through the window.

"The cops," Tracey said to him. "What was that, Momma? I missed that last part."

"There were two detectives here to talk with Calvin," Vanessa told her. "They said they had questions for him about Garrison."

"Shit," she said into the phone.

When Vanessa didn't ask her not to swear, it was apparent how scared she was.

"What?" Calvin said, sitting up in bed.

Tracey shushed him and listened. "I told them you went to the grocery store," Vanessa said. "It's all I could come up with, I don't have experience at lying, especially to the police. Who goes to the grocery store this early in the morning? Lord."

"It's fine, momma. Are they still there?"

"Girl, I don't know. They was sitting in their car out front for a while, but I can't look out the window again to check. I already told them what I could about Garrison, that he was a good kid mixed up with the wrong people. Which is the truth, so that don't count as a lie."

"No, it doesn't," Tracey agreed. "They ask anything about Calvin?"

"Only that they're looking to talk with him. They gave me a number to call, but also said they might swing back around when you're back from the store. Lord have mercy, I'm about to get sick sitting right here."

"Breathe, Momma. Is Singletary there?"

"He's still asleep. You don't need to worry about him, he don't know nothing about all this. I didn't want to burden him with it."

"We're gonna come home and take care of it. If the police come back before we get there, you tell them you called me and I said we would be right there."

"Girl, don't you think that'll look suspicious? Me calling you so quick?"

"It don't matter, because you did call me and if they look at your phone they'll know it."

Vanessa sighed heavily into the phone. "Jesus help us."

"You pray all you can, Momma. We'll be right there."

By the time she hung up, Calvin was already dressed.

Agent Luelle and Detective Sutherland sat in the unmarked sedan across the street from the small house in Inglewood where Garrison Russell's cousin, Calvin, lived with his wife, Tracey, son, Martin, and mother-in-law, Vanessa. In the past forty-eight hours they'd visited eight houses just like it and had left each one after hearing the same thing—nobody knew anything.

Agent Luelle flipped through the file in her lap, going over the records she had pulled on Calvin. No gang affiliation. Six months' time served for grand theft auto three years ago, but nothing since. A few other minor blips prior to his stint in County—one for tagging the wall of an Arby's restaurant when he was fourteen, another for underage drinking when he was seventeen, and a third arrest at twenty-three for taking part in a nine-person fight during a neighborhood barbecue at Edward Vincent, Jr. Park. Garrison Russell had been involved in the fight as well, but both were released and all charges were dropped when it was determined the fight began over a perceived slight over to a girl.

Agent Luelle had shown Calvin's picture to all the eyewitnesses outside the bank, but none of them had gotten a good enough look at the driver of the Toyota to say one way or the other. The same could not be said for the witnesses at the scene of the accident involving the Camaro and the telephone pole fifteen blocks from American Federal. Several people said it looked like the man who had talked to Gavin Hendricks as he lay dying on the hood of the getaway car, but they couldn't be one hundred percent positive. A man by the name of Scott Terrell, whom the mystery man had threatened with bodily harm if he didn't put down his phone, had initially claimed that the photo of Calvin was definitely the same man. But then Mr. Terrell added, "I could be wrong though, I mean, they all look alike, right?"

"That must be them," Detective Sutherland said.

Agent Luelle looked up from the file in her lap as the Honda pulled into the driveway across the street. Calvin and Tracey parked and pulled a few bags of groceries out of the trunk. They were halfway to the house when Detective Sutherland called out to them.

"Mr. and Mrs. Russell?" he said, walking with Agent Luelle across the street. "Detective Kevin Sutherland with the LAPD, we'd like to ask you a few questions."

Calvin and Tracey stopped, turned back.

"Yeah, we figured you would," Calvin said, switching his grocery bag from one arm to the other. "Surprised it took you this long to get to me."

"Lot of balls in the air with this one," Detective Sutherland said. "This is Special Agent Grace Luelle with the FBI."

"FBI?" Tracey asked.

Agent Luelle gave a friendly smile. "It's a joint task force."

Calvin nodded toward a few of the neighbors out on their porch, watching them. "You mind if we go inside?"

"Of course," Agent Luelle said.

When they entered the house, Tracey immediately took the bag of hastily purchased groceries from Calvin and disappeared into the kitchen.

Detective Sutherland asked, "Where's your son, Mr. Russell? Your mother-in-law mentioned he was with you."

"We dropped him at a friend's house," Calvin said, leading them to the couch. "Vanessa called Tracey and told her you guys were looking to talk. It's better if he ain't around listening to this."

"Of course," Sutherland said. "Why don't you have a seat and we'll try to get through it as quickly as possible."

"I ain't in no rush," Calvin said, sitting. "And you don't have to keep calling me Mr. Russell. Calvin's fine."

Tracey returned from the kitchen and sat beside Calvin on the couch. Vanessa and Singletary were nowhere to be found.

"I'm sorry about your cousin's death," Agent Luelle began, taking a chair opposite them. "I understand you two were very close."

"He was more like a big brother to me," Calvin said.

"A big brother who was involved with some pretty bad people," she said, the warmth in her smile fading.

"He did some bad things," Tracey said, "but Garrison wasn't a bad person."

"Fair enough. But one of those bad things got him dead and we'd like to find out who killed him."

"So would we," said Calvin.

"Where were you on Saturday morning, Calvin?" asked Detective Sutherland.

"I was here until about nine-thirty and then I went to help a friend with a car."

"Delvon Jenkins," said Detective Sutherland.

"That's right," Calvin said, his voice clipped. "If you already knew that, why'd you ask?"

Tracey put her hand on his leg.

Agent Luelle said, "I understand this a difficult situation for you both. And I don't blame you for being wary of us. But if you really want us to figure out what happened to your cousin inside that bank, then you need to tell us everything you can about it."

"There's nothing I can tell you," Calvin insisted.

"Did you hear anything leading up to Saturday morning? Any rumors about the job?"

Both Calvin and Tracey shook their heads.

Agent Luelle said, "No? With Garrison and you being so close, like brothers you said, it's a little odd that he wouldn't have said anything to you."

Calvin took a deep breath, either from guilty nerves, or irritation. "Ain't nothing odd about it," he said. "He knew I wasn't about that sort of thing, so he kept it from me."

"Garrison was always protecting Calvin," Tracey said, taking hold of he husband's hand. "When he got involved with Sollo and the others he didn't want Calvin anywhere near them."

Detective Sutherland looked confused. "But you knew Sollo, too," he asked Calvin. "Didn't you?"

"Yeah, I knew him. Everyone around here knew him."

"But in fact, you knew him very well. When you were

arrested three years ago for grand theft auto, it was Sollo you were working for, wasn't it?"

Calvin gave him a tight smile. "You gonna keep asking me questions you already have the answers to?"

"I need you to be straight with me, Calvin. Were you still working for Sollo as of last week?"

Another deep breath, this one most definitely nerves. "I saw him around, but after those six months in County, I figured I already did enough time for the man."

"So, that's a no?"

"Yeah, that's a no."

"Are you completely out of the car-stealing business or just the car-stealing for Sollo Gibson business?" Detective Sutherland asked.

Calvin shook his head. "You tryin' your best to jam me up, huh?"

"I'm not looking to cause problems. If you lie to me, that's going to be on you, not me."

Agent Luelle noticed Tracey squeeze Calvin's hand.

Calvin said, "I might have worked for him a little bit over the past year. Running errands for him, that sort of thing. But I ain't stealing cars anymore. That's the truth."

Detective Sutherland nodded and wrote in his notebook, then took out a photograph of the Toyota from the bank job. "Ever seen this car before?"

Calvin took the photo, glanced at it. "Yeah, it's a Toyota."

Agent Luelle noticed Tracey's eyes flick in her direction and then quickly away.

"No," Detective Sutherland said. "I mean this specific car. Does it look familiar to you? Ever see anyone in Sollo's crew driving it?"

Calvin handed the picture back. "No," he said. "For sure not Sollo. That ain't his style."

"You figure he likes a higher end ride when robbing banks?"

"I don't have any idea. Far as I know, that was the first bank he ever robbed."

"And the last," Detective Sutherland said, tucking the photo back into his notebook.

"It's gotta be hard making ends meet with a kid," Agent Luelle broke back in. "Since you haven't been working for Sollo that much, do you have a regular job?"

"I sometimes help Delvon in his shop, like I said."

Agent Luelle kept her eyes on Tracey. She was so poised, so nurturing, the way she continued to hold Calvin's hand. It was interesting, too, that he let her. Most men his age, with his background, wouldn't have. "How's nursing school going?" she asked.

Tracey looked startled. She finally let go of Calvin's hand and wiped the perspiration from her palm across her thigh. "You sure do have a lot of information about us."

Agent Luelle's warm smile returned. "When your husband's name came up in the investigation, we did our due diligence. You can understand that, I hope?"

"Of course," Tracey said.

"Must be difficult to find the time to study, while working down at Target."

Tracey shook her head. "Damn, that's some deep due diligence you got there."

"Actually, it was your mother who mentioned how hard you work."

Tracey shrugged. "I do what I have to do."

"Where is your mother?" Detective Sutherland asked.

Tracey hesitated, then said, "She's probably down at the

church praying. She's upset enough as it is with Garrison dying, but now that you're here asking about Calvin, she's about to lose her mind."

Agent Luelle shook her head. "To be clear, your husband is not a suspect. We're only doing everything we can to figure out what happened inside that bank on Saturday. To that end we're looking at every angle to get a clearer picture. That's the only reason we're here. There's a lot of pieces to the puzzle we don't yet have."

"I can assure you we aren't any of those missing pieces," Tracey said. "Calvin was with me in bed on Saturday morning before he went to help Delvon."

Agent Luelle continued to size her up. "Were you close to Garrison?"

Tracey took a moment to formulate her answer. "I loved him because he was family," she said. "But he and I didn't see things the same way. All I can say is he did the best he could with the little he was given. Life can be hard on people and sometimes that makes them hard back, you understand?"

Agent Luelle nodded. "Yes, I do."

A few more questions were asked, mostly about all the rumors floating around the neighborhood concerning who that second crew was inside the bank, but the answers were as vague as the rumors themselves. Everything from white supremacists, to a bunch of meth heads who had no idea what the hell they were doing.

"I'm sure we haven't heard anything you haven't," was all Tracey could say.

Agent Luelle wrapped things up by offering her card. "If anything comes up that might be of value, I'd appreciate you calling me."

They all stood and walked to the door.

"There is one thing I forgot to ask," Detective Sutherland said. "What time was it that you left Delvon's place on Saturday?"

Calvin thought for a second too long. "Bet you already know the answer to that one, too."

"What time, Calvin?"

He shrugged. "Job took a couple hours. I wasn't paying much attention, to be honest. Somewhere around noon, maybe?"

The detective wrote in his notepad and then offered his hand. Calvin had no choice but to take it. When they let go, Sutherland curled his fingers to his palm and wiped at the perspiration Calvin had left there.

"Nervous?" he asked.

Calvin hooded his eyes and said, "I don't trust the police."

As Detective Sutherland and Agent Luelle drove away from the house, he asked, "You believe them?"

"No, not particularly," Agent Luelle said. "He was clearly still working for Sollo, but I guess with his record it's expected he'd lie about it."

Detective Sutherland snorted. "That's not all he's lying about. I have no doubt they know more than what they're saying."

"Seems to be the way of things for everyone around here."

Sutherland waved his hand out the driver's side window. "Three things you can count on in this neighborhood. The Lakers, not the Clippers, are the home team, Obama was the best President ever, and nobody trusts the police."

Agent Luelle squinted into the sun. "She was interesting, though. Smart. If Calvin is wrapped up in this, I'm guessing she wasn't directly involved, not with her profile. Did you notice the way she held his hand?"

"Yeah. Keeping him in check."

"It was more than that. She's scared for him and she's doing everything she can to hold it together."

"You peg Calvin as one of our missing drivers? That crack about the Toyota was bullshit, he was only trying to buy time to figure out how to answer."

"What time did Delvon Jenkins say Calvin left his shop?"

Sutherland shook his head. "He said he couldn't remember."

Agent Luelle looked out the window at the city, glowing white under an unforgiving sun that cast no shadows, as if to remind everyone there was no place to hide.

"Interesting," she said.

CHAPTER FOURTEEN

THE GOLDEN TRIANGLE is a section of Beverly Hills bounded by Wilshire Boulevard to the south, Little Santa Monica to the west, and Cañon Drive to the east, with Rodeo Drive running through it like an artery, circulating fame and fortune as if they were white blood cells keeping up the city's immunity. Though the same tourists from Hollywood Boulevard flocked to the area to gaze into the windows of stores likes Louis Vuitton, Prada, Fendi, Dolce&Gabbana, and Gucci, the two meccas weren't just on different planets, they were on different planes of existence.

Richie and Calvin parked in one of the three-hour-free lots and hustled down the sidewalk. The unexpected interview that morning with the police had screwed up their schedule, but they were intent on not letting it screw up their plans. A cursory internet search had left them without any clear picture on what the coins were worth, the numbers had ranged so widely that all they could do was hope for the best. They'd agreed the best they could hope for was one hundred thousand dollars. But they would settle for half that if push came to shove.

"Jabba's got some nice digs," Calvin said as they approached the Victorian Building on Brighton Way, a few blocks south of Rodeo.

"I told you he was the real deal," Richie said.

They rode up to the ninth floor and arrived exactly forty-five minutes late for their meeting with Chad Richards and his mystery client. The space was not particularly large, but not so small that it didn't impress. This was no full-service firm with dozens of partners, associates, and paralegals quietly overcharging hours to thousands of clients. Richards & Hawthorne was a boutique operation that specialized in providing personal legal advice to clients with an often tenuous grasp on personal ethics. The lobby was decorated with faintly Asian decor, its red and black walls and bamboo floors polished to a high shine. Down a short hallway from the lobby was a conference room that could comfortably accommodate fifteen and two smaller offices with arched entryways. A hallway on the opposite end of the lobby led to Chad's inner office.

"May I help you?" Chad's executive assistant Jennifer asked, closing a Marie Claire magazine on the uncluttered oak desk. Behind her, a large window framed the Beverly Hills skyline. She was in her late twenties, with pale skin, thick auburn hair, and a starkly angular face that was not quite symmetrical enough to be conventionally pretty but had a certain appeal.

"We're here to see Mr. Richards," Richie said.

"Tell him it's Lenny and Squiggy," Calvin added.

"Of course," she said, with no indication she got the reference. "He's been expecting you."

"We're a little late," Richie said, taking off the backpack that held the box of coins.

"I'll let him know you're here," she said, picking up the phone.

"Tell him it couldn't be helped," Richie went on, anxiously.

"We had car trouble. Had to wait for a tow. Probably the radiator or something, maybe a hose."

"I'm sorry for the trouble," she said, smiling.

"Pump the brakes," Calvin whispered to Richie as Jennifer announced them over the phone. It was not a prudent strategy, they had agreed, to inform a prospective buyer of your stolen property that the deal was briefly delayed because the police where questioning you about said stolen property.

Richie let out a long breath and rechecked the inside of the backpack.

Hanging up, Jennifer rose from the desk and sauntered toward the hallway with a slightly pigeon-toed gait. "Right this way," she said. "Can I get you something to drink?"

"I'm good," Calvin said.

"I'll have a water," Richie said as they reached the frosted glass door at the end of the hall.

"Would you prefer cold or room temperature?" Jennifer asked as she showed them inside Chad's inner office.

"Cold," Richie said. "No. Room temp—wait, cold. Thanks."

"And here I was worried it was your feet that got cold," Chad said, stepping up with an extended hand.

"Car trouble," Richie babbled nervously as they shook. "Had to wait for a tow. Not sure what the problem was, but—"

"It's all good now," Calvin said.

"I certainly hope so."

As they shook, Calvin gave Chad a curious once-over. "And who the hell are you?"

Chad laughed good-naturedly. He was clean shaven, dressed in a conservative brown suit and his hair was combed with a well-defined part. "Good to see you, Mr. Russell," he said.

"Oh, it's Mr. Russell now?" Calvin said. "Last night you was lying around lookin' like Hugh Hefner on crack, talkin' about cutting off ears and shit and now you're…this."

Chad's professional graces remained unchanged. "Last night I was at a business meeting until quite late. Otherwise I would have been home watching the Discovery Channel with my wife."

"Whatever," Calvin said. "It's your world."

"That it is, so let's share the wealth it contains. Gentlemen, this is Mr. Winslow."

They all turned to the white-haired slab of beef jerky rising off the couch. He was somewhere in his early sixties, though age had not softened him. He was about six-foot-two and he used every bit of it as he stood, the zippers on his brown leather motorcycle jacket jingling. By way of greeting he said, "I used to ride with a colored son-of-a-bitch named Aldo who also could never figure out how to tell time."

An awkward silence filled the room.

"It was probably the radiator," Richie said, anxiously filling the hole created by Winslow's observation. "Got too hot."

Calvin's eyes had remained steady on Winslow. "C-P time, right?" he said.

Winslow let loose a grunt that fell short of a laugh. Weathered lines crisscrossed his deeply tanned face, though none of them appeared to run deep. In fact, everything about him seemed to be right out on the surface.

"Richie Glass," he said, turning to look directly at Richie, his expression constantly shifting between light and dark. "Chad's told me he used to do business with your father."

"Yes, that's right."

"He vouches for you."

"Okay. That's good."

He tossed a thumb at Calvin. "So who the hell's vouching for this guy?"

Richie looked like he couldn't tell if Winslow was joking or not. He certainly wasn't smiling, but why the hell would he have come this far if he wasn't convinced they were to be trusted?

Winslow clapped his hands twice, as though Richie had fallen asleep and needed waking. Richie looked helplessly to Chad, who sat on the edge of his desk and spread his hands as if to say, "What can you do?"

"If Chad vouched for me," Richie said, sounding unsure of the protocol. "Then I suppose I'm vouching for Calvin."

Another grunt from Winslow. "You are, huh? And what exactly do you know about him?"

Richie shot Calvin an uncertain look. "Enough, I guess."

"Oh, you guess? Is that what we're doing here, *guessing*? I don't operate on guesses, son. Someone I don't know from Adam comes out of the woodwork asking to make a deal, I tend not to be interested. How do I know he's not wearing a wire?"

"Hey, fuck you, man," Calvin said.

"It's not like that," Richie tried.

"No? Why don't you tell me what it is like then?"

"Chad," Richie said, leaning over to get a better angle on the lawyer. "Tell him we're cool."

Chad shrugged. "I've given him all the information I have."

Calvin continued to stare at Winslow. "What's it gonna take for you to stop trippin'?"

Winslow sat on the arm of the couch and crossed his arms, the zippers again jingling as he sized Calvin up. "Calvin Russell from Inglewood, California. You from the 'hood?"

"That's right."

"You know who else is from Inglewood?" Winslow sat there, arms still crossed, waiting for a response.

Calvin shook his head. "I ain't got any idea what the hell you—"

"Tyra Banks. America's Next Top Model."

More silence.

"So what?" Calvin said, eventually.

"So, you know her? Ever spend an afternoon drinking forties with her down in the hood?"

Calvin had come up against all sorts of puffed-up assholes, but this dude had a touch of crazy he had no experience with. It took another moment for him to realize Winslow was actually expecting an answer about his possible acquaintance with Tyra fucking Banks. "No, man. I don't know her," he said.

"That's too bad. So I guess she can't vouch for you either. So why don't you go ahead and strip down to your underwear, so we can see how clean you are."

Calvin considered the request, then said, "You first."

This time Winslow's grunt turned into an actual laugh. "Good for you, boy."

"I ain't your boy."

Winslow's laugh faded, but his smile remained. "You're not taking my shit, huh? I guess those six months in County a few years ago toughened you up, whetted your appetite for robbing banks and staring down old men."

Calvin and Richie exchanged another glance.

"I'm gonna start thinking you two are in love, the way you keep looking at each other." His face grew harder as he stared. "That's right, I did my homework on you, Calvin Russell from Inglewood. I gotta say, I'm offended that you two morons didn't bother to do any homework on me. You don't have any goddamn idea who you're dealing with, do you?"

His eyes pierced Calvin like hooks, reeling him in. Damn. Even though they were the ones with the coins, they'd given up all control to these two crazy white men, all because he had no choice but to trust them more than they trusted him. Sollo had once told him to never trust anybody; once you did, they owned you. Trying to salvage some pride, he said, "Little hard to do homework on you when we was never given your name until we walked into the room."

Winslow stood from the arm of the couch. "And you still haven't been given my name. In fact, you never even walked into this room at all. You have no goddamn idea what my name is or what the hell I look like. Because whatever might come your way from whoever stashed those coins in that bank, if so much as a rumor of my involvement comes back to me, I'm gonna send some of my friends to straighten things out between us. We clear on that?"

Richie cleared his throat and nodded.

"Say the words, Richie," Winslow said.

"We're clear."

"What about you, Calvin? You don't have to say anything if your ego can't handle it, but I am going to need you to nod, so I see you understand the situation."

Calvin clenched his jaw and did what he was asked.

Winslow's reptile smile returned, exposing a gold incisor. "All right, let's see what you brought me."

Calvin hung back as Richie pulled the box from the backpack and set it on the coffee table. Winslow used both hands, seven out of ten fingers covered in turquoise rings, to open the lid. "My, my, my," he said.

"You like what you see?" asked Chad.

Winslow stared into the box a moment longer. "They're exactly as you described."

"I'm happy you're pleased. So, we're in business?"

Winslow took out several coins and held them close to his left eye as he closed his right. "We're definitely in business."

"Excellent."

Winslow continued to pull coins from the box, examining each one with a quiet reverence. "You boys are so far out in the deep end that you have no idea what you have here, do you?"

"Some old Greek coins?" Richie said.

Winslow looked over his shoulder at him. "Your ignorance would be cute if you were a ten-year-old. Yes, they are coins. Greek and Roman, to be precise. From the looks of it, most of these date to five hundred years before the birth of Christ."

"Jesus," Richie said, more than a little impressed.

"Exactly," said Chad, patting him on the arm.

Winslow handed one of the coins to Chad. "Don't you love the irony?"

Chad studied the image on the coin. "Dikaiosyne," he said, and Winslow chuckled.

"You gonna let us in on the joke?" asked Calvin.

Chad handed the coin back to Winslow. "Dikaiosyne is the Greek personification of justice and fair dealing."

Calvin stepped close to get a better look. "And how much are she and her friends worth?"

Winslow closed the box. "Whatever I choose to pay for them."

"What kind of bullshit is that?"

"It's not bullshit." Winslow said. "It's supply and demand. I'm the only one here willing to buy."

"And we're the only ones selling," Calvin countered.

Winslow looked from Calvin to Richie with a smug confidence. "Are you really gonna let this low-rent asshole ruin things for you?"

Calvin squared his shoulders toward Winslow. "Who you calling low-rent? You the one looks like you was eaten by termites."

Richie slid in between them. "Come on," he said. "Let's not be so confrontational here. I'm sure we can make this work for all of us if we stop measuring each other's cocks for a minute, and try to come to a—"

"One million dollars," Winslow interrupted. "Cash."

Richie and Calvin stared in stunned disbelief.

"Gentlemen," said Chad helpfully, coming off the edge of the desk. "Do you have a counter offer?"

Richie licked his lips, looked at Calvin. "No, I, ah…Calvin? Do we have a counter offer?"

Calvin was quiet for a moment longer. "One point five," he said, finally.

Winslow remained unfazed. "How bout we go with just the five hundred?"

"We'll take the million," Richie said quickly.

"Calvin?" asked Chad. "The ball looks to be in your court. Do you agree to the terms?"

Calvin narrowed his eyes, trying to appear as though he wasn't shaking with electrified nerves. He considered pushing the issue and calling Winslow's bluff, but before he could muster the confidence to do so, the word "Deal" was already out of his mouth.

Chad opened a wall safe, removed a black bag by its strap and set it on the desk. As he unzipped the outer layer to reveal the interior pouch holding the actual cash, he said, "One million in US banknotes, all one hundred dollar bills, all pre-circulated. The bag is made of SDRT grade composite fabrics twice the strength of Kevlar at half the weight. The lining of the interior pouch also contains nickel, copper, and silver fabric designed to block RF tracking, so you have no cause to worry about being followed by Mr. Winslow or any of his associates when you leave the office. Once you take possession of the bag, our business is complete."

Calvin and Richie peered into the bag like children on Christmas morning who couldn't believe Santa had been so generous, and Winslow tucked the wooden box under his arm as though it was an unneeded umbrella, rather than something he'd traded a million bucks for.

"You can take this," Richie said, holding out the backpack.

Winslow ignored the offer and shook Chad's hand. "I'll be in touch."

"Flying back right away?" Chad asked.

Winslow's gold-toothed smile returned, his mood clearly elevated. "Me and the boys rode out."

"After all these years, still playing Easy Rider."

"I like the wind in my face. Keeps me young."

With that, Winslow left without so much as a glance in the direction of either Richie or Calvin, walking out as if they weren't even there.

"Asshole," Calvin said to no one in particular.

"Forget him," Richie said, zipping up the bag of money. "Let him run off with the rest of the Retirement Village People. He's old, he'll be dead soon. Come on, man—we win."

Calvin draped the moneybag over his shoulder, but the twenty-five-or-so-pounds felt like a hell of a lot more. It felt onerous. Like it was alive, an animal clinging to him. It had all gone too smoothly. Even with Winslow's racist goading and threats of impending violence if they ever spoke of him, it had been too easy. Nothing in his life had ever come easily, and as he shook Chad's hand, something told him they still hadn't won a damn thing.

CHAPTER FIFTEEN

NEITHER RICHIE NOR Calvin had ever pushed a shopping cart holding a million dollars down the frozen food aisle of a supermarket before. But as they looked for mint-chip ice cream to go with the chocolate sheet cake he'd bought for Martin, Calvin imagined there would be lots of new things he'd now be able to do.

The unsettled emotions Calvin felt leaving Chad's office in Beverly Hills had dissipated once he called Tracey. Her soft voice was like deep shade on a scorching day. "It's over, baby," he had said, not getting any more specific than that on the phone; the visit from the *joint task force* that morning was still a bothersome consideration.

"I hope so," Tracey had said. "I hope it's all done with now."

Martin's muffled voice had trickled into the conversation then, and Tracey told him that daddy's business meeting was all finished. Martin asked another question and Calvin heard his wife say, "Yeah, baby, he's coming home right now."

And that's when the sense of displacement—if that's what it was—returned. Despite the score of a lifetime, nothing was as he'd expected. He wanted to say the words that would bankroll their future, shock her with the crazy amount of money they could now use to get Martin far away from the likes of Randall Washington. But Tracey hadn't even asked about the damn money. Of course she hadn't. She cared only about him, and about their boy. The instant they hung up, he realized the score he'd always dreamed of wasn't as important as his family was.

Richie closed the freezer door and dropped the pint of mint chip into the cart, while Calvin imagined Martin asking how they could suddenly afford all of the things his father had promised him. What lie would he infect his son's innocence with? Winning the Lottery? Inheritance from some dead great uncle he'd never mentioned? Martin was still young enough that he would believe anything his father said. Whatever Calvin told him, it would have to be a lifelong lie. A lie that would always be between them. But he had no choice but to do it. Telling his son who he truly was would be even worse.

"We gotta get some champagne or something," Richie said. "This place must have something we can crack open."

"I'm not feeling it," Calvin said, moving on with the shopping cart.

"What do you mean?" Richie said, catching up. "We gotta celebrate this!"

"This ain't a party situation for me, dog. You gonna have to wait for Tracey and me to ghost before you call up your friends and start raging."

Richie looked at him as though he didn't understand the joke. "Come on, Calvin," he said. "One drink. This is a good thing that happened today."

Calvin gave no indication he agreed as he continued to push the shopping cart toward the check-out line.

Richie pulled up the driveway to his house, parked the Subaru in the garage, draped the bag of money over his shoulder, and carried the grocery bag of ice cream through the back yard, toward the house. Calvin carried Martin's cake, balancing it on his outstretched hands as he took careful steps, irked that some of the icing got rubbed off on the plastic lid. Richie smiled at the sight. It was the first time he fully saw Calvin as a dad.

"So where you gonna go now that it's all done?" he asked.

"That's up to Tracey. She wants her mom to sell the house and move with us to some fool place like Arizona, but we'll have to see. What about you?"

Richie hitched the bag further up his shoulder and fumbled to get the keys from his front pocket with his free hand. "No idea," he said.

"What happened to Fiji?"

"Maybe for a vacation."

"Tracey might even go for that. We ain't ever been anywhere nice but San Diego."

Richie pictured Calvin, Tracey, and Martin on a white sand beach in the South Pacific, sitting under a palm tree. There were many things Richie had anticipated he might feel once the deal was made, but lonely wasn't one of them. "Wherever you end up," he said, "it's nice you're not gonna be alone once you get there."

"You ain't got no family at all?"

Richie stuck the key into the back door. "I've never had a family," he said, using his foot to push the door open for Calvin.

"Yo, little man!" Calvin called out as they headed for the kitchen. "Come check out what I got for you." He set the cake on the center island and tossed the plastic lid on the counter behind him.

Richie lifted the black bag from his shoulder. "Where should I put this?"

"Hide it somewhere," Calvin said, licking green icing from his thumb. "You got any candles?"

"What for? It's not his birthday."

"So?"

"So it's weird blowing out candles if it's not your birthday."

"You got any or not?"

"Why would I have candles?"

Calvin shook his head and picked up the sheet cake. As he walked from the kitchen, Richie took the bag of money to the pantry. He used a foot to shove over a couple water bottles on the floor and dropped the bag.

Down the hall Calvin called out for Martin, and then for Tracey. "Where you at?" Calvin asked a third time, but there was only silence.

When Richie closed the pantry door and turned, a fist caught him directly in his left eye socket, momentarily blinding him. His knees folded and he crumpled to the floor. How long he lay there before becoming aware of the buzzing in his head, he did not know. It sounded like a fly caught in a jar, zooming back and forth in fits and starts. And then the fly broke free and the buzzing went away. He looked around, saw nothing but the bottom third of the refrigerator.

"You must be Richie Glass," Christos's voice came from somewhere above him.

Richie didn't move. It occurred to him that he probably had his second concussion in the past few days, and among all of his immediate concerns, his mind strangely focused on the specter of brain damage when he was older.

"Come on, idiot, let's go," Christos ordered.

It was the same accent Richie had heard in Connor Weeks' living room, right after Connor's head exploded. Okay, so it wasn't Russian. But he still couldn't place it. "Who are you?" he asked.

"Get up on your feet," Christos said, grabbing Richie by the shirt and yanking him up.

The room shimmied as the blood rushed from his head; he leaned his hands on the island to keep from falling back to the floor.

"You've been causing us problems, Richie," Christos said. "You should not have taken what did not belong to you."

"How did you find me?" he asked, his head still swimming.

Something landed with a loud thump on the island in front of him. It took a moment to realize what it was. Sam's betting ledger.

"Your friend Sammy sends you his best," Christos said.

Richie looked at him for the first time. He was big, but not as big as he'd imagined a person that strong being. "What did you do to him?" he asked.

"Don't worry about Sammy. We did him a favor, saved him from a life in that shithole, selling crap. He's better off. Come with me, we'll have a talk with the others."

"I don't think I can walk yet," Richie said, the sparkling white dots in his field of vision still swirling.

Christos punched him in the ribs. He grunted as the pain radiated through his torso. It was like being sucked into a vacuum, all the air leaving his body at once.

"You stayed on your feet," Christos said. "So you can walk. Let's go."

With a viselike grip on the back of Richie's neck, he yanked him away from the island and walked him into the living room, stepping over the fallen sheet cake, which lay upside down on the floor. There were two other dark-haired men wearing slacks and pressed shirts, one standing by the window looking bored, and another with his back to Tracey and Martin, who sat on the couch, their distressed faces shiny with either sweat or tears, Richie couldn't tell.

The man Richie was being delivered to had a smooth, olive-skinned face. His eyes were dark under heavy brows and his black hair was cut close to his scalp. He nodded as if answering a question and the vise came off Richie's neck.

"You fucking guys," Stavos said, sounding exasperated.

Richie stared down at Calvin's body on the floor, beside the couch. He lay there exactly as you'd expect a dead body to, halfway turned over onto his stomach, his left arm bent underneath his hip, his legs spread wide. "Jesus Christ, did you kill him?" he asked.

Stavos didn't answer. He stared like a disapproving P. E. instructor, his shirt tight to his muscular chest, his arms at his sides. "You should be concerned about what I will do to you," he said. "Not about what I have done with him."

Richie leaned to the side and caught Tracey's blank stare. Her hand continued to soothe the back of Martin's head, which leaned heavily on her shoulder. The man snapped his fingers, bringing Richie's attention back around.

Then Calvin's legs moved and he shifted fully onto his back as he regained consciousness. He lay there, staring up at the ceiling, blood trickling from his nose and mouth like molasses, and Martin started to cry. Tracey tucked the boy's face into her chest, shielding his eyes.

Stavos then asked, simply, "Where are my coins?"

"We don't have them anymore," Richie said.

Stavos took a switchblade from his back pocket and flicked it open with a metallic swishing sound. Tracey let out an involuntary yelp and Martin's cries grew louder.

"He's not lying," Calvin said from the floor. He rolled over onto his side and spit blood, his swollen right eye now visible.

Stavos spun and kicked Calvin in the chest. "Stop lying to me," he raged.

Calvin coughed and wheezed. "I just said I *wasn't* lying, dumbass."

Stavos squatted in front of him, the knife dangling in his hand as if he had forgotten he was holding it. He stared into Calvin's beaten face. "Mr. Tough Guy," he said. Grabbing Calvin's wrist, he pressed the blade against his index finger. "How tough are you?"

"No!" Tracey screamed.

The blade sliced into Calvin's flesh a half-inch above his knuckle and blood trickled down his hand.

"They sold them!" she cried. "I swear to God, that's the truth. Please stop. Please."

Christos looked to the man standing by the window and asked in Greek, "Why is he cutting off everyone's fingers?" The man by the window shrugged.

Martin pulled his head free from his mother's chest, tears falling down his face. "Daddy!" he cried, his little voice coming out low, as if it was afraid to draw too much attention. "Daddy! Please don't hurt my daddy!"

Stavos looked up at Martin and the knife came off Calvin's fingers. For a moment he stared into the boy's wet face as though he recognized something. "You are afraid?" he asked.

Martin sucked moisture back up his nose.

Stavos's voice softened. "You need to be strong now, yes? No more crying."

Martin nodded, his eyes wide with fear.

"We have the money," Richie said. "A million dollars."

Tracey gasped at the amount.

Stavos looked at her, then to Christos as if to ask, *how stupid are these people?* "You fucking idiots sold my coins for a million dollars?" he said, standing.

"We didn't even know what they were when we took the box, I swear. All we did was drive for the bank job. It was Connor who was behind all of this. He's the one who stole them from the bank, we were only a distraction. We were set up, so we took them from him, not from you. We didn't know anything about you."

Stavos stepped close to Richie, looking at him as though he couldn't comprehend such idiocy. "Who did you sell them to?" he asked.

"Some guy."

"Some guy?"

"He wanted to remain anonymous."

"I don't blame him," Stavos said, and then he flicked the knife on the underside of Richie's chin, taking out a thin slice of skin. He yelled into Richie's face, "He paid *half* of what they are worth!"

Richie pressed his palm to his chin, felt the wetness between his fingers. His heart raced, the wound pulsing faster and faster, more and more blood dripping onto his shirt.

Calvin lowered his head, as though his stupidity and greed had become too heavy a burden to bear. "We can get them back," he said.

Stavos wheeled around. "If you don't even know his name," he yelled. "How are you going to find him?"

"We made contact through another man," Calvin told him.

"We can find him through him. We'll give him his money back and we'll give you the coins."

Stavos calmed as he considered his options. Reaching down, he wiped the knife clean on Calvin's shirt before tucking it back into his pocket. "You're cornered now, an animal in a trap, trying everything you can to break free. Maybe instead of finding this anonymous man, you will do something stupid, like call the police."

"No," Calvin insisted. "No cops."

"I do not believe you," Stavos said, patting Calvin's head. "That is why I'm taking the woman and the boy."

"No fucking way," Calvin snapped.

Stavos nodded at the man by the window, who obediently moved to pull Tracey from the couch. She yelped and pleaded for them to leave Martin, but her pleas were ignored. Their cheeks were slippery with tears, their mouths twisted with anguish as the man pulled them toward the front door.

Their screams reverberated in Calvin's ears, stabbed at his heart. With every bit of energy he had left, he made a desperate attempt to get to his family. His feet shuffled, trying to find purchase on the hardwood floors, his upper body stretched forward as he rose up. His face was wet with blood, his eyes bulging in panic. He let out a primal yelp, a wail of anger and fear, that was cut short as Stavos kicked him in the head, knocking him out cold.

Stavos took out a business card with only a phone number printed on it and tucked it into Richie's shirt pocket, saying, "I'm tired of chasing you all over this fucking city. I'll give you twenty-four hours to find this anonymous man who has my coins. If I don't hear from you by 2:00 tomorrow, the little boy and his mother will be mailed to you in tiny pieces. If you call the police, they will be mailed to them in tiny pieces. Either way, they end up in tiny pieces. And then, we will come find you and finish what we started here today. Do you understand?"

Richie nodded, the pain in his chin asserting itself, sending pulses up both sides of his jaw. He looked helplessly to Tracey, a gun shoved into her neck to keep her quiet.

And then a leather strap was wrapped around his own neck.

Christos pulled the strap taught. Richie's hands instinctively came up to his throat, but there was nothing he could do. His feet kicked up and he dropped to his knees. The strap was pulled tighter and tighter, and the sparkling dots returned to his field of vision.

And then there was only darkness.

CHAPTER SIXTEEN

TRACEY AND MARTIN rode in the back of the SUV, next to one of the Greek men who had snatched them. She knew they were Greek from their accents. They sounded like characters from *My Big Fat Greek Wedding*, a movie she'd seen as a kid and caught parts of several times on cable over the years. But the characters in the movie were all funny, warm people who exuded charm even when they argued. These guys exuded a coldness that made it difficult to draw a breath. She wrapped her arm around Martin, who was so quiet it were as though he'd fallen asleep. But when she looked down at him, his eyes were wide open, frozen in place.

Before the SUV reached Fountain Avenue at the bottom of the hill, they were blindfolded. Martin tensed as the world went dark behind the cloth covering his eyes, and Tracey imagined all the horrors dancing in his mind's eye. Whatever he could imagine, the reality was worse. Even though she could see nothing behind the blindfold, she closed her eyes. It was all too surreal. There was a whole world going on outside the car, normal people doing normal things—complaining about traffic, walking their dogs, wondering what to have for dinner. And they were no longer a part of it. They were suspended above it, a separate form of life, no longer the people they had been when they woke up that morning.

The men spoke freely, but their words were all in Greek. They laughed a few times and Tracey wondered how such a thing could be possible. How could they find anything humorous in what they had done, what they were planning to do? She didn't try to imagine what they had planned for them; to do so would send her spiraling down. She concentrated on the warmth of Martin's body, his tiny hand in hers. When he began to cry, she leaned her head down until it touched the top of his. She began to hum "Let Your Light Shine On Me," a gospel song her mother used to sing when she was a little girl. Martin raised his chin when his ears caught hold of it and he burrowed into her, though his body continued to shake and did not stop.

It was difficult to tell how long they rode in the SUV before they reached their destination. An hour maybe. The men had stopped their chatter after a while and the minutes drifted by in blackness. And then suddenly they were being pulled from the car. The man beside Tracey climbed out, bringing her out one door as another of the men pulled Martin through the other. Tracey let loose a scream at being separated, but was jabbed in the back, told to shut up and keep walking. She reached blindly for Martin and a moment later he was again beside her, their hands finding each other as they walked the rest of the way inside—inside where?

"Take them to the study," one of the men said.

Tracey had imagined all sorts of places they might be taken— an isolated warehouse, a garage perhaps, even, during her darkest moment, a hole in the ground, but never once did it occur to her that they were to be held in a place that had a *study*.

"What the hell have you done?" a man's voice raged.

"Put them in there," another voice ordered, and Tracey and Martin were shoved inside a room, the door pulled closed behind them.

They had not been instructed to remove the blindfolds, so they left them where they were, clinging to each other as they listened to the two voices beyond the door.

"Why would you bring these people into my home? Where is your judgement?"

"It was the best option," the familiar one said, sounding defiant and defensive at the same time. "It is the only way to guarantee the coins will be returned to us."

"It is your fault the coins were taken to begin with!"

"No, Papa."

There came a loud smack of hand against skin and then a moment of silence before the voices returned, this time in Greek. Even in a language Tracey couldn't understand, she understood their intent. The violence in the words was clear. Martin squatted down and grabbed at her legs, a defensive posture he had never before taken. He huddled beside her as the angry voices continued a few feet away, only the closed door keeping them clear of the storm.

"Everything's gonna be okay, sweetie," she said, crouching down to blindly hug her son.

Martin cried and Tracey lifted off her blindfold and then his. It was an instinctual move, her motherly need to calm her child overriding all other considerations. Their faces were only inches apart, so close she could see his brown irises constrict as his eyes lit up.

"I'm right here with you," she whispered, running her hand down his cheek.

"I want to go home," Martin whispered back.

It took everything she had to keep from crying. "I want to go home, too," she said. "But until we can, we're going to stay together, okay?"

Martin nodded and she pressed her forehead to his. It was a lie, she knew. She had no control over anything and could not guarantee the angry men beyond the door would keep them together. Perhaps she should not have said it, but the words were there and they were the words he needed in that moment, so she used them.

"Put them back on," a man's voice came from the opposite side of the room, startling them.

Martin jolted as Tracey stood quickly, realizing for the first time they were not alone. The man was sitting in a high-backed brown leather chair beside a floor-to-ceiling bookcase. His legs were splayed and his head hung heavily on his neck, his arms resting on the arms of the chair. It was the same man who had beaten Richie, though now he looked nothing like the animal he had been at Richie's house. Now he looked tired, sitting there like a teenager who didn't want to go to class. His boss had said they were tired of chasing Richie and Calvin all over the city, and the effort showed on his face. His eyes were heavy and he clearly hadn't the energy or desire to get up and make her do it himself.

Tracey glanced around the room. It was large, with high-end furniture and several oil paintings, one of a spotted dog with a pheasant in its mouth. It was certainly nicer than anything she could have imagined. Nicer than any place she'd ever been, as a matter of fact. Mob money, she figured. There was a window on one side, heavy drapes pulled back, allowing the late afternoon sun to spill through. She wished she could look out the window, get a better sense of where they were, but she stayed still, holding Martin.

"Hey, woman," the man said, flexing his hand as if to work out a bruise. "Listen to me. I said to put the blindfolds back on."

Tracey nodded and reached for the fallen blindfolds. She was used to his type. The type of man who wouldn't use your name, even if he knew it. She had grown up with those men. She once had an old boyfriend blithely say to some male friends as they discussed going to a party, "She gonna bring some of them other bitches with her." It was all so tiring. All the posturing. All the bullshit bravado and the demand for respect, when they didn't respect anything themselves. All of it—the dismissive attitudes, the flashy cars, the built-up bodies, even the three-hundred dollar sneakers—were nothing but garish feathers on a bunch of goddamn peacocks strutting around like they owned the world, when in fact they were all scared shitless of getting eaten.

That's why she had fallen in love with Calvin. He at least acknowledged the problem, tried to break free from the expectations of being young and black with no money and limited possibilities. But he had failed, there was no doubt about it. And now his weakness had dragged them all down into this pit they might not ever climb from. As she lowered the blindfold back onto Martin's eyes, plunging him back into the darkness, she hated Calvin for what he had done to them. And as she lowered her own blindfold, covering her own eyes to the cruel world, she could not stem the silent prayer that if someone had to die for Calvin's actions, let it be him instead of their perfect little boy.

Calvin was the first to regain consciousness. He awoke to a world of suffocating silence and laid there staring at the closed front door, beyond which, somewhere, his family had been taken. The dull ache in his ribs made moving difficult, but he pushed himself to his knees and used the back of his hand to scrape the crusty blood from his lower lip. He stared a long moment at Richie, who was face down on the floor, not moving.

And then he cried.

Deep sobs tightened his stomach and knotted his throat. His mind conjured images of Tracey and Martin with the men who had taken them. Thoughts of rape and torture slipped through the cracks as he tried to put up a mental wall. Squeezing his eyes closed, his focus came and went, his ability to operate sputtering like an engine unable to gain traction. He took deep breaths that felt like jagged rocks filling his chest, his lungs never able to fully expand. Slowly he regained control, the sobs becoming shallower, the shaking subsiding, until he was strangely calm. His body lightened and for a moment it was as though he was floating before he dropped down quickly, refilling his own skin, heavy as cement.

"You dead?" he said aloud.

Richie didn't respond. Didn't move.

Calvin wiped the tears from his face. "Richie," he said, this time louder.

Richie's left arm twitched and then his right foot. Calvin struggled to his feet and shuffled over to him. Richie rolled onto his back, blood crusted to his chin. "I'm sorry," he said, his voice a painful rasp.

"It ain't your fault. It's mine."

"What the hell are we gonna do?"

"We gotta call Chad."

Richie climbed to his feet and immediately sat back down on the chair beside him. He drew in a breath, his finger exploring the inside of his mouth. "I got a loose tooth," he said.

It were as though the men had stopped the beating just short of putting them in the hospital, as if they had practiced exactly how much a body could take and still remain functional.

"Call him," Calvin said.

Richie pulled the phone from his pants pocket and dialed.

"Global Consulting," Chad's assistant, Jennifer answered.

"I have to speak to Mr. Richards," Richie said, his eyes remaining closed.

"Who's calling please?"

"Richie Glass. We were there this morning."

"Yes, of course, Mr. Glass, one moment."

The line went momentarily silent. "It hurts to talk," Richie said, gingerly touching his throat and the imprint of the leather strap. "You're bleeding, by the way." He tapped beside his right eye and Calvin mirrored his action, wiping at the open cut next to his temple. "He must have been wearing a ring or something."

"Richie!" Chad's voice was suddenly in his ear, happy as a voice could sound. "What can I do for you?"

"We have a problem."

The line went silent for a second and then Chad's voice returned, decidedly less enthusiastic. "What's the issue?"

"We need the coins back."

There was another silence, this one even longer, before Chad said, "What coins?"

"What do you mean, what coins?"

"I apologize, but I don't know what you're talking about. I have no knowledge of any coins you may be missing."

"Okay, I get it, but can we cut the bullshit? We have a problem with the men from the bank and we have to get them their coins back. We still have all of the money, so we need to get in touch with Winslow and trade them back. Even though you *screwed* us on their value. No harm no foul, right?"

The line was silent yet again. And then Chad said, "Son, are you okay?"

"No, not at all. We just had the shit beat out of us."

"My God, that's horrible. Have you called the police?"

"The police? You know we can't call the cops about this."

"Why not? If you've been assaulted, you should file a police report."

Richie looked up to Calvin, helpless to comprehend what was happening.

"What?" Calvin asked.

"He said we should file a police report," Richie told him. He returned to the phone, saying, "What the hell are we supposed to say to the police? We robbed a bank a couple days ago and now we need your help protecting us from the psychos we stole from?"

Chad's voice turned ever more serious, parental even. "Son, if you're in some sort of trouble that requires counsel, I can refer you to a criminal attorney, but this is not the sort of law I practice, so I would be of little help to you. Now, I don't know anything about any bank robbery or missing coins and I'd like to keep it that way, you understand?"

"No, I don't understand at all," Richie yelled.

Calvin yanked the phone from him. "Yo, asshole, we ain't playin'. We need to get those goddamn coins back from your boy."

"Okay," Chad said. "I'm finished with this conversation. Whatever problem you two have found yourself in, I have no involvement, is that clear? And please keep in mind that the types of people I represent are not inclined to be as forgiving as I am. In fact, if they were to be harassed in the same manner, I have no doubt it would be resolved with extreme prejudice. Is that clear to you? Now, I wish you luck, but don't ever call my office again."

The call disconnected and Calvin hurled the phone across the room.

Richie stared, dumbfounded.

Calvin slowly digested the reality they found themselves in, then turned to Richie and said, simply, "Let's go."

The Subaru pulled into the cracked cement driveway leading to the small house in Inglewood, its occupants looking like a couple of zombies who had wandered off the set of *The Walking Dead*. Their faces were swollen, with matching purplish-yellow bruises around their eyes and mouths, Richie's sliced chin covered with a Band-Aid.

Calvin winced, his hand pressed to his bruised ribs, as Richie slammed the car into park.

"You okay?" Richie asked.

"As long as I don't breathe, I'm fine," Calvin said, still not reaching for his door.

"I can go in alone and get it," Richie suggested. "Tell me where it is."

"No, I'm good," Calvin said, blowing out a slow breath and opening the door. "I'll be right back." He was halfway up the porch stairs when the sound of the Subaru trunk slamming closed turned him around. Richie put the bag of money over his shoulder and started across the front lawn towards him.

"It's fine, man," Calvin said. "Leave it in the trunk and wait for me."

Richie hustled up the steps. "Honestly, I'm a little scared to be out here alone."

They went inside together, having decided to keep quiet about Tracey and Martin. If they told Vanessa about her daughter and grandson there would be lots of screaming, crying, and police calling. She was already praying for them; that was all they needed from her at the moment. Vanessa had no trouble believing in evil—she was a true believer in the Devil and all his wicked ways—but she had no experience with the sort of violence they'd been through and would not be able to comprehend the ramifications of getting the police involved. As it turned out, it wasn't Vanessa who greeted them in the living room, but her boyfriend, Singletary. He was sitting on the couch watching Laker highlights on ESPN as Calvin closed the door behind them.

Singletary was the poster child for black-don't-crack. He was sixty-three, but looked fifty. His hair had only a faint dusting of gray, and his shoulders were as wide and muscular as they had been for the past thirty years. But it wasn't his appearance that Vanessa had fallen in love with after her husband died of diabetes complications three years before; she'd fallen in love with Singletary because he was as solid on the inside as he was on the outside. When he wasn't working as a Water Utility Supervisor for the LADWP, he was volunteering with Vanessa down at the First Baptist. The only reason they hadn't gotten married is that the Alzheimer's that ravaged his wife was crueler than the diabetes that ravaged Vanessa's husband, and she hadn't physically passed until seven months ago, even though the woman he once loved had disappeared four years prior.

"What in God's name happened to the two of you?" he said, looking up, his eyes wide.

"Nothing good," Calvin said.

"I can see that," he said, silencing the TV. "You look like you got turned inside out."

"We got jumped. Couple of homeless dudes over in Venice."

Singletary stood and extended his hand to Richie. "My name's Dennis, but everyone calls me by my last name, Singletary."

"Nice to meet you," Richie said as they shook. "Richie."

"Okay, yeah. Vanessa mentioned you the other day. So did you guys call the police?"

Richie shot Calvin a look. "The police?"

"Yeah, did you file a report on the guys that lit you up?"

On one hand they were glad for the question, it meant he was in the dark about everything and there was no chance of him putting anything together, but on the other hand, they had no idea how to answer his question.

"No," Richie said, eventually. "They ran off, so…"

"Is Vanessa home?" Calvin asked quickly, before the questions got any more specific.

"She'll be right back, went over to Kimmie's house to help her with some craft booth she's putting together for her grandkid's school." He lowered his head to get a better look at Richie's throat. "Damn, son, you get choked?"

Richie ran his fingers over the wound, now purple and further on its way to black with each passing minute. "Yeah, one of them came up behind me with a belt or something."

"Sweet Jesus," Singletary said, shaking his head. "That looks painful."

"It looks worse than it feels."

"Wait here," Calvin said to Richie. "I'll be right back, I gotta get that thing from my room."

Singletary stopped Calvin with a quick hand. "Hey, we haven't had a chance to talk, but I'm sorry about Garrison. I still can't get my mind around it."

"Thanks, man," Calvin said, giving in to Singletary's hug. "It's been a rough few days."

"No doubt, no doubt at all," Singletary said, letting him go. "Vanessa's pretty upset, can't even bring herself to talk about it, even with all them chatty women down at First Baptist. But for you, what with how close you and Garrison were, I can only imagine. Having to deal with all that and now this. Lord Almighty."

Calvin tried to hide his impatience with a deep, cleansing sigh. "Right now I'm trying to stay focused on Tracey and Martin," he said. "In fact we gotta get back to them, so—"

Singletary nodded and took a half-step back. "I understand, yeah, yeah. Go ahead."

Calvin nodded and left the two of them alone as he went to his bedroom.

Richie and Singletary stood awkwardly beside each other.

"You a Lakers fan?" Singletary finally asked, gesturing toward the TV.

"Sure, yeah. Grew up watching them. Bet on them a few times too."

"I don't mess around with that."

"Neither do I, not anymore."

Singletary rubbed his chin. "I used to go all the time when they were up at the Forum, but I don't go but a couple times a season now. Too pricey. Especially these playoff tickets, it's crazy."

"Yeah, it really is," Richie said, choosing to keep quiet about the time he got courtside seats.

"They doin' okay now," Singletary said, brightening. "Especially after losing that first game the way they did."

"I haven't been keeping up," Richie admitted. "How'd they lose game one?"

Singletary looked at him out the corner of his eye, the way a person might look at someone who said they weren't sure about the earth being round. "Big fan, huh?"

Calvin returned from the bedroom, the .9mm pistol they came for tucked into his belt under his shirt. "Okay, let's hit it."

"Where are Tracey and Martin, anyway?" Singletary asked.

"Huh?" Calvin said, not sure how to answer.

"They still at your place?" Singletary asked Richie. "Vanessa told me that punk Randall came by here the other day trying to start some trouble."

"Oh, yeah," Calvin said. "It's like a little vacation for them."

Singletary nodded. "I can understand that. But I'm gonna be staying over here tonight, so if y'all wanna go to Roscoes for dinner, it's on me, if you're up to it."

"Yeah, maybe," Calvin said, emotion making the words catch in his throat. They were standing there talking about having dinner as if nothing much had changed. But he was in an alternate universe now, his old life—Singletary, Vanessa, Garrison, the too-small house, Mount Olive preschool—all of it was a dream he couldn't quite recall, his new life a perpetual fall over a thousand-foot cliff, the ground coming up faster and faster to greet him. His wife and son were falling behind him, and the tension in his swollen skull was a constant reminder than he was the one who pulled them off that cliff. "Tell Vanessa that—tell her we'll see her later."

"Will do," Singletary said.

Richie shook Singletary's hand. "It was nice meeting you."

"You too, Richie. You want some ice or something for that throat before you go?"

"No, I'm fine."

Calvin opened the door and froze, his hand remaining on the screen. He pushed out a foul breath that growled in his throat before he pushed the squeaking screen door wide and stepped out on the porch. Richie stepped out beside him and then took a step back.

"What do we do?" he asked.

"I have no idea," Calvin answered.

The whale-like blue Thunderbird sat at the end of the drive-way, blocking the Subaru. Randall leaned on the hood, arms crossed, legs spread wide. Big Mike stayed at the wheel in his usual spot, and a third man—a Crip named Ghosty, whom Calvin had been friends with in elementary school when his name was Leonard—leaned against the Subaru as if he owned it.

Randall called out, "Damn nigger, I told you to be straight with me and now we got a situation."

"There ain't no situation," Calvin said, staying on the porch.

"Fuck there ain't," Randall said, coming off the Thunderbird. "In fact, judging by your face lookin' all busted, looks to me like you already into some shit over all this."

"Ran into some bad luck, is all."

"And I'm guessing the bad luck ain't over either, that's why you hangin' with whitey all of a sudden."

"He's my kid's tutor," Calvin casually lied.

A small smile momentarily creased Randall's face as he took a few steps toward the porch. "Is that what you told the cops when they was here?"

Calvin shifted his weight from one foot to the other. "They tryin' to figure out what's up, same as you are. Couldn't help them any more than I can you."

"Keep lyin', nigger. I been asking around 'bout that bank deal and word is you came away with some serious money."

"Can't help what people say."

Randall held out his hand to Richie. "Lessee what's in the bag, snowflake."

Richie readjusted the bag of money on his shoulder, regretting his decision to take it from the trunk. "It's only school supplies," he said. "Tutoring stuff, pens, books."

Randall looked over his shoulder at Ghosty. "You believe this shit?"

Ghosty spit on the ground by way of answer.

Randall raised his chin at Big Mike and the silent mountain moved out from behind the wheel to stand beside the Thunderbird.

The screen door squeaked behind them and Singletary came out onto the porch.

"You're gonna have to move that car," he said.

"Get your ass back in the house, old man," Randall said with a dismissive wave.

"Hold up," Ghosty laughed. "He about to tell us to get off his damn lawn."

Big Mike smiled at that one.

"We have a problem out here?" Singletary asked Calvin.

"Hell, yeah, we got a problem," Russell said. "What you gonna do?"

"Me? I'm not gonna do nothing." He took a cellphone from his back pocket and held it up like a shield. "But I can get the police on the phone right now and maybe they can do something about your problem, how's that?"

Russell waved another dismissive hand. "This ain't your business."

Singletary defiantly stepped off the porch. "You standing on my property makes it my business."

"Singletary," Calvin said. "Forget it, we don't need the cops here. You should go back inside."

Singletary ignored the suggestion. "How's that parole going,

Russell?" he asked, walking closer. "I'm guessing you don't want a violation, so why don't you reconsider your attitude."

Randall's expression slackened as he absorbed the challenge. And then he dropped Singletary to his knees with a short jab to the kidney. Singletary gasped for breath as he fell forward onto his hands, the phone flying free.

Calvin jumped off the porch, but got no closer.

"I'm guessing there's a reason you don't want the cops here any more than I do," Russell said to him. "So let's stop fucking around about it."

Calvin looked back at Richie, his eyes wide and afraid. "Get back in the house," he said. "Lock the door."

But Richie didn't move. He glanced at Ghosty and Big Mike as they stepped forward like a couple of wolves about to pounce. Then he, too, stepped off the porch.

"What the hell you doing?" Calvin said.

"The only thing I can do," Richie said, putting the bag of money on the ground at their feet.

"Richie, no," Calvin snapped.

As all eyes moved to the bag, Richie reached behind Calvin and pulled out the gun tucked into his belt. He pointed the pistol at Russell's chest, holding it steady less than a foot away.

"You think you hard now?" Russell said. "I'm gonna kill you, motherfucker."

"Yeah, well, get in line," Richie said.

As Russell eyed him like a dog trying to break free from a muzzle, Calvin reached around and took Russell's Glock from his belt, pointed it at him.

"You done fucked up, boy," Russell said.

"Yeah, I know," Calvin said. "Toss your gun over there," he said to Ghosty, flicking his wrist.

Ghosty tossed a nine-millimeter ten feet away and Big Mike shrugged when Calvin's gun landed on him. "Don't have one, cuz," he said.

Calvin had heard that about Big Mike, that his last parole violation broke him of the habit, so he didn't question him further. "Singletary," he said, not looking at his mother-in-law's boyfriend, his eyes now bouncing like a pinball between Ghosty, Big Mike, and Russell. "Go back in the house, we're cool."

Singletary stood, his cellphone back in his hand, now pressed to his ear. "I have a couple gang bangers threatening me," he said into the phone. "I need you to send a unit to Parks and 111th—"

"Singletary!" Calvin shouted at him. "Hang up—I said no police!"

Singletary's mouth hung open as he tried to work out the dynamics. "They're already on their way, son."

"Shit," Calvin said, moving to pick up the gun Ghosty tossed. "Richie, get the bag. Singletary, just go back inside the house."

Russell hooded his eyes as Richie picked up the bag and they moved toward the Subaru. "Go inside!" Calvin yelled at Singletary, who still hadn't moved.

This time, Singletary did as ordered.

As Calvin and Richie climbed back into the Subaru, Richie leaned out from behind the wheel and said, "By the way, when people ask why we can't all just get along? It's because you guys are dicks."

He then pulled the door closed, locked it, and turned over the engine. The car was thrown into reverse and it rammed the Thunderbird with a loud crunch of metal. It took an extra bit of engine power to push the bigger car back far enough to get out of the driveway, but once they were clear, Calvin rolled down the window. "And that gun the white boy pulled?" he said to the three men standing impotently on the lawn. "It wasn't loaded."

"I'm sorry, what?" Richie said.

"Just drive," Calvin said, and then he used Russell's Glock to shoot out the rear left tire of the Thunderbird.

Singletary watched from the front window of Vanessa's house, the gunshot still reverberating. "What in Jesus's name are you boys involved in?" he said aloud.

As Russell, Big Mike, and Ghosty ran to the disabled Thunderbird and drove off on three good wheels, making sure to be clear of the area before the police arrived, Singletary's cell-phone rang. It was the 911 dispatcher calling back. But he let it ring, having no idea what to tell them.

CHAPTER SEVENTEEN

IT WAS CLOSE to five by the time Calvin and Richie reached the lobby of the Victorian building on Brighton Way in Beverly Hills. They stepped into the elevators with a young lawyer in a brown suit. The brown suit pressed three and Richie pressed four.

"I thought maybe you were coming up to see us," the brown suit said.

"Excuse me?"

"I was only joking," the brown suit said with a shrug. "We represent a lot of accident victims."

"We weren't in an accident," Richie told him.

"Got it. First rule of Fight Club: don't talk about Fight Club."

The door dinged open, the brown suit walked from the elevator and the doors closed.

Richie shook his head, the bag of money heavy on his shoulder. "It's only after we lose everything that we're free to do anything, right?"

"What the hell you talking about?" Calvin asked.

"*Fight Club*. It's a line from the movie. It seemed apropos."

The doors dinged open and they stepped into the hallway,

facing the door to Global Consulting. With a quick look down the deserted hallway, Calvin said, "Give me my gun."

"Don't you have the one you took from Russell?"

"I left it in the car. Mine's a hell of a lot safer. All I need is to accidentally shoot this asshole in the face."

Richie gave his own furtive glance up the hallway, then handed the unloaded .38 to Calvin.

They entered Global Consulting to find it empty. No Jennifer at the reception desk.

Richie moved toward the silent conference room. "Maybe they left."

"With the door unlocked?" Calvin headed toward Chad's inner office. He gently pushed the door open to find Chad's desk chair turned away, toward the wall. Chad was in the chair, with the back of his head pointing up, as if he were looking at the ceiling; only, he didn't move. A shudder ran the length of Calvin's body as he realized that somehow, the men who took Tracey and Martin had already been there.

"Oh, shit," Richie said, as he looked over Calvin's shoulder, taking in the scene.

With a startled reflex, Chad's head ducked forward and then his entire body disappeared from view behind the desk. "One second," he said, before standing back up.

He turned to face the unexpected visitors, his hands busy buttoning his pants and fastening his belt as Jennifer climbed from her knees and came into view behind him. There was no trace of embarrassment on his flushed face, only a flicker of irritation. "I thought I made myself clear on the phone," he said. "There's nothing I can do for you." He squinted at them. "Other than perhaps refer you to a doctor. If your insides are as bad as your outsides, I'm afraid you might only have a few minutes to live."

Richie stepped fully into the room. "You're not far off, if we don't get those coins back."

Chad took a deep breath that filled his chest up with every last bit of his annoyance. "As I told you, I don't have any idea what coins you're talking about."

Calvin pulled the gun and pointed it at him. "This ring any bells?"

Jennifer let out a sharp squeal.

Chad held up both hands. "Take it easy, son."

"My old man died in prison after shooting a dumb-ass crook like you, so call me son one more time and you're gonna end up just as dead."

"Understood," Chad said, his cold, lawyerly exterior melting. He turned to his assistant, who had begun to cry. "You can go."

Jennifer came around the desk, but Calvin blocked her exit. "You can stay, actually."

Chad said, "She doesn't need to be here for whatever business we have."

"And I don't need her out there calling security because you've suddenly developed amnesia." He shook the gun in her direction. "Wipe off your knees and have a seat."

Jennifer took a few halting steps backward and sat on the couch.

"The gun is really not necessary," Chad said.

"Bullshit!" Calvin said. "You cheated us."

"No, it was Winslow who did that."

Richie jabbed an accusing finger at him. "We trusted you."

"Oh, don't give me that *poor me* shit," Chad said, turning to Calvin. "Wasn't it you who said there was no difference between a businessman and a thief? You had to expect I was going to make a deal that best served my client's interests."

"We were your clients, too," Richie said. "Damn, after all my father did for you."

"Playing the dead father card is beneath you, Richie."

"Oh, really, *Chad?*" Richie yelled in his face. "I should let him shoot you right now. Shoot you right in the knees, you lying prick. Or maybe shoot that little pecker off so Jennifer doesn't have to keep brushing her teeth in the middle of the day."

"Hey!" Chad barked. "I looked out for you, too. I did. Whether you choose to believe it or not, his first offer was half of what you got."

Calvin walked the gun forward, until it was pressed to Chad's forehead. "I don't give a shit about the goddamn money."

Chad's right cheek quivered. "I assure you that Mr. Winslow will not feel the same way."

"Then I swear to God, I'll kill him."

Richie's voice softened. "Chad, listen. The men who owned the coins took Calvin's wife and son."

Chad sagged slightly. "Jesus. I'm sorry to hear that."

"Then you'll help us, right?" Richie pleaded. "We still have all the money, all of it. Even though it's not what they're worth, it's still an even swap back."

"I'm telling you," Chad said. "He'll never agree to it. All he'll do is hang up in my ear, then send some of his biker friends to convince you of his position. Judging by the condition of your face, you've already learned how convincing those sorts of conversations can be."

The gun shook in Calvin's hand. "Then give us an address," he said. "We'll take care of it ourselves."

The drive from Los Angeles to Las Vegas can take anywhere from three and half hours to ten, depending on traffic. Leaving at five in the afternoon meant it would take somewhere in the middle of that range, but Calvin and Richie had no choice but to suffer the slow desert trip in the busted-up Subaru. It was fortunate—all things considered—that Winslow was a desert rat. A man of his means could have flown in from Monte Carlo or some other far-flung location, and Richie and Calvin would be screwed. Flying was out of the question, as there was no way to sneak two guns and a bag stuffed with a million dollars past the TSA.

When they reached the freeway heading east, they had nineteen hours left to find Winslow, make the exchange for the coins (either by agreement or by force), get back to Los Angeles, and make the second exchange of coins for Tracey and Martin.

During the first hour and a half of the trip—spent in bumper-to-bumper traffic on the 10 freeway—Calvin didn't say a word. When they reached Highway 15, the road that would take them north to Vegas, he spoke for the first time since leaving Beverly Hills. "If I get killed," he said, his eyes fixed on the world outside the car. "You gotta give me your word you'll do whatever it takes to get Tracey and Martin home safe."

Richie's nerves were like exposed wires, and Calvin's request shocked him to attention. "Damn, Calvin," he said. "Nobody's gonna die. Maybe Winslow's an asshole, but he's not gonna kill us. Chad's gotta be wrong about him. He'll bitch and moan, maybe threaten us a whole lot, but ultimately he'll see it's the right thing to do."

Calvin looked down at his hands, flexing them. "People are blind, man," he said. "They can't do the right thing when they can't see what the right thing is."

"Then we'll make him see. We'll pry his fucking eyes open."

Calvin stared out the window at the desert slowly being consumed by darkness. "Right."

And that was the last of the conversation.

By the time Richie refilled the tank in Barstow, halfway to Vegas from LA, the whole endeavor had long taken on a surreal quality. Standing under the bright lights of the gas station, an oasis amid the impenetrable darkness of the Mojave, he pondered the task they had set themselves on, unable to decide if it was fear that made him shake, or mere exhaustion. Either way, he needed to fight off the nausea turning his skin moist and his tongue dry.

Despite his assurances to Calvin that nobody was going to get killed, the possibility weighed heavily on him. The more he thought about it, the more it struck him as probability rather than possibility. After all, they were not special, not immune to the deathly chaos assaulting them from all sides. They were no different from the doomed hipster Amir-Ali, dead at the bottom of the ocean, or Gavin Hendricks, Gonzo, and the other men dead on the floor of American Federal, or cousin Garrison dead on the sidewalk, or Connor Weeks dead in his wheelchair, or David Perlstein and Connor's men dead in his living room, or Sammy, dead in his shop in Hollywood. They, too, had all refilled their gas tanks and made plans, casually assuring themselves that tomorrow was theirs, the full tank of gas was going to get used, it was the other guy who had to worry, not them.

Richie had seen death before, both a slow ending with his mother and a quick one with his father, but those had come naturally. Death by disease was a different animal, one that could be understood, its emotional affects tamed. But what he'd experienced over the past few days was impossible to put into context, impossible to emotionally absorb.

He put the pump back into the cradle and screwed on the cap. Climbing back behind the wheel, he could not bring himself to speak to or look at Calvin. Any casual conversation would be a lie, a low whistle past a graveyard.

After Barstow it was all desert, an expanse of darkness that remained hidden from view; only the road directly in front of them was illuminated. As the engine hummed and the tires thumped in the silence between them, it was as though they were already dead, ghosts trying to figure out a way back into the physical world. Richie drove on in a trance. Who would care if his life truly ended? Certainly none of his ex-girlfriends, who had all moved on long ago. He had no extended family to speak of, at least none who would bother to travel further than across the street for a funeral. And even if they did, there would be no tears spilled on his account. They'd only gossip about what a screw-up he'd been and wonder what the hell happened to all of the money he must have squandered. A few gambling buddies might notice his continued absence, but they wouldn't miss him, only his bad luck at the table. Sam would have cared, maybe, if he wasn't dead himself. But what would that amount to? There's always another gambler to take his place.

But Calvin. Calvin would be missed. Even if Tracey and Martin hated him right now for what he'd put them through, they would miss him. Jesus. Tracey and Martin. What was happening to them? They weren't immune either. Death could swallow them up just as easily. In fact, they might be in the greatest danger of all.

What would happen to them if Winslow wouldn't play ball? If he didn't believe their story about foreign gangsters and family kidnappings. Or he might believe them and not give a shit, deciding it was much cleaner to kill the two idiots who'd sold the coins for half their value and then impudently demanded them back. If that was the case, then no more coins and no more Tracey and no more Martin. Richie imagined Vanessa and Singletary down at the Baptist Church crying and praying over them, insisting that Calvin was a good man, despite what the papers were saying about him being a criminal, a thug. They were a good family, they'd say, more than just another statistic to be added to a lost society's ledger. They were valued, worth crying over.

He glanced to his right, catching only Calvin's profile as he stared straight ahead, undoubtedly lost in his own ghost world.

"You really think Winslow's crazy enough to kill us?" Richie asked.

The road behind them disappeared into the darkness.

Calvin said, "Yes."

Chad's professional stance on keeping no daylight between himself and his client's secrets had been softened by the gun Calvin pressed to his forehead. In fact, he became quite talkative once he stopped shaking and sweating, his cock getting smaller and smaller in his pants as Jennifer helplessly looked on. Despite Winslow still having no first name, they had learned enough about him to understand they were driving into the den of the lion. Chad had made it clear that Winslow was more than your garden-variety asshole, and far more than merely eccentric. He was crazy, and crazy was impossible to predict. Assholes reacted within certain parameters, Chad had argued, but those with his type of crazy had no limits on their behavior, because they *chose* to be that way. Yeah, he could control it, but it was more fun to let it run rampant. While some poor bastard off his meds might strip naked and walk down the street yelling about UFOs, Winslow might stab a guy in the leg out of curiosity to see how he would react. Controlled crazy was much more dangerous. And Winslow's crazy was fed by unlimited funds. "Not a good combination" was how Chad put it.

But Chad had no concrete ideas about how Winslow had

made his money. Something to do with South America was all he knew. He'd learned other things, like the fact that as a younger man, Winslow had spent two years in prison for beating a woman with a croquet mallet. And that fifteen years ago, he had done business running guns in Tampa with a mobster connected to the Lucchese crime family. That brief but highly profitable arrangement had come to an end when the unnamed mobster turned rat and ended up wearing his tongue as a necktie. Once his connected associates started getting rounded up by the Feds and Winslow saw that he'd somehow swum free of the fishing net, he left the guns behind in Florida to set up shop in Vegas, where he took up motorcycles and collecting pretty things made of gold. He had mellowed a bit in the intervening years, sure, but the crazy remained.

It was ten-thirty by the time Richie and Calvin arrived at the Vegas Strip, five and half hours after leaving Beverly Hills. Their wracked bodies were stiff with pain, their bruises having deepened all the way to the bone. The specific mechanics of the exchange had not been decided, as it had been agreed the plan would present itself once they got the lay of the land. Maybe break into his house. Maybe kidnap him. Maybe plead for mercy and understanding. There was no playbook when dealing with a madman. So for now, they focused on the fact that, somehow, the money was going to stay with Winslow and the coins were going back with them. To even entertain the possibility of failure was to entertain the idea of Tracey and Martin being killed. Find Winslow. Make the exchange. Drive back to LA and make the phone call by two o'clock tomorrow. Get Tracey and Martin home safely. Keeping it in those general terms made the drive bearable. Try to fill in the gaps with too many specifics and you'd lose your lunch.

Waiting to turn left on Flamingo Road, the eight-mile-long

street that intersected the heart of the Strip, Richie said, "If you'd told me a week ago I'd be sitting here, this close to all those casinos, with a million dollars in cash…" He shook his head and they inched forward in the line of red brake lights.

Calvin turned from the crowds that streamed down the street like frenzied ants swarming a buffet, their neon-lit faces glowing with excitement beneath the behemoth hotels that, by their ostentatious enormity, promised all who entered a chance at finding sudden wealth. "It just hit me what you're giving up," he said.

"It's no big deal," Richie said.

The light turned green and the Subaru moved forward.

"Half a million ain't a small deal either."

Richie rolled his head toward the window. "No, I guess it isn't."

They followed the map on Calvin's phone eastward for another twenty minutes, to a hilltop community of large homes with large lots, each with a sweeping view of the surrounding desert.

"Turn here," Calvin said, looking up from the glowing phone.

Richie turned at the quiet intersection and they drove down a wider street with fewer homes, set even further apart. Most were brightly lit in the moonless Mojave night, deep shadows contouring landscaped yards full of shade trees and gurgling fountains.

"Left," Calvin said at an intersection.

Richie turned the wheel, each throb of his pulse felt in the scabbing wounds on his face.

"Right," Calvin said after a couple hundred feet.

Leaving the other homes behind, the world outside got darker and darker, matching their moods. The Subaru's headlights now illuminated a long, dark cul-de-sac, with only one home at its wide-mouthed end. It was like the street was swallowing them down its gullet.

"Slow down," Calvin said, the phone in his lap finally going dark.

An uneasy duet of shallow breaths filled the car as they eased up the street and the Subaru came to a stop. They idled in silence, staring at Winslow's home.

Its architecture was modern, two stories of squares and rectangles of varying dimensions stacked at odd angles, some turned slightly off axis, giving the impression of a Jenga tower turned on its side. Powerful uplights glinted off the preponderance of glass and steel in some places, while downlight cast shadows from the eaves and balconies on the second floor, giving it all a sinister aura. Danger seemed to lurk in the dark crevices, ready to pounce on anybody foolish enough to get too close. Where the other homes they passed had pruned cacti, fruit trees, fountains, and flagstone hardscape, this home had no trees at all, no bushes, only a polished cement driveway that splintered off from two massive steel garage doors taking up the western edge of the main, ground-floor rectangle, on its way to the blood-red front door.

"Doesn't look like anyone's home," Calvin said at last.

"No," Richie said. "It doesn't."

"Any ideas?"

Richie put the car in reverse and backed up a hundred feet. He pulled off the paved street and shut off the lights, shrouding them in the desert darkness. He opened the car door. "I gotta take a leak."

Calvin followed him out of the car and they stood beside each other, peeing into the dirt.

The night hummed warmly in their ears, invisible insects scratched their skin. They both shook, gooseflesh rising on their arms.

"I'm scared out of my fucking mind," Richie said, zipping up his fly.

Calvin finished up and turned back to look up toward the house. "You don't gotta do this. You've done enough, giving up that money like you did. This is on me now. You wait here, I'll go up there and deal with him myself."

Richie rubbed his eyes. "Turning me back into a getaway driver, huh?"

Calvin grinned, despite himself. "I guess so, yeah."

"And that turned out so well for me the first time."

"Better than it did for Garrison and anyone else that went inside."

Richie's eyes narrowed at a pinpoint of light approaching from far down the road. "Hey, we got company."

As the distant headlights grew larger, more distinct, the two frightened men ran for cover, hiding in the soft ground behind the Subaru.

"Shit," Calvin whispered.

"What?"

"I left the gun in the car."

"You can't get it now. You open the door and the light will go on. Damn it, maybe we should run."

"Run where?"

"Anywhere." Richie nodded into the darkness. "Out there. So what if he sees an abandoned car?"

Calvin's frustration came to full boil. "The money's in there too. If he stops and finds that bag, we're done."

Their breathing turned shallow, expectant, as the car made its way up the dark street toward them. It moved quickly, the hum of its engine not slowing as it passed and continued on toward the house.

"Holy crap, I don't think they saw us," Richie said.

Once they were sure they couldn't be seen in a rearview, they moved back to the road, looking after the car, its red brake lights barely visible in the distance.

"At least we know someone's home now," Calvin said, opening the door to the Subaru to retrieve Randall's .38 from under the seat.

Richie stretched his neck. "I guess that means we're not gonna be breaking in."

"We?" Calvin asked, looking sideways at him as he tucked the gun under his belt at his lower back.

Richie shrugged. "I was a crappy getaway driver anyway."

"You sure? Ain't no light poles around here to crash into, you'll be all right."

"I'm sure," Richie said. But he said it like he wasn't sure at all.

The distant brake lights disappeared and the headlights washed over the terrain beyond the cul-de-sac as the car turned around, heading back toward them.

"Oh, shit," Richie said, ducking back behind the Subaru.

Half a second later, Calvin crouched down beside him. "Forgot the money again," he whispered.

"We really aren't very good at this," Richie whispered back.

This time the car slowed as it approached and then stopped, its engine idling in the still night.

And then the horn honked.

Richie and Calvin remained where they were, holding their breath.

"Hello?" a man's voice called out.

Calvin let out a long, regretful sigh and then started to stand. Richie tried to stop him, but Calvin pulled his arm free and stood, exposing himself. Richie stayed where he was.

"What up?" Calvin said, his right hand behind him, ready to pull the gun.

"Everything all right?" the man asked. He was Middle Eastern, his eyes bright, friendly.

"We're waiting for someone," Calvin told the man.

"Oh, yeah, he's home," the man said. "I just dropped off his girlfriend, at least I'm guessing that's who she was."

Calvin glanced at the Uber sticker in the car's windshield and brought his empty right hand forward, waved it at him. "Thanks for the information."

The driver jabbed a thumb back toward the house. "He asked me to tell you to come on up."

"He what?" Calvin asked.

Richie shot upright behind the Subaru, stared at the driver.

"Oh, hey," the driver said. "How's it going?"

"What did he say to you?" Richie asked.

"He said he's tired of waiting for you two fuck-sticks to make up your minds what you're gonna do and that you should tuck your balls back into your pussies and go inside. Sorry for the language. He paid me an extra twenty bucks to say that. Have a good night."

The Uber driver gave a small wave, rolled up his window and drove off.

After five minutes of debate over how screwed they were, they decided whatever plan they might have come up with didn't matter now, so they climbed back into the Subaru and drove back up the road.

"It had to be Chad that tipped him off," Richie sighed. "After all my dad did for him. Sent him all that legitimate business, made him a small fortune, and this is how he repays us. I actually believed him when he said he'd stay out of it."

"People tend to lie when they have a gun pointed at them," Calvin said. "Evidently he's more afraid of Winslow than he ever was of us."

The massive house again rose up to greet them, and they were momentarily silenced.

At the end of the cul-de-sac, Richie put the car into park and shut off the engine. "Guess Chad assumed we weren't gonna live long enough to pay him back for lying to us."

Calvin looked down at the gun in his lap. "Maybe it's Winslow who's not gonna live long enough."

"You really think you have it in you to shoot him?"

Calvin nodded. "All I gotta do is remember that he's standing in the way of me and my family. If it comes down to him or them, I'll put a bullet in his head. I swear to Jesus I will."

"I'm sure Jesus appreciates you bringing him into this, but promise me you'll let me talk to Winslow first. You can't go in there and start firing at everyone."

Despite his stated convictions, fear widened Calvin's eyes. "How many guys you think he's got in there?"

"I have no idea, but even if it's only him and his lady, adding double homicide to our resume isn't gonna help things."

Calvin looked seriously at him. "This shit's for real, you understand that, right?"

"Yeah, I got it." He pointed at the wounds on his chin, nose, and neck. "Those bastards imprinted real all over my face."

"I'm just saying if you go in there with me, you gotta be prepared to do whatever it takes." He reached under the seat and pulled out the .9 mm.

"That thing loaded this time?" Richie asked.

"Compliments of your old friend, Ghosty."

Richie hesitated, then took the gun. "Okay," he said. "But give me a chance to talk to him first. If he tries anything, then we blast away and we'll plead self-defense if it comes to that."

Calvin conceded to the plan and they climbed from the car.

"I think we're gonna be okay," Richie said as they slowly walked to the fifteen-foot-tall front door looming over them like a drawbridge.

"Yeah?" Calvin asked. "Why?"

Richie reached for the doorbell. "Because if he wanted us dead he'd have killed us already."

The doorbell rang and they waited.

"You're forgetting one thing," Calvin said, the bag of money draped over his shoulder.

"What's that?"

Calvin looked up at the video camera pointed down at them, a pool of sweat developing between the gun and his lower back. "This motherfucker's choosing to be crazy."

CHAPTER EIGHTEEN

"YOU GUYS MADE good time," the woman said as she closed the door behind them. "That drive can be a real bitch."

She was tall, about five-ten, with thick brown hair that fell all the way to the top of her wide hips; a brown cloth bandana held it back from her round face. She wore a faded Black Sabbath t-shirt that revealed her thick arms, neither of which had any space left to add to her collection of tattoos. She could have been thirty-five or fifty-five, it was hard to tell with the deep tan and heavy makeup around her eyes. Though if you went only by the throaty voice, you'd guess somewhere around eighty.

"He's been expecting us, I take it?" Richie said.

The woman's laugh came up from her throat as if riding on a tide of phlegm. "Yeah, he called me hours ago, said you two idiots were on your way from LA." She led them down a single step, directly into the warehouse-like living room decorated with a mishmash of spare decor that was not without a certain elegance. Original artwork with a modern sensibility hung on the walls, and leather club chairs mixed in nicely with Art Deco sofas underneath a starry canvas of recessed lighting. Floor-to-ceiling windows on the eastern exposure looked out on a brightly lit pool, its water glowing aqua green amid a seemingly eternal expanse of desert.

"Are you Mrs. Winslow?" Richie asked.

"Mrs. Winslow," she repeated with a derisive grunt. She lifted a pack of unfiltered cigarettes from her shirt pocket and put one between her dry lips. "You shouldn't have come."

Calvin remained silent as she lit it.

Richie said, "We didn't have a choice."

"Of course you did," she said. "But you chose wrong. Coming at him like this was a mistake. It shows a lack of respect."

"We mean no disrespect to anyone," he said.

"Mm-hmm," she shrugged, blowing out a thick stream of smoke that shrouded her weathered face.

The house was quiet, eerily so. There were long hallways off both ends of the living room, leading to distant darkness. The entry hall and living room were evidently the only illuminated spaces in the whole place. Richie craned his neck to see past the woman, as if worried there were assassins hiding in the shadowy recesses behind her.

She leaned to the side to catch his eye. "Looking for something?"

"Where's he at?" Calvin asked.

Her eyes flicked over to him as another laugh came out sounding like a shoe scraping across a bed of pebbles. "He's right behind you."

They whipped around to see Winslow standing under the archway leading into the entry hall. He was still dressed in his Easy Rider getup, black work boots and leather pants, though he had lost the leather jacket, with all its jingling zippers. A tight beige shirt that was only a few shades darker than his skin was left unbuttoned to the middle of his hairless chest, exposing his own menagerie of faded tattoos. A glass of dark liquor sloshed in the lowball glass in his hand.

"I told you two what would happen if you ever came looking for me," he said. "What part of that did you not get?"

Calvin had one hand clutching the money bag strapped across his chest, the other hand tucked casually behind his back.

"We can explain," Richie said.

"Please do."

Richie spoke quickly, before Calvin had the time to decide the conversation was useless and moved on to plan B. "I don't know what Chad's already told you," he said.

"He told me you're having a situation with the men you stole from. And I can see by the condition of your goddamn faces they mean business."

"Yes, that's right," Richie said.

"Don't you two know how to fight?"

"There were more of them."

"And it looks like they did some of the work I had planned to do myself."

"So how 'bout we call it even?" Richie asked.

Winslow stepped fully into the room as the woman blew more cigarette smoke, fouling the air. "I gotta be honest with you. When Chad called me, I was beyond pissed, lost my shit for a while. Hell, I was ready to send some of my friends to kill you both before you reached the state line, keep you as far away from me as possible. But Heather here talked me off the ledge, said the circumstances warranted a new perspective."

Richie nodded at her. "We appreciate that, Heather," he said to the woman and she smiled back, waved her cigarette at him.

Winslow took another sip of booze, eyed Calvin. "You agreed to let him do all the talking, didn't you?"

"I know you got a problem with me," Calvin said. "So we figured it was better that way."

"Sounds reasonable," Winslow said. "Though it's not as if I have any great feelings for either one of you."

"And we don't blame you for that," Richie said, his confidence building. "But we hoped you would understand that we had to come, despite the risks, and that you would be open to discussing our options."

Winslow gave him a confused stare. "Options?"

"Yeah, ways to work this out."

"And exactly how many ways do you see for us to do that?"

Richie immediately recognized his error. The gun he had tucked into his belt felt like a hot coal burning his skin and he was sure Winslow could smell it from across the room. "Only one, really," he said. "We still have all the money."

Winslow asked Calvin, "But what you don't have is the wife and kid, that it?"

"That's exactly it," Calvin said.

Winslow nodded as though he were dealing with a couple of idiot children. "Like I said, Chad explained all of this to me already. Said you'd like to give me the money back."

Richie licked his lips, cleared his throat. "Well, trade it back for the coins."

Winslow frowned encouragingly, as though this was all a misunderstanding to clear up, so they could go on their merry way. "That way you can exchange the coins for your family?"

Calvin nodded once.

Winslow finished his drink. "Even-Steven."

"Even-Steven," Richie said, his shoulders finally relaxing.

Winslow looked to Heather. "What do you think about all this?"

"It is what it is," she answered.

Winslow was quiet for a long moment, then said to Calvin, "I'm not looking to jam you up. After all, I have a family too."

Heather tamped out her cigarette in a stone ashtray on the coffee table.

"So where does that leave us?" Calvin asked.

"It leaves us with some business to take care of," Winslow said, simply. He held out his hand. "Give me the money."

Richie and Calvin read in each other's eyes the wary possibility that maybe this dude was crazy enough to defy all their expectations.

"Where are the coins?" Calvin said.

"They're in my office."

"Maybe Heather can go get them for us," he suggested.

Winslow smiled. "I'm sure she'd be more than happy to do so. Go ahead and give her the bag and she'll swap them for you."

Calvin shook his head. "No coins, no money."

Winslow smiled, flashed his gold tooth. "For someone with a face like a rotting plum, you sure don't lack for confidence."

A distant hum unsettled the room's atmosphere. At first it seemed like an earthquake with barely enough energy to reach them, but soon after their ears caught hold of it, the hum turned into a rumble that vibrated in their chests. Closer and closer the rumbling cacophony came, like an avalanche filling that mouth-like cul-de-sac out front, loud enough to rattle teeth. Perhaps twenty motorcycles could make such a racket, but maybe it would take thirty, fifty, it was impossible to tell. The noise from the engines echoed off the walls as the bikes idled in front of the house.

Richie's face paled. "I don't suppose that's the Vegas chapter of Bikers for Christ?"

"Afraid not," answered Winslow. "That's the *family* I told you about."

"Sounds like you have a lot of mouths to feed," said Richie. "I hope they aren't here to feed on us."

Winslow laughed, but there was no amusement in it. "Don't worry, I'm a man of my word. We still have a deal."

Richie again licked his lips. "So why don't we do this, so we can be on our way?"

"Good idea." Winslow's joyless smile slowly faded. "Give me the two million right now and I'll give you the coins."

"C'mon, man," Richie said. "You know we don't have that kind of money."

"Did you come here to make a deal or not?" Winslow asked.

"Yes, but—"

"And I'm sure Chad explained that's what the coins are worth."

"They're worth a lot more than that," Calvin said.

Winslow turned. "You still don't understand supply and demand, do you?"

Richie said, "It doesn't have to be like this, man."

"Sure it does."

Calvin made a move to pull the gun from his belt, but only got it halfway out.

"Take it easy, Midnight," Heather said, the gun in her hand only a few inches from his right temple. Evidently he wasn't the only one hiding something. "Keep moving and what little brains you have'll be splattered all over the floor."

With no other choice, Calvin raised his hands and she took the Glock from him.

"If I didn't just have the place cleaned," Winslow said, "I'd let her go ahead and blow your head off."

"Yeah, these things can get messy," Richie said. He aimed Ghosty's .9mm directly at Winslow's tattooed chest.

"Option number two," Winslow said, his voice calm as ever, his eyes two dark holes, endless in their depth.

"We didn't want it to come to this," Richie said.

"How many bullets you got in that thing, boy? Enough for all my brothers out there? Because if you pull that trigger, that's what you're gonna need."

"Put the gun down," Richie said to Heather.

"Sure. Should I shoot this nigger first?" she asked.

Calvin's eyes were bloodshot with emotion. Sweat dripped under his lids.

"No," Richie answered. "No one needs to die here."

"You sure?" Winslow asked. "Because I sure as hell don't see option number three."

"Shoot him," Calvin said. "Shoot his ass. We're fucking dead anyway."

"He's got a point," Winslow conceded.

Heather did not take the gun off Calvin, letting Richie decide which of them would die first, her man or his. Richie's eyes flicked her way—whatever happened, she didn't seem too concerned about who would die third. Richie's finger trembled on the trigger as it eased forward, but it would go no further.

The front door swung open and a sickening menagerie of bikers came inside, each one larger than the one before, some with hair down their backs, others with shaved domes, too many of them to count. Whatever the number, there were more than Richie could ever shoot, even if he had four guns. He lowered Ghosty's .9mm and let it drop.

Heather brought her gun down on the side of Calvin's head, dropping him to his knees. She swung the gun back at Richie, who raised his hands, helpless. She waved the barrel of the gun toward the floor. "Join your friend," she said, and Richie obediently knelt. One of the arriving bikers, a bald behemoth with a thick mustache that bent like a horseshoe around his mouth, kicked Richie in the back with the heel of his cowboy boot, sending him onto his face.

The other men laughed.

Winslow crouched beside Calvin, who was struggling to stay conscious, his eyes glassy, his mouth hanging open as if his jaw had been knocked off its hinges. A long string of saliva dripped from his lower lip. "I told you I'm a man of my word," Winslow said, his breath hot in Calvin's ear.

"Please," Calvin said, staring through the white spots in his field of vision.

"Don't beg," Winslow said, lifting the bag of money from Calvin's shoulder. "It's annoying."

"They're gonna kill my family," he said.

"Yes," Winslow nodded. "They are."

He stood with the money bag clutched in his ringed fingers.

"Any ideas how we can dispose of these two?" he asked his newly arrived guests.

"Nice night for a bonfire," the bald biker who had kicked Richie suggested, eliciting more laughter.

"Looks like you two already went to work on them," another voice chimed in.

"Nah, they walked into the place looking like that," Heather said. "I'm guessing in their condition it isn't gonna take much to finish them off."

"No fun in that," the bald biker said, followed by yet another round of laughter.

Richie trembled as he listened, afraid even raise his chin to get a good look at his executioners.

"Get 'em outside, before they mess up my floors," Winslow ordered, swinging the bag of money over shoulder. "And one of you go bury their guns somewhere. I don't want any trace of these two left behind."

As Winslow left to deposit the bag into his safe, Richie was yanked to his feet and hauled across the room in a crush of denim and leather that smelled of sweat, booze, weed, and cigarettes. Most of the men surrounding him sported some unkempt brand of facial hair, many spotted with grey, with only a handful who looked to be under forty. From the bits of conversation Richie could decipher, a few of the men were cracking jokes about sodomizing them with a cactus, while others talked about unrelated business, unfazed by the violence of the moment. "It's that crappy cam-chain system, it's grinding all the time," one voice complained about his motorcycle, as if it was merely another day around the water cooler. Another voice answered, "Brother, you need to get a new gear set. That shit's a problem that's only gonna get worse."

Richie listened to them, struck by the notion that tomorrow he was going to be dead and these two were going to be down at Pep Boys complaining about the lag time in getting new parts. It was like being caught in a riptide, no matter his effort, the tide would not let him go. He relaxed into it, allowing it to carry him where it would. Perhaps he'd become numb to the violence over the past week, but none of it seemed real anymore. As they reached the back door and the desert night air slapped his face, his vision blurred. He realized he was crying. Tears dripped down his cheeks as knotted hands squeezed tighter under his armpits, dragging him along, his legs worthless to him, like streamers trailing a parade car.

The procession stopped a few yards beyond the glowing pool, its submerged lights casting aqua blue shadows, softening the rough faces standing around it. A thumb ground into his armpit like a screw a size too big, and he yelped in pain. Then his voice cut off in his throat when the biker to his left slammed a forearm across his cheek and he was shoved to his knees. Surrounded by a tangle of legs, he heard Calvin's voice, full of anger and belligerence, screaming to be let go so he could kick their asses.

Richie wiped the blur from his eyes. Leaning first to the left and then to the right, he caught sight of Calvin between two sets of grease-stained jeans. He stood on the opposite side of the pool, three men restraining him; one had him in a chokehold. An odd sense of pride welled up to see Calvin fighting so hard that it took three men to restrain him. Then his pride gave way to shame that nobody held him, that he'd already given up.

Winslow and Heather stood beside Calvin, facing the pool and the thirty or so men surrounding it, like it was an altar on which they would place their sacrifice. Heather smoked another cigarette, the smoke rising like an offering to the god of destruction they all worshipped.

"This is not personal," Winslow's voice announced, silencing the men around him, but not Calvin, who let out another primal scream of anguish, a stuck pig sound. But the chokehold around his neck grew tighter, and after the initial explosion of protest, his vocal chords were now barely able to vibrate enough to make any sound at all. Everything he ever was—a son, a husband, a father—was slowly being snuffed out.

"I'm sorry about your family, Calvin, that's not a lie," Winslow said to him, unmoved by his suffering. "But you should have done more to protect them, and that's on you, not me. That's all this is about—protection. You failed to protect your family, but I'll be damned if I fail to protect mine. You should never have brought me into this if you couldn't keep your end of the deal. I told you the first time we met, I would do whatever it took to protect myself, and, well, this is what I meant." He twirled his index finger in a small circle. "And that goes for all you sons-of-bitches. We have a code, and if anybody here breaks it, you're gonna end up buried in the desert right alongside these two Twinkies. Where's that sniveling white boy at anyway?"

The man with the screw-like thumbs again jammed them into Richie's armpits and hoisted him to his feet. Others then pushed and pulled him forward to the pool's edge. He stood there like the sacrificial lamb he was, shaking in the warm air, trying like hell not to start crying again. He stared across the glow of water at Calvin, who was barely hanging on under the force of pressure to his throat.

"Anything you'd like to add, Sunshine?" Winslow called to Richie.

Richie considered making one last plea for leniency. But there were no words left to use. "I'm sorry, Calvin," he said. "I should have shot this racist piece of shit when I had the chance."

The air was once more thick with laughter. They were all having such a good time, drunk on the adrenaline of surrendering to their basest impulses.

All resistance drained from Calvin's eyes. He had no hope left. In his defeated posture, Calvin acknowledged that Winslow was right after all. He hadn't done anything to protect his family. In fact, he had caused their destruction with his own selfish bullshit. He had lived on the street instead of in his home, and this is where the street ended. He'd been running up a cul-de-sac his entire life.

"Five hundred bucks to anyone willing to get wet and drown these assholes!" Winslow called out.

Another cheer rose up amongst the bikers as a few started to strip down to their underwear. Heather draped an arm around Winslow and happily pointed.

"All you gotta do is throw the black boy in!" she shouted. "They can't swim anyway."

Amid the whoops and hollers, four men won the race down to their underwear, two of them forgetting to take off their socks as they jumped into the water like kids anxious to play a game of Marco Polo.

"That's it!" Winslow called out. "No more of you in the water! They aren't worth more than two grand!"

The outlaw's pool-party intensity grew to a fever pitch as Winslow flicked a quick arm across the water, indicating the time had come for the sacrifice to begin.

Richie had barely a moment to take a breath when he was violently pushed into the pool. His mouth was open when he hit the water and the chlorinated distaste washed down his throat. He thrashed back to the surface, his clothes weighing him down, his eyes stinging as his lungs expanded. He caught sight of Calvin being shoved under the water across the pool, his legs kicking up, impotently splashing those cheering on the carnage from the pool's edge.

And then there was only darkness and the muffled sounds of his own terror. He kept his eyes closed as the water enveloped him, everything getting heavier and heavier. Sturdy hands pressed on his shoulders, curved his head down into his chest, sending a jolt of pain up his spine. He bent his arm behind him, trying to make contact with the men he could no longer see, but the arm was grabbed, twisted behind his back. It felt as if it would break, snap right off at the elbow, as he was bent further forward at the waist, his chest now closer to the bottom of the pool than his shoulders. The force focused on his body was otherwordly, as though gravity itself was in on the drowning.

He fought hard, a frantic survival instinct taking over, but he could not break free, could not so much as raise his chin. A spasm went through his body, and then he went limp.

This time there would be no unexpected bullet through a window to stay the execution.

No reprieve from the darkness they had immersed themselves in.

This time, only the God of Chaos himself could reject the sacrifice being offered in his name.

CHAPTER NINETEEN

CHAD SAT IN his office, alone. Jennifer had gone home over an hour ago. It had taken him the hour before that to convince her not to quit. She had cried and whimpered and, on two separate occasions, screamed at him. But she had calmed, eventually, after he gave her a raise of a thousand dollars a month and promised he would no longer do the sort of business that ended with guns pointed at them.

Once Jennifer was gone, he poured a glass of Scotch and, less than five minutes later, poured another. He continued to drink, despite the lingering sensation of nausea. The prospect of immediate death certainly had a way of upsetting the stomach.

He was starting on the third glass when the little boy came to sit with him. At first Chad invited him in, sat with him in silence and tried to reminisce about the happy times. But the boy was not there for a friendly visit and would not play along. He had no interest in playing back the memory tapes of their brief time together, before the cruel world decided they'd had enough. Chad tried to trick the little boy into a better mood by telling him about his mother, who was home, probably fixing dinner and wondering what movie they were going to watch that night on HBO. We're still together, he told his dead son. He'd kept the promise he made all those years ago. But his son's ghost only sat there, staring at him with wide, judgmental eyes—forever nine years old, forever silent.

Chad finished his third glass of Scotch and had the bottle of Macallan hovering over his glass before he decided he'd had enough. One more and he might do something stupid. He went to the bathroom down the hall and closed the door.

He splashed cold water on his face, let it drip off his chin and nose into the sink as he studied his fat, pale face in the mirror, pinkish pads under his eyes the only color to be found. It was like looking at a cadaver. And he was sure the inside was even worse than the outside. There was no doubt his organs—distended after sixty-seven years of too much booze, too many drugs—were worthless. Even his cock no longer worked, unless, of course, he popped yet another pill. After decades of taking all sorts of pills for pleasure, now he mostly took them to remain upright, penis and everything else. This one for the heart, this one for the blood, this one for the joints. God, he was falling apart. Who the hell would want any part of him?

His son, relentless, now sat on the counter beside him as Chad splashed more water on his face and tried to ignore him. A shiver ran up his legs, through his chest and into the head he held in his hands, as if to make the point that his body was functioning quite well, that it wasn't his body that was in crises. It was his soul. He looked his son dead in the eye, challenging him to speak, then left the bathroom when all he got was more silence.

Despite the three glasses of scotch, Chad climbed behind the wheel of his silver Mercedes and headed for home. His wife had left two messages, both of which he had ignored. He glanced at the dashboard clock: eleven minutes past eight.

They wouldn't even be there yet, he said to his son, who was sitting in the passenger seat beside him. The boy turned away, looking out the window.

Instead of heading north toward his house, Chad drove west down Wilshire Boulevard. He hadn't planned on it. When he left the office, he had every intention of going home and putting the day behind him, climbing into bed and sleeping it off. But he couldn't face his wife if their son was there, haunting him. So he drove. He ran out of continent when he reached Santa Monica, so he turned north along the Pacific Coast Highway and kept on going. Traffic was light at this hour and the going was smooth. For a while he hypnotized himself with the vibrating hum of tires, the setting sun glistening a waning path of light toward the ocean's horizon, but reality crept back in soon enough. When he arrived in Malibu, he stopped at a liquor store to buy a fifth of Scotch, then parked and walked down to the beach.

The breeze stung his face as he looked out over the waves to the dark horizon, but the booze warmed him. He sat on the cold, damp sand and drank, listening to the waves crash and recede, crash and recede. He sat and shivered and listened for a long time.

He asked his son how long he would continue doing this, staring at him without saying anything. He got no answer, of course, so he did all the talking himself. He told his son that in all the years he'd aided and abetted various schemes and diversions of dubious ethics, he had always hung his hat on the notion that nobody was getting hurt. Sure, *financially* some people were dinged, but that was the nature of business, there was always going to be winners and losers. The deal between Winslow and the boys was business as usual, the same as every deal he'd brokered over the past thirty-five years. Even better than most, in fact. Both sides had left happy. Richie and Calvin had been content with their windfall, and Winslow had made a cool million in profit for the cost of gas and a small bite to the man who'd made it all possible. What difference did it make that they could have made a better deal if they'd understood the true value of the coins? Being bad at business was their own damn fault, not his.

And then his son finally spoke. But getting them killed is your fault, he said.

Chad didn't argue. He had called Winslow to warn him. And when he picked up that phone and told him the boys were coming to see him, there was no other possible outcome. Richie and Calvin were going to die because they could no longer surprise him, possibly get the drop, get out with their lives and disappear to live a new life somewhere beyond the reach of Winslow's psychotic ego.

If he had done as they asked, if he had called Winslow on their behalf, maybe he could have diffused the situation. Maybe he could have talked him into a compromise, possibly even thrown in another deal with one of his other clients to help soften the sting. Perhaps he could have convinced him that if Calvin lost his family it would only motivate him to call the cops. Anything, *anything* would have been better than what Chad had done.

It was the fear that had decided. He'd been too afraid of Winslow's paranoid nature. If he'd sided with the boys, at best, Winslow would never have trusted him to do business again; at worst, he would have included him in his paranoid need to tie up loose ends. It had been self-preservation, that's all.

I warned them, Chad said to his son, the top third of the Scotch bottle gone. I told them what would happen if they went to Vegas.

But they didn't go for themselves, his son answered.

Chad closed his eyes for a moment and when he opened

them, his son was gone. He stared at the little black boy sitting where his son had been. He was as silent as his son had been. He didn't even look at Chad, his wide brown eyes moving slowly across the dark sky, over the dark ocean, as though searching for someplace he might be safe. He was young, only five, and Chad knew that, like his own boy, he would never get any older.

He looked at his watch. Ten-thirty.

Chad thought he might throw up. And then he did. He leaned to the side and deposited a belly-full of Scotch onto the sand and wiped his mouth.

What the hell. You win.

He pulled the encrypted burner phone from his pocket, the one he'd taken from his office, the one that a paranoid former client with several accounts in the Cayman Islands had insisted he use. But he wasn't going to call the Caymans. He fumbled around in his other pocket for the piece of paper with the ten-digit number Jennifer had given him, her last bit of penance for occasionally having her mouth on the penis of a man who participated in a world of psychotic gangsters and the people they would kill.

He shook his head as if to shake away any dust of doubt that might have settled in his addled brain and carefully pressed the ten numbers on the phone's keypad.

How do you feel about your old man now?

He got no answer.

And then a voice answered on the other end of the phone and Chad began to speak, committing his final crime of the day.

CHAPTER TWENTY

THE CHEERING BIKERS around the pool were so focused, so full of blood lust, that none of them heard the approach. But when the high-powered search light popped on beneath the helicopter and swept over the backyard, they realized what was happening. Eight Las Vegas Metropolitan Police units had answered the anonymous call reporting the active shooter and the possible kidnapping and torture of a family of five visiting Vegas from Orem, Utah, but it was the SWAT team that took the lead. They arrived at the home at the end of the cul-de-sac in an Armored Rescue Vehicle, wearing full body armor and carrying AR15 assault rifles, flash-bang grenades, and ballistic shields.

The plan was for them to contain and assess upon arrival, and with thirty-two motorcycles filling the street in front of the house, there was evidently much to contain and assess. But when the eye-in-the-sky radioed in, detailing the strange activity around the pool out back, the decision was made by the SWAT team commander to overwhelm and subdue.

With light from the hovering chopper swirling and officers swarming the yard, the poolside bikers scurried like cockroaches caught on a kitchen floor at midnight. But every hole had been sealed off. The panicked cockroaches turned and bumped into each other before falling into a stunned silence as the desert came alive with ever more flashing lights and men. The AR15s and Remington shotguns led the charge, the men holding them yelling commands to raise hands and get on the ground. The orders were obeyed without resistance.

As police entered the dark house, looking for the poor, kidnapped family from Utah, and the helicopter kept a moving spotlight on the thirty bodies now lying face down on the deck, hands folded behind their heads, fingers interlaced as instructed, a SWAT officer yelled at the six men in the pool.

"Keep your hands where we can see them!" he ordered, his Sig Sauer 9 millimeter trained upon them.

The four men in their underwear obeyed, but the two men who were fully dressed had a harder time treading water. Perhaps it was nerves, the officer surmised, but for some reason they were having a hell of a time catching their breath.

Calvin and Richie made their way to the side of the pool and hoisted themselves up. It took Richie two tries to find the strength in his arms to make it out of the water. Eventually he came to rest next to Calvin, both of them on their hands and knees, panting and shivering like wet, beaten, dogs.

"Lay down," a SWAT officer ordered. "On your stomachs, hands behind your backs."

Both collapsed to the deck, lungs burning, the muscles in their arms and legs so depleted of oxygen that it made it difficult to comply with the last part of the order. It was as though the bones in their arms had been replaced with lead as they brought their hands to the back of their heads. More shouts and commands whipped through the air, but the helicopter remained overhead and it was difficult to understand specific words as hands patted them down, looking for weapons. The intent of the words was clear though—move and we will shoot you.

Calvin's body slowly settled back into the weighty world he had been convinced he was about to leave behind. The white spots slowly faded from his vision as the oxygen reached his brain and the hypoxia from the near-drowning dissipated. After a few more minutes, he lifted his cheek from the damp deck and looked around. Richie was beside him, his eyes still closed, looking like he'd fallen asleep. If the cops came here to save them, he wondered, why were they making them lie there like that? It wasn't as if they would be hard to find; there weren't any other black guys, and Richie didn't exactly blend in with the biker boys. Calvin's mind slowly came around to the realization that whatever the hell was happening, it wasn't about them.

Seven or eight officers stood at various locations between the bodies around the pool, shotguns now resting on their hips rather than trained downward. Calvin wiped away a few drops of water and looked back toward the house where more police congregated. The beam from an officer's flashlight landed in his eyes like a warning. He twisted his head around and was suddenly staring directly into Winslow's dark eyes. They were no more than five inches from each other. Winslow's gaze remained hard and unrelenting, though somewhere deep in the foul darkness that ran all the way down to the pit of his demented soul, there was a flicker of light.

"You do this?" Winslow asked him.

Calvin shook his head slightly; he didn't yet have the energy to push out any words.

The faint light in Winslow's eyes grew brighter.

"Then keep your mouth shut until we get a handle on what

the fuck is going on," he said. "You leave our business out of this and I give you my word, you'll get what you came here for."

Before Calvin had the chance to respond, to even calculate all the angles of the offer, a SWAT officer grabbed Winslow, yanked him to his feet, and dragged him away.

Calvin stared at the now vacant spot, but all he saw was Tracey. She sat with her legs crossed, Martin tucked into the pocket between her thighs, her ankles crossing over each other in front of him, as though she were a fortress keeping him locked away and safe. Martin had his eyes closed, his head tucked into her chest, but her eyes were wide open, frantic. They searched for something, a way to safety perhaps, but they found no relief. Calvin stifled the impulse to jump to his feet, to call out to the SWAT officers standing above him, tell them they were needed elsewhere, that his family was in danger and they were running out of time. He twitched but remained where he was, cheek pressed to the ground, mouth screwed shut.

He had no doubt that the men who took his wife and son would do what they promised if they involved the police. Those packages they promised to send, filled with various body parts, would arrive at his doorstep and he would be lost forever.

He turned his head back toward Richie. "Richie?" he said. Repeated it when he got no response.

Richie's right eye popped open, the left one still slammed tight. The open eye wandered a bit before finding focus. Bloodshot lightning bolts, suspended mid-strike, filled the white parts, the corner nearest his nose a pool of collecting blood. He didn't speak as he stared at Calvin.

"Don't say nothing to the police about why we here," Calvin said.

Richie's eye narrowed in confusion, then slowly closed.

An hour later, Calvin and Richie sat in Winslow's living room, surrounded by the men who had tried to drown them. The cops were still there, fewer now, but enough to keep everyone nervous. The SWAT team had left only moments before, as a statement was given to the media gathered behind the yellow tape, beyond the police cruisers and motorcycles in front of the house. Winslow had turned on the 75-inch flat screen television above the fireplace. Captain Harold Monroe of the Las Vegas Metropolitan Police, a middle-aged man in an ill-fitting uniform, stood in front of a bank of local reporters, warning any residents in the western half of Nevada who might be tuned in to their local news station at one in the morning, that SWATing, the practice of prank calling emergency services in order to trick them into dispatching a SWAT team to raid the home of an unsuspecting person, is a crime.

"While there are no current federal laws to address this issue," Captain Monroe explained, "individuals can be charged with conspiracy to provide false information and reckless endangerment, both of which can result in serious jail time." An off-mic question was thrown out at the Captain. He shook his head and said, "No indication the alleged missing family from Utah exists at all. However, out of an abundance of caution, we are currently contacting all the hotels in the area to ascertain if they have any information regarding any families matching the description." Another question was called out. "Not at this time," Captain Monroe answered. "But we are doing what we can to trace the call back to the responsible party. Unfortunately, these callers have the ability to mask their location quite effectively." He listened to a reporter on his left and nodded. "There are any number of reasons, sometimes it's merely done as a prank, while other times it's used as retaliation against a real or perceived issue with the victim." Captain Monroe listened to another question, then said, "No, not in this case. The owner of the home was here, having a pool party, and was taken completely by surprise." He shook his head at another question. "There are no ongoing issues between the owner of the home and any of his neighbors."

Calvin and Richie looked across the room at Winslow, who stood, back erect, drink in hand, staring at the television.

"What's going through his mind, you figure?" Richie whispered, readjusting the Egyptian cotton bath towel around his shoulders, supplied by Winslow himself.

"He's trying to figure out who did this to him," Calvin whispered back. "Going through his list of enemies."

"Man like that's gotta have a hell of a list. I'd help add them up, but my phone was in my pocket when I got thrown in the pool, so the calculator doesn't work."

"My money's on Chad."

"No fucking way."

"Gotta be. Doesn't make any sense that it's a coincidence and you said yourself that God don't care for us enough for it to be a miracle."

Richie lowered his voice even more. "Why would Chad risk getting involved after he warned him we were coming in the first place? Even if he did give a shit, he doesn't have the balls to go up against him like that." He tugged at the inseam of his Levis, still tacky and stiff from the water. "Speaking of balls, my sack is itching like crazy."

Richie realized the biker closest to him, a stocky dude of about fifty with a scorpion tattoo running up the side of his neck was taking a particular interest in what they were saying. He leaned closer to Richie and nodded, as though some truth had passed between them.

"You wanna switch seats?" Richie asked Calvin.

But Calvin was no longer paying any attention to him. He was looking off to the four officers in the entry hall. He'd given them a bullshit story about coming to Vegas to do some gambling and hopefully see the Blue Man Group perform, courtesy of Winslow, who was an old friend of Richie's deceased father. The cover story had been worked out in about twenty seconds, once it was determined that the kidnapped family from Utah was a hoax.

"That's all the information you need to give them," Winslow had said as he handed Richie and Calvin the Egyptian cotton bath towels to dry off. "We have a deal?"

"Yeah, we got a deal," Calvin had said.

When Winslow walked away to pour himself a drink, Richie had checked for any lingering cops and then whispered harshly at Calvin, "You get too much water up your fucking nose or something? Swamp your brain? Half an hour ago he was trying to kill us, remember?"

Calvin wiped his face with the towel. "He gave me his word."

"Oh, his fucking *word*?"

"He gave us his word once before," Calvin reminded him. "And he followed through."

"Hold up," Richie said, incredulous. "You're giving him points for following through on the promise he'd *murder* us?"

"Ain't no different than the street mentality I see every day," Calvin insisted. "All that bullshit about respecting a code. About being true to the family. Just like them bangers out there in Compton. He understands you gotta be real with your homies or shit falls apart."

"Yeah, that's stupendous, but we're not his *homies*."

"If we don't hang him out to dry with the cops, that means we're protecting him. In his eyes that *makes* us his homies."

"You're willing to risk your life on that?"

"It ain't about *my* life. We say something to the cops now and we guarantee they save our asses, but we'd be risking Tracey's and Martin's for sure. All we need is those coins back and if there's any chance of that, I'm going with it. It's your choice how to play it, I ain't gonna make you stay. If you don't trust him, you can walk out when the cops leave. But I'm staying."

But now, sitting there surrounded by his would-be killers, Calvin wondered if all his planning was for nothing. He looked at the cops in the entry hall, waiting there to make sure nobody left before the all-clear was given. They must have run his name through some police database, figured out that he had done a stint in prison a few years back. That in itself was no big deal. He wasn't on parole; he could go wherever he wanted and do whatever the hell he pleased. But what if his name had also come up as being connected to a recent bank robbery in Reseda, California? The fucking LAPD and FBI had interviewed him about Garrison, so it wasn't that big a leap. The moisture returned to his scalp. That's all he needed, for it to get back to the goddamn FBI that the man they interviewed thirty-six hours ago was now involved in an incident in Las Vegas at the home of another ex-con, one with ties to the criminal underground and a notorious biker gang.

Captain Monroe came through the front door and talked quietly with the four officers in the entry hall. One of the officers, a black man around Calvin's age, turned to look into the living room, his eyes immediately finding Calvin's. It was hard to say if he'd intentionally sought him out or if Calvin was the only one looking his way to catch his eye. He tried to read the officer, but was met only with the blank condescension of authority. The officer's hand rested casually on the butt of his holstered revolver, his muscular shoulder rounded forward. Calvin's paranoia reached its apex as Captain Monroe finished speaking and four more officers came through the front door.

Captain Monroe turned to the collection of agitated men sitting around the room and said, "Remain seated a moment longer. We'll wrap this up and you'll be free to go. Right now there are some issues with a few of you we need to take care of."

Irritated glances and a few swear words were passed around the room, but nobody stood in protest as the eight officers spread out into the room, winding this way and that through the crowd like rats through a maze. Calvin's heart climbed past his Adam's apple and jackhammered up his neck as the officer who'd been staring at him headed his way. His eyes were alert, snake-like, ready to strike. But as he arrived, the eyes twitched over to one of the bikers to Calvin's left, a badly pock-marked man with dirty hair tied off in a ponytail halfway down his back.

"Jeff Connelly," the officer said, his hand back on the gun in its holster. "I need you to stand up and put your hands behind your back."

"What the fuck for?" Jeff asked.

The officer stuck his hand under his arm and pulled him to his feet. "There's a bench warrant for your arrest."

"This is bullshit," Jeff complained as the cuffs were employed.

"Next time you have a court appearance, make sure to put it on your calendar," the officer advised as they headed for the front door.

In total, five men were taken away, three on bench warrants and two for missing parole hearings, but Calvin's name was never called.

"Gentlemen," Captain Monroe said to the room, "our investigation is complete and those of you remaining are free to go."

That was it. No apology. No further explaining. Good night, have a nice life.

It took a few moments of grumbling and head shaking for the maze of men to break apart. A few of them tossed the middle finger at the departing officers, but, their fever long broken, nobody raised too big of a complaint. Certainly none of the bikers questioned Winslow's change of heart toward Richie and Calvin. The fact that they were all heading home to their beds rather than to a jail cell on charges of attempted murder made his reasons clear enough.

The cops still out front watched them all closely, making sure no problems arose as the men made their way to the bikes filling the cul-de-sac. A few media trucks idled, no doubt waiting to get the money shot of outlaw bikers rumbling away into the dark night.

Richie turned back to Calvin and offered his hand. "I can't take anymore of this."

Calvin shook his hand. "We're cool, Richie. I'll be right behind you."

Richie raised an eyebrow. "You better be. I'll wait in the car." As he walked through the front door, he tried to convince himself it was the smart thing to do, a sort of insurance policy against Winslow having yet another change of heart. The truth was, he was leaving because he was afraid. He stepped outside amid the deafening rumble of bikes and only when the last bike had disappeared would he start the slow walk back to the Subaru, in case any of the departing bikers saw things differently than Winslow.

Back inside, Winslow poured a whiskey. "And then there was one," he said to Calvin. "You need a drink?"

A shot or two would definitely calm him, but Calvin had been up for twenty-four hours and, if all went well, he was minutes away from embarking on a four-hour car ride back to L.A. Likely, the booze would knock him out completely. "It's a little late," he said, shaking his head.

"You're in Vegas," Winslow said. "Time has no sway here."

Heather lit another cigarette between her pale lips.

"You want one?" Winslow asked her.

She shook her head and took a seat on the sofa, blew smoke out her nose. Her eyes stayed on Calvin like hooks he couldn't pull free.

"You got something to say?" he asked her.

She was silent for a good ten seconds before saying, "No hard feelings?"

He looked sideways at her. "No feelings towards you whatsoever."

The reverberating earthquake of noise out front retreated as the motorcycles departed. For Calvin it was like slowly waking from a nightmare, unsure how awake he was, and if safety had truly returned.

Winslow brought his drink to the sofa and sat beside Heather, his free hand landing on the ample thigh squeezed into her faded jeans. "Hell of a night," he said, taking a deep sip. "I'm still trying to figure out exactly what happened here. You must have someone watching over you, the police swarming in here like that."

Calvin shrugged. "That was lucky, yeah."

"Lucky, my ass. Somebody *out there* decided to take control of the situation *in here*. Kicked my ass, too. I will give them credit. But I'm gonna find out who it was and pay them a little visit, that I can guarantee. You got any ideas who it might be?"

Calvin was in no mood to discuss revenge strategy. He shook his head.

"Bullshit, you don't. Give me a name."

"Santa Claus."

"The balls on this guy," Winslow said to Heather. She blew more cigarette smoke. He looked back to Calvin. "Had to be Chad, right?"

"Sounds as likely as anyone," Calvin conceded. "Look, you mind if we get this done?"

Winslow's face darkened, as though feeding off a wellspring of rage that lived deep within him. But then his features softened. "Can't blame you for the rattled nerves," he said. "But we're all good here."

"If it's all the same to you, I'd rather be all good someplace else."

Winslow's playful smile returned. "So what's the deal on these guys who took your family?" Winslow asked him.

"They're pissed we have their coins. That's about the extent of it."

"They're not Russians are they?"

"I got no idea."

"Well, I hope for your sake they aren't. I've done business with a few of them. Those sons-of-bitches don't fuck around. So, what's your plan?"

"What do you mean?"

"I mean, what's your fucking plan to make the exchange? You can't walk into some place of their choosing and expect them to let you walk back out with an appreciative tip of the hat. You need to have some leverage to make sure they let your old lady and your kid go first."

Calvin had no real answer. "It's under control," he said.

"It's under control. Right. Like things were under control when you came here, huh? It'd be a pathetic move for you to hand the coins over to these guys, whatever the fuck nationality they are, only to have them kill you anyway and see my two million dollars float away like a fart in the wind." He swallowed more of his drink. "You could really use someone like me looking out for you."

Calvin studied him a moment. "So what are we talking about here?"

"You just said it."

"Man, I don't know what the hell you're—"

"*Control*," Winslow snapped, as though the word was a swinging club, the chemical anger again exploding in his eyes.

Calvin hesitated. "Are you saying you wanna help me control what happens to the coins and my family?"

"I only care about the first half of that equation."

"You offering your assistance?"

Winslow sipped and stared, eased back into the couch. "I'm not offering dick, yet."

Calvin's jaw tensed. "Except the coins, right?"

Winslow nodded as he finished off his drink. "That's right. Your coins, my money. Even-Steven. But perhaps there's a way for us to both get what we want, yes?"

Calvin imagined all sorts of scenarios involving Winslow and his biker brothers dealing with those fucks who took Tracey and Martin. "Could be interesting," he said.

Winslow stood. "Could be better than interesting. Could be fun." He walked from the room, laughing.

"He's intense," Heather said with a small chuckle of her own as she squashed her cigarette out in the stone ashtray. "Real freak about being in charge, needing to run the show. Even when he's not in any position to do so. I wouldn't trust him if I were you."

Perhaps it was only the residual distaste left in his mouth

when she'd taken such racist glee at the drowning party, but there was something about her that unsettled Calvin even more than Winslow. While Winslow's crazy was right out there in the open for all to see, with her there was a disconnect, as though she was perpetually demonstrating an absence of all empathy. He had no doubt she wouldn't cross the street to aid a two-year-old who'd fallen out a window. "Thanks for the advice," he said, finally.

Beneath the dead-eyed gaze peeking from under hooded eyelids painted black, a grin came to her narrow mouth. The grin made clear that, whatever was passing between them, she had the upper hand. She said, "Nothing's changed since the moment you first walked through that door. I told you, you shouldn't have come."

"It's Vegas," Calvin said, his voice thin, despite his act of confidence. "Looks to me like the gamble paid off."

Her grin expanded into a full-tilt smile that briefly brightened her eyes. "Did it?" she asked.

Calvin squinted at her. "What the hell you talking about?"

"Aren't you paying attention? We're still talking about control."

He took a step back, looked down the hallway.

"He was right," she said. "That's all this is about."

Calvin glanced down the hallway again. "Winslow?" he called out.

Heather stood from the sofa. "Who has it," she continued on, "Who doesn't."

"Sit your ass back down," Calvin said, taking a step away from her. "Yo, Winslow!"

"Go ahead," Heather said. "See for yourself."

"See what for myself?"

The light in her eyes dimmed. "What control really looks like."

"Winslow!" he called out, inching his way toward the hallway.

His voice echoed off the polished cement floors, but the house remained as quiet as a tomb. It was as though he and Heather were the last two people on earth, battling over whose reality would survive. In Calvin's reality, Winslow was down that hallway with the box of coins, waiting to discuss the plan to get his family back. He tried to conjure the image, to trust in it. They were messing with him, that's all. This was Winslow being Winslow, the crazy bastard. He was using Heather to control his emotions, to make it clear that they owned him, that they controlled the narrative, not him.

But as he moved slowly down the hallway, every frayed nerve, every spike of instinct told him to turn around and run, to bolt for the front door and keep on going. Halfway down the hallway he looked back over his shoulder. Heather was there, standing at the opposite end. The bandana was gone and her long, brown hair framed her face. She said nothing.

The police had left every light in the place on, and white light glared off the white walls. He passed a media room, empty and silent, big enough to seat twenty comfortably. He walked on. Reaching the open study door on his right, Heather's footsteps now approaching quickly behind him. Her boots landed on the cement floor like tiny explosions.

But he did not turn. Could not look away as he stared into the room.

Winslow was there all right. But he wasn't alone. Calvin recognized the man standing beside him right away, the scorpion tattoo winding its way up his neck, its bulbous black claw opened wide as if about to clamp down on his ear. He'd spent the last hour sitting next to Richie as the cops had investigated the bogus kidnapping of the white-bread family from Utah, waiting to see how the long night would end. But Winslow, for all of his talk of control and respect for some mythical code, had never considered the night would end as it had.

Because he lay on his stomach in front of the open safe, his throat slashed to the bone, a lake of blood spreading like warm molasses on the polished cement floor.

CHAPTER TWENTY-ONE

RICHIE WALKED DOWN the dark road, the mouth of the cul-de-sac yawning behind him. The bikers were long gone, their screaming engines not even a lingering echo across the desert. The media vans had driven past him, followed by the long line of police cruisers. The last of the cruisers had stopped and asked him where he was going. Richie explained that he had parked his car down the road to make room for the motorcycles. The officers didn't seem to care; their demeanor suggested the whole damn thing had been a colossal waste of their time, and they sped off.

When the last of the police were in front of him, he looked back toward the house, so big and imposing. Damn, he wished he was tailing the cops right now, all the way to highway 15, heading west. Didn't matter that he'd been up for twenty-four hours, that his body was freshly bruised, a new layer upon the day-old layer, that every time he moved his jaw the pain rippled through his temples and spread all the way to the top of his head like it was tying a bow. If he could, he would get in the car and drive all night, put Vegas forever in his rearview.

But when he arrived at the spot where they'd left the Subaru, he realized the fantasy of heading home was exactly that, a fantasy.

Not because Calvin was still back at the house, risking his life on the word of an insane person, but because the Subaru was gone.

"Are you fucking kidding me!" he screamed into the darkness.

Of course they'd taken the car. Winslow knew it was there, knew he was going to kill them, knew he had to get rid of all traces of them. And this was the man whose word Calvin trusted. Richie checked his phone but the waterlogged screen remained as dark as his mood. Shit. No Uber app. No way to call for a taxi. No options. Even if Calvin survived, got the coins, then what? Walk to the goddamned airport? Hope the TSA didn't question two severely beat-to-hell guys carrying nothing but a box of gold coins? Why don't you tell us a little bit about the coins, they'd say. Win those in a poker game? Can you give us the previous owner's name? No? That's fine, why don't you step over here while we look into this.

Shit. Shit. Shit.

His legs were already walking back to the house before his brain gave the okay. It was a though his body was too tired to put up with any more planning and strategizing, it'd had enough pain, didn't want to hear any more ideas from the great mind above. As the numbed, mindless legs continued to move, the great brain attempted a return to power, formulating vague ideas involving asking Winslow to borrow a car to take back to LA. But even Richie's brain calculated the worthlessness of that endeavor and shut down the operation immediately. He plodded along slowly, on autopilot, like a zombie. But as he reached the center of the cul-de-sac, his brain again sprang to life, the motor neurons in his spinal column firing all at once, sending savage impulses down every axon until the body was again under its control.

Richie's eyes focused on the glint of light coming from the far side of the driveway, near the garage. What is this? his brain asked. Why the hell is there a motorcycle parked out front? Winslow had told everyone to leave, hadn't he? Richie's eyes narrowed and his stomach clamped down on the biting worry in his gut as he moved from the street into the shadows along the side of the house.

Chad's gonna be relieved he doesn't have to worry about Winslow anymore.

It was a strange consideration in light of the fact that Heather now had a gun in her hand, aiming it at the back of his head, but Calvin was still in a state of shock and unsure how to process the heinous sight before him.

"Never saw it coming," the dude with the scorpion tattoo on his neck said as he pulled off his black gloves and stuffed them into the pocket of his jeans. "Had no idea I was even in the room. Soon as he had the safe open, I came up behind and opened up his neck. Blood came out like a fucking breached dam. This shit's disgusting."

Calvin gagged at the thickening liquid that continued to spread out across the floor, a high tide lapping at the base of the tall, white cabinet that housed the safe. Winslow's body was twisted into the shape of an S. His torso was on its side, with his legs flopped one way and his left arm flopped the other. His right hand was up near the gaping wound across his larynx, as if it had tried to scoop up the blood and return it to its rightful place after he fell. His tan face had taken on an ashy complexion, his eyes open but vacant.

Scorpion Tattoo stepped aside to avoid the blood and then jumped slightly to make sure he cleared another slowly forming tributary. Calvin noticed the blood had spewed, covering a good portion of the cabinet. His stomach lurched and he stepped back-wards, but Heather's gun kept him from moving more than a few inches. He blinked several times, anticipating the bullet that was about to travel through his brain and exit through his forehead.

"You came here for a reason," Heather said. "So let's go." The barrel of her gun pressed with more urgency against his head, to make clear what it wanted of him.

Calvin instinctively raised his hands. "I don't understand."

Scorpion Tattoo sniffed impatiently through his hairy nostrils.

Heather said, "Go get what you came here for."

The gun to the back of Calvin's head continued to push him toward the open safe. He took a tentative step, trying to avoid the blood.

"You gotta step in it, OJ," the biker said. "We're gonna need those footprints."

It was clear now what their game was. Calvin had to hand it to them, it was a hell of a scheme. He stepped into the blood and the sole of his black Nike went squishy. He brought his opposite foot forward and left another waffle-like impression for the police to find in front of the soiled cabinet. The safe was on the bottom shelf, about three feet off the ground. He crouched down next to Winslow's body, noticing the long, serrated-edge knife lying near his soggy hair, its rubber handle partly submerged. He blew air out of his open mouth and looked inside the safe.

The box of coins rested on the top shelf, along with a pass-port, a pile of documents, and seven Rolex watches. The bag of money filled the bottom shelf.

He looked back over his shoulder at Heather. She stood back, the gun lowered slightly, but still aimed in his general direction. "Hand them over," she said. Calvin pulled the coin box from the safe, using both hands, and held it out to her. She shook her head and flicked the gun toward Scorpion Tattoo.

"How long you been planning this?" Calvin asked, leaning across the space between them.

"About an hour," Scorpion Tattoo said, taking the box with a cocky smile.

"Not you," Calvin said. "Her. I'm guessing it was her idea, right?"

Scorpion Tattoo opened the box and his eyes practically spun. "What can I say, she's got brains and beauty," he laughed, shutting the lid with a solid pop of wood. He placed the box on a cabinet shelf, high enough to avoid the flecks of blood.

Calvin said, "She's also the only one with a gun. You want help doing the math?"

Scorpion Tattoo looked as though he'd swallowed a fly. His eyes darted to Heather.

She raised the gun. "Both of you shut up. Get the bag of money, Midnight."

"What about the watches?" Calvin said. "Don't you want those too?"

"Yeah, man, grab 'em," Scorpion Tattoo said. "Winslow always had good taste."

Heather shook her head. "Just the money."

"No, man, the Rolexes too."

Calvin crouched back down and pulled the million dollar bag from the bottom shelf. Standing, he said to Heather, "Should I give this to you now, or you gonna take it from him after you put a bullet in his ass?"

"Give it to her," Scorpion Tattoo said. Then to Heather, as he held out his hand for the gun, "In fact, why don't we trade?"

"Relax," she said to him, her glassy eyes staying on Calvin. "Toss it over there."

Calvin tossed the bag to the floor beside Scorpion Tattoo, but the biker made no move to retrieve it.

"Now pick up the knife," Heather ordered.

There was no longer any doubt—as soon as Calvin had the knife in his hand, he'd have a bullet in his head. "You sure you don't want those watches?" he asked. "They probably worth another quarter-million."

Heather said, "I'm not as dumb as he looks. I don't need anything that can be traced to Winslow."

"You hear that, moron?" Calvin said to Scorpion Tattoo. "That includes you."

Scorpion Tattoo's mouth opened as if it was waiting for something smart to fall out.

"Pick up the goddamn knife," Heather barked, the first indication she had any emotions.

"Enjoy these last few minutes," Calvin said to Scorpion Tattoo. "I'll be sure to meet you on the other side so we can discuss what an idiot you were."

"Would you please shoot this nigger right now," Scorpion Tattoo said.

But Heather only stared at him, shaking her head.

"What kind of bullshit is this?" he snapped at her. "We had a deal."

"Actually, we never had a *deal*," she said to him. "All we had was a plan."

Calvin was looking at Scorpion Tattoo, so he saw the exact moment the outlaw biker fully realized he'd been played. It was when his chest exploded and the look of fury on his face was replaced with one of shock. It was a look Calvin had seen too much of recently to take any joy from. Besides, what was the use of being pleased about being smarter than a dead man, when you were about to join him? Scorpion Tattoo sputtered a few incoherent words as he stumbled backward, his heart shredded into crab meat, and fell to the floor, no longer concerned with avoiding the blood.

When Calvin looked back to Heather, she said, "You're next. And if you don't put that knife in your hand, I'm gonna make your death as painful as—"

The remainder of the threat got stuck in her throat as her head bent sideways on her neck, her eyes rolling back to show all white. She seemed suspended in space for a flash before the gun fell limply from her hand as she collapsed to the floor.

"I thought for sure you were dead when I heard the shot," Richie said, standing in the spot vacated by Heather, the stone ashtray from the living room still raised up in his hands.

"You and me both."

Richie looked down at the unconscious body at his feet and expelled a sharp breath. "We really gotta stop doing this."

They found two rolls of duct tape in a kitchen drawer and used them to bind Heather's hands behind her back and her legs together. The deep cut on the side of her scalp where Richie had struck her with the ashtray continued to bleed and when they lifted her dead-weight body into the chair, they discussed varying uses for the all-purpose tape. Calvin told him about the time when he was eight years old and saw a guy from the neighborhood use duct tape to keep some dude's leg from falling apart after he was shot in a drive-by. There was no such compassion for Heather though, as they used the remainder of the roll to fasten her bound legs to the chair and then the bound hands at her lower back around the back of the chair. It was Calvin's idea to leave her tied up in the study, so when she regained consciousness she could enjoy the silent company and fetid aroma of her two companions.

"We gotta hurry," Richie said as the procedure dragged on. "This is taking too long."

"We're good. We got time," Calvin assured him. "We'll be back in L.A. before traffic even starts."

"I'm not sure about that," Richie said, breathing heavily, his skin pale and clammy. It wasn't only the physical exertion of moving Heather that had him in such a state, it was the emotional toll from sharing the space with two dead men who had more of their blood outside their bodies than inside. "The car's gone," he told Calvin.

Calvin shot his eyes up from Heather's ankles as he ripped the last of the tape from the roll. "What do you mean, gone?"

"I figure the bikers took it earlier, evidence they needed to get rid of. We're the ones who're supposed to be dead, not these two, remember?"

Calvin took a few breaths, then squeezed the last of the tape around the leg of the chair, making sure Heather's legs were held secure. "We'll figure something out."

"What about her? We gonna leave her like that?"

Calvin stood and admired their handiwork. "Ain't no way Winslow cleaned this place himself, so eventually someone, a maid, a gardener, is gonna come back and find her."

"And then we're screwed, right?"

"Well, she's definitely gonna go with a bullshit story about us killing Winslow, and we already lied to the cops about why we was here, so it ain't gonna look good. All they'll have to do is tie us to that bank job to make us out to be a couple hardcore gangsters. That's twenty-five to life right there."

The two men stood there, lost.

Finally, Richie shrugged and said, "We could kill her."

Calvin nodded.

"I was kidding!" Richie said. "What the hell are you nodding for?"

"I'm not saying we're gonna do it, I'm only saying it's an *option*."

"No it's not!" Richie yelled in his ear, "We aren't gangsters!"

"That's good to hear," Heather said, her glassy eyes looking up at them.

The two men took a surprised step back.

She winced as she tried to raise her chin to get a better angle on them. "What the hell you hit me with anyway?"

"Your ashtray," Richie told her. "Didn't you ever learn cigarettes'll kill you?"

"I could use a smoke about now," she laughed.

"Damn, you're one cold bitch," Calvin said.

"Not really," Heather said, stretching her neck to the side and flexing her jaw, seeing if it was still in working order. "If I'd loved either one of them, you'd have a point. But they used me just as much as I used them. Neither of you are going to prison, by the way, so you can stop worrying about it."

Calvin said, "How you figure? You gonna forgive and forget?"

Heather nodded at Winslow. "I'm afraid that ship has sailed. There's gonna be too many questions asked amongst the brother-hood. Most of them are barely smart enough to wipe their own asses, but I don't pin this on you two, eventually they'll come around looking at me."

Riche stared. "Well, then, shit. We're gonna have to kill you."

She smiled slightly. "Better do it quick. The man I was supposed to call when this was all taken care of is no doubt on his way here right now to make sure I'm okay."

"Bullshit," Calvin said.

Heather grunted. "Whatever. He's gonna kill you whether you believe me or not."

Richie said, "I can't decide if she's bluffing, but I vote we don't stick around to find out."

Calvin tried to read her. She certainly sounded sincere, didn't look the least bit unsure of herself, but she was a sociopath, so who could really tell? "What if we leave you the million bucks?" he asked her.

Richie held up his hand. "Wait, what?"

Calvin ignored him. "Would that be enough to keep you quiet?"

Heather's glassy eyes had cleared. "Only one way to find out." The phone in her pocket dinged with a text message. She said, "And that's the sound of you running out of time to decide your next move."

Calvin pushed his shoulder into her chest and dug out her phone. The message was from somebody named S.D. It read: *All good?*

She said, "I don't answer that and there's no way you walk out of here without five or six extra holes."

Calvin said, "But you could stop him if you wanted to?"

"Of course."

Calvin looked at Richie, then back to Heather. "A million dollars," he said. "We take the coins, you get the money."

"Interesting offer," she said.

"And you can be damned sure we ain't gonna say nothing to the cops about any of this," Calvin said.

She angled her head and spit on the floor. "You willing to put that in writing?"

Richie asked. "Can we talk about this?"

"It's the only way we walk out of here alive," Calvin said to him.

It was difficult to argue with the logic, and Richie relented.

Calvin turned back to Heather. "We have a deal or not?"

She stared up at him for long moment, then said, "What the hell. Sure."

Richie brought his hands together with a loud clap. "Well, hallelujah. We're broke, but still breathing." He grabbed the coins from the cabinet shelf. "Now let's get the hell out of here."

"Though, to be honest," Heather said to Calvin. "What we have is really less of a *deal*, and more of a *plan*."

Richie had already moved for the door, but Calvin stood motionless, exhausted.

"C'mon, man," Richie said. "We don't need to waste time arguing semantics. We're good to go."

Calvin's shoulders dropped as the weight of the world became, all at once, too much to bear. He tossed the phone into Heather's lap.

"No," he said. "We're not."

CHAPTER TWENTY-TWO

"IF SHE'S NOT gonna honor the deal, then why the hell you still want to leave the money?"

Richie was following Calvin back up the hallway, the black money bag swinging in his hand. Calvin turned back to face him, said, "You're the one said we ain't gangsters."

Richie raised the bag up as exhibit A. "But I never said we aren't thieves."

"Don't you get it by now? We take that money, it's never gonna end."

"That's right, it's not," Richie hissed. "Their little brotherhood's gonna follow us anyway."

"I'm not talking about them. I'm talking about all of it, all the shit we've been swimming in since we pulled up in front of that damn bank." Calvin flashed on Tracey. Her face full of pain and regret, so close he could smell her scent, her eyes searching his for some hint of understanding. "All I want is my family back," he said. "I'm done with the rest of it. I'm done getting shit on everyone around me." His eyes watered and he shook his head. "Man, all I want is to get clean."

Richie considered him, not giving an inch. "I'm broke. You

understand that? I got *nothing*. I take this money and I can start fresh someplace else."

"Yeah, I understand that." He pressed his index finger into Richie's chest. "Because you got no other *options*, right? No rich daddy to call on, no rich friends to crash with. Man, you now the same as all them boys from the hood."

"That's right. I've been kicked out of the Beverly Hills White Boy Club and I'm fucking lost. That's why I need this money, so I have someplace to go."

"And what happens when that money runs out? Because the money *always* runs out. But when it's gone, you're still gonna have that thief mentality, looking for the next score." Tracey's face returned to Calvin, as silently resigned as his own. "You take that money and it doesn't matter where you go with it, because it's always gonna be the same damn place."

The next few moments would dictate his fate, so Richie used them all to mull over his next move. His whole life he had looked for the easy way, the path of least resistance, and it had always failed him. It had been so long since he'd done the right thing, it was as though he couldn't recognize what the right thing was anymore. He said, "You realize that once Tracey and Martin are free, this isn't gonna be over. What happened tonight isn't gonna go away. We're gonna have to answer to either the brotherhood or the cops as to what happened here."

Calvin nodded. "And someday I'm gonna have to answer to my son about all this, too. Which ending you figure's best for him to hear?"

Richie took a deep breath, let it out slowly.

"C'mon, Richie. No more shit," Calvin said.

Richie's body sagged. He looked down at the bag of money in his hand. "No more shit," he said. Then he dropped it on the floor.

They were quiet a moment, measuring the weight of their decision, before Richie said, "We gotta be smart about this, then. It'd be a hell of a thing to get shot before you had the chance to tell Martin what an upstanding citizen you've become. We should lock the doors before we go, cops left them open. That's how I got back in to save your ass, which you still haven't thanked me for by the way. At least it'll buy us some time before the brotherhood can get to Lady Sasquatch in there."

An idea lit up Calvin's face. "Get started on the doors," he said, picking up the money bag.

"Where're you going?"

"I gotta get something from the kitchen and take care of some business."

"What business?"

Calvin ran for the kitchen, saying, "I'll explain when we're out of here. When you finish with the doors, meet me in the garage."

"What about my thank you?" Richie called after him.

"Missed me?" Heather said from the chair as Calvin rounded back into the study.

He took the phone he'd left in her lap. Heather shifted her ass in the seat, but the duct tape was holding. There was a second message from S.D. saying: *We're coming up.* "Shit," he said under his breath, turning the phone for her to see. "Whose *we*?"

"I told you, my man and a couple of his brothers."

"You can stop with the *brotherhood* shit, considering you just killed two of them."

Heather gave him another soulless smile. "His *actual* brothers, his blood. They're my true family and they're gonna fuck you up real good."

She jerked her head to the side as he crouched down beside

her, using a sharp elbow to push her shoulders forward. He then grabbed her bound hands at her lower back. Twisting her right thumb as far as he could without loosening the duct tape, he pressed it to the home button on the phone and the screen unlocked. Opening the text app, he asked, "You have any pet names for S.D.? Sugar-Bear Sweetie-Pie? Or, Baby-Hitler?"

Heather said nothing.

"Not the nickname type, huh?" He sent S.D. a return text: *Still working on it. Don't come yet.* Then he opened the camera app. "Smile," he said as he snapped her picture. He then took a photo of Winslow's body. Then Scorpion Tattoo's.

"What the hell you doing?" she said.

"Documenting the crime scene for when I tell the police what happened here."

He got a good angle on the knife partially submerged in blood. Finally, he took a picture of the gun that Heather had dropped when Richie slammed the ashtray against her head. For good measure, he even took a pic of the ashtray.

Her gravelly voice deepened. "You ain't gonna talk to no cops, you fucking nigger. You already lied to them once tonight, so they aren't gonna believe shit about what you have to say."

"But you figure they will believe your bullshit that I killed these two in cold blood and then tied you up to live another day?" He pulled a plastic Ziplock bag from his back pocket. "That makes about as much sense as me being able to fire that gun, leaving nothing behind but your fingerprints."

Heather's face fell as she caught up to the play.

Calvin used a pen to lift the gun by the trigger and drop it into the Ziplock, followed by the phone.

She thrashed against the tape holding her to the chair, almost tipping over. "You'll be dead before you have the chance to say anything at all."

He bent close, his face inches from hers. "I wonder what the brotherhood's gonna do when they find out you killed their cash cow. I'm guessing they're not gonna be pleased." He straightened back up. "You were right about one thing, though. Sometimes a plan is better than a deal." He then picked up the million-dollar money bag and tossed it back into the safe. "But you still should have taken the deal."

He slammed the safe closed, spun the dial, walked out of the room.

Winslow's garage was bigger than the house Calvin shared with four people. It was a showroom. The floor had a wall-to-wall shine, covered with a light grey epoxy that didn't have a stain on it, despite housing seven motorcycles and four cars—two Porches (a red 911, and a black Panamera), a metallic blue Range Rover, and a banana-yellow Lamborghini Aventador.

"Let's take the Ferrari," Richie said.

"First of all, that's a Lambo, not a Ferrari," Calvin said, walking between the bikes, touching them with an appreciative hand as he went. "And second, we should take the motorcycles. Better maneuverability to get through traffic or go off road to avoid S.D. and his brothers."

They had their choice of a Harley Davidson that was too heavy to seriously consider, two Triumphs, a BMW, a motocross dirt bike, a screaming red Ducati, and a squat, Indian Chief Scout power cruiser.

"Don't like it," Richie said. "Better to stick to the main road, outrun them in the Lambo."

"We need to blend in," Calvin pointed out, "not draw more attention to ourselves."

"The clock's ticking though. We can get back to L.A. a hell of a lot faster in that thing."

"Depends on how many times we get pulled over by the highway patrol. And what do you plan on telling them when they ask for the registration? The bikes are better, trust me."

"Okay, then I'll take one of the other cars and you take one of the bikes."

Calvin stared him down. "You don't know how to ride a motorcycle, do you?"

Richie shrugged. "I rode a moped in Hawaii once."

After another tactical discussion, they decided they'd take the Range Rover, though Richie continued to stare at the Lamborghini like a diabetic kid in a candy store.

"Can you hot-wire it without any of your tools?" Richie asked.

"It's not nineteen-eighty-five, you can't hot wire these things," Calvin said, waving him off. "But I guarantee you I can get any one of these rides started in under five seconds."

"I appreciate the confidence, but let's not get carried away with the ego."

Calvin pointed to the back wall and the row of eleven tiny hooks with eleven keys all lined up for the taking.

The plan was to head for the strip, until they were sure they weren't being followed, then back to L.A. If they were followed, they could dump the car and run into any one of the casinos to lose the tail. Lots of people on the strip and lots of cameras in the casinos that good old S.D. and his brothers wouldn't want any part of.

"You all set?" Calvin asked as he slid behind the wheel of the Range Rover.

Richie had the coins in his lap, the Ziplock bag with Heather's gun and phone at his feet. A weariness slid over his face and he tried to hide it with a quick smile. "All set to be either in prison, homeless, or dead."

Calvin started up the car. "I don't know about the first two, but a lot of people have tried to kill you in the past few days and ain't none of them succeeded."

He reached up and pressed the garage opener and the massive door slowly rose, revealing the dark night outside. The garage was only a third of the way up when a man ducked inside at the far end.

"Hey!" Richie yelled.

But the biker was already firing his gun before either of them fully understood what was happening.

The passenger side window shattered, showering glass like confetti. Calvin jammed the Rover into drive and clipped the top of the car with a loud crack on the rising garage door as he tore outside. Another bullet spiderwebbed the rear window with a sickening pop, but the bullet made it no further than the backseat head rest. The Rover swerved through the cul-de-sac as Calvin flattened the accelerator, his head so low he couldn't see over the dashboard. Another gunshot rang out, but there was no answer of metal. Whoever was firing at them was too far away to be accurate.

When Calvin finally raised up, he spotted two men running for a red and black Dodge Charger parked near the mouth of the cul-de-sac. "You hit?" he asked Richie.

Richie touched his face and neck. His right cheek had taken the most damage, though enough glass pocked-marked the side of his neck to draw plenty of blood there as well. "It's glass from the window. Holy crap, how many are out there?"

"I only saw two, plus the asshole from the garage."

"No bikes, that's why we didn't hear them."

"And the one from the garage is now in the house."

"So much for locking the doors."

"Shit, once he finds Heather, it's gonna be war."

The Dodge Charger's headlights lit up behind them, two fire-balls gaining in intensity as the car rapidly ate up the space between them.

"It's already started," Richie said.

After a few more unanswered texts, S.D. had evidently lost patience and gone out of his mind. Whether he was more interested in saving Heather or the money and the coins was beside the point. Now, they only had to avoid getting killed. Richie looked over his left shoulder, then the right, like he was sitting behind a fighter pilot, scouting for bogies.

"Which way to the main road?" Calvin yelled as they approached a four-way stop.

Richie continued to spin in his seat, trying to get his bearings. "Hold on, I think it's—"

Calvin slammed the brakes, dropping from ninety to thirty-five with a scream of rubber as he yanked on the wheel and chirp-turned the Rover around the corner, the rear end fish-tailing as they shuddered back into alignment.

"Nice driving," Richie said, "but that was supposed to be a left."

"How the hell do you know?"

"I was driving and I remember. You gotta turn back at the next corner."

Calvin accelerated to the next block and made the turn, the Dodge making it with him.

"Okay, maybe I was wrong," Richie said, straining to see a signpost.

"I'm not leading a fucking parade here," Calvin barked. "We gotta get this right."

"Hold on," Richie said, his face toward the hot wind sweeping in through the shattered window. In the distance he saw a faint glow of light rising like mist into the dark sky, and then a singular beam, shooting into space. The Luxor Casino.

"That way," he said. "The Strip's that way."

The Rover's V-6 engine roared, using every last bit of its 340 horsepower, the passing houses a blur as they finally found the main street leading back to civilization. There were no other cars on the road, but even at three-thirty in the morning, there would be enough crowds on the Strip to get lost among—if they could outrun the rest of S.D.'s bullets. As powerful as the Range Rover was, it was no match for the Charger. At each vehicle's top speed, the Charger would have to slow down or pass right by. On the straightaway, the Charger quickly caught up to the Rover's rear bumper and a dark figure leaned out the passenger window. Three quick blasts rang out, and two of the bullets found their target. The spiderwebbed back window shattered completely and a second later, the passenger side-mirror exploded and then dangled like a partially severed limb.

"Christ," Richie said, lowering himself further in the seat.

"You might want to put on that seatbelt," Calvin suggested.

Richie reached back and struggled to pull the belt across his chest and click it into place as another bullet pinged the Rover somewhere near the roofline on the driver's side. Calvin swerved back and forth, blocking the Charger from getting alongside, keeping the shooter from having a clear path to his head. More miles passed in a blink and the road widened to four lanes. A couple hours earlier, there would have been twice as many people on the street, but as it was the street was lit with enough restaurants, bars, and after-hours clubs for them to make out the faces of gawking tourists too drunk or too amped or too depressed to return to their hotel rooms. More than one of them waved a disapproving hand and yelled at the street racers howling past.

"We're not gonna lose them," Calvin said glancing into the rearview as they approached another intersection. He raised his eyes to the mirror for only a few seconds, but that was enough to keep him from noticing the green light change to yellow and then red. But even if he had seen it, they were going way too fast to stop. He leaned on the horn and blew into the intersection, nearly colliding with a taxi that needed to skid sideways to avoid getting t-boned. A short line of other cars came to a swerving stop behind the taxi, tires squealing in protest. "Whoa!" Richie screamed, the word coming out as a desperate reflex, his legs coming up to his chest. Behind them the Charger slalomed between the stopped cars, refusing to give up the chase as a chorus of blaring horns trailed after them.

They moved around a pickup truck piled high with old furniture, making its way along Flamingo Road, heading toward the Strip. In front of them was another intersection and a line of cars idling at a red light. Calvin said, "I'm gonna burn it to the right at the corner and then stop. We're gonna have to make a run for it into the Palms Casino right there, all right? When you get out, keep running."

Richie's throat was tight, holding down the contents of his stomach, and he could not speak.

"You with me?" Calvin screamed, his voice as revved up as the Rover's engine.

Richie's eyes briefly closed. "Yes."

Neither heard the gunshot that found the right rear tire, only the conclusive blast as the tire went supernova. The Rover vibrated on its three good tires, and all at once it were as if they were dragging an open parachute behind them.

"Crap," Calvin yelled, the car torquing clockwise, his hands gripping the wheel like it was about to break off from the steering column.

Under normal circumstances, he was adept enough behind the wheel to keep his foot off the brake, to allow the car to slow on its own, but he had no choice. With cars stopped in front of him and no control to swerve around them, he stood up on the brake pedal before he plowed into them. The rear end fishtailed wildly and the Rover spun as though they were on a lake of ice, before it found air and flipped twice, crashing back to earth with a sickening crunch of metal and flying glass. It continued sliding and rammed into the trunk of a Honda Civic, crushing its rear end like an empty aluminum can.

The five-thousand pound Range Rover finally came to rest on the driver's side, its three remaining wheels spinning, the stuck horn blaring like a mechanical scream of pain.

Inside, smoke vented from the spent airbags sagging white under the dashboard, filling the cabin with an acrid chemical scent, as Calvin and Richie regained their bearings. They were both still strapped into their seat belts, Calvin's left shoulder and cheek only a couple of inches from the pavement, Richie hanging limply above him. Panicked voices approached, though it was impossible to understand what they were saying above the howl of the Range Rover's horn.

Richie's breathing was surprisingly slow, calm even, when he turned his head to see a man's face appear at the space where the window used to be. The man was sweating, his eyes wide. "You're still alive," he said, sounding more surprised than pleased.

It was difficult for Richie to keep his eyes open with the haze of smoke burning his nostrils. The man shimmied his way into the car through the blown-out window, his belly on the door frame above him, only a heavy denim jacket, buttoned to the chin, between him and the broken glass. His hands shot downward, as though trying to unlatch the seatbelt.

"Give me a second," Richie said, the words floating weakly from his throat.

But the man's jarring hands kept moving, reaching so deeply into the car now that his elbow pressed into Richie's chest.

"Wait," Richie said, his hands rising in front of his eyes like half-filled balloons, until the weight of the man's torso pinned them back down. His brain had turned to paste, every thought only half-formed and sticky, none cleanly separated from another, and it took another second for him to realized the man wasn't trying to unlatch his seatbelt at all. The man gave a final effort and then lifted the box of coins that had been stuck between his left hip and the center console.

"No!" Calvin yelled from below Richie, his voice a live wire that jarred him.

Calvin's left arm flailed upward, aiming for the man's face, but the seatbelt kept him from breaking free and his fingers scratched Richie's chin rather than their intended target.

"Fuck you," the man said. He pulled back and disappeared from view, like an eel retreating into a cave.

And then the paste broke apart in Richie's mind and it all became clear.

The coins were gone. They were stuck. And the approaching sirens were for them.

CHAPTER TWENTY-THREE

AFTER RICHIE AND Calvin were dragged from the Range Rover and it was determined the damage to their faces had not been caused by the car crash, they were thrown into the backs of two separate cruisers and brought to intake at the Clark County Detention Facility—an establishment with roughly the same ambiance, Richie noted, as Christmas morning in hell. "Where Santa brings everyone hepatitis," he said to nobody in particular as they were placed in metal chairs on opposite sides of the room.

A nurse came by, a chubby, gruff woman in her late fifties wearing latex gloves and a silver cross necklace. Her task was to make sure they weren't going to die anytime soon, thus leaving the good state of Nevada susceptible to any lawsuits. After supplying abbreviated medical histories and assuring her that their impressive collection of wounds weren't terminal, Calvin and Richie were left alone, surrounded by an ever-rotating assortment of bottom-feeders.

There were miscreants of every stripe, including rank-smelling vagrants who appeared as content being there as anywhere else, and a wearying menagerie of desiccated prostitutes of both genders, sitting next to Johns caught with them (including a middle-aged man, wearing a Stanford sweatshirt and a gold wedding ring, who wouldn't stop crying). Those who complained the loudest were placed into windowless holding cells until they calmed down and accepted who was in charge.

Moments after the nurse left, Calvin was in danger of being dragged into one of those holding cells. His insistent concern about his kidnapped wife and son grew louder and louder every time it was ignored by one of the passing officers, until it turned into a full-force rant. Richie looked on helplessly from across the room as two officers tried to settle Calvin down with professional tones that only made him more agitated. "Call the fucking FBI," he screamed, his arms flailing, spit flying from his mouth. "Tell them I have information they need. I gotta get the hell out of here!"

"You're not going anywhere at the moment," one of the officers said in a tone you use for the mentally disturbed. "So you need to lower your voice and take a seat."

"No! You gotta listen to me," Calvin screamed into his face. "My wife and kid were taken and I have to talk to the FBI right now!"

The officers all looked bored, as if inured to any and all drama after years of dealing with endless delusions and lies. There were protocols in place and, to keep their sanity, they were programmed to follow them. "You'll have a chance to explain everything once you've been booked and processed," one of them said.

"Look, the FBI's already interviewed me once, okay? They'll know who I am."

A third officer stepped close, holding a Taser. "Sir, we will look into everything once you're booked, but until then, if you can't sit quietly, we're gonna have to restrain you in one of the cells. Do you understand that?"

"I'm running out of time. Why can't you get that?" Calvin cried. He made a move around the officers, toward the intake desk. "Give me the fucking phone and I'll call them myself."

The officers swarmed, dropping him to the floor, the metal chairs around them toppling like bowling pins. The fifteen or so prostitutes, Johns, drunks and lowlifes waiting to be booked took in the action as if they'd seen it all before, nothing to get excited over. The officers cuffed Calvin's hands behind his back and dragged him to a holding cell.

"He's telling you the truth," Richie called out, as Calvin continued to scream about stolen coins and the gangsters that kidnapped his family. "Make the fucking call and you'll see."

But both of them were ignored and the clock continued to tick, the minutes piling up on each other. Ninety minutes later, Calvin had calmed enough to be brought back out and he retook his seat without so much as a glance in Richie's direction. He sat with his head buried in his hands and stared at the floor. Eventually they were photographed, fingerprinted, and booked on charges of reckless endangerment and vehicle theft; the police clearly had not been able to confirm their story of the double homicide inside Winslow's house.

Calvin and Richie were moved to a large concrete holding tank, with two metal benches affixed to the walls on either side, filled with sleeping men who smelled of cigarettes and urine. The only other seat was a toilet in the corner that was currently occupied by a sweating fat man, fouling the air in a grey t-shirt that failed to reach his bellybutton, and chino pants around his ankles. More men lay on the floor, curled up like rats in the bowels of a sinking ship, while others leaned against the walls, talking in hushed tones.

Richie and Calvin found a spot to sit in the opposite corner from the man on the toilet and Richie pulled his shirt up over his nose. They were quiet for a moment, before he said, "I have an idea where we can get some help."

Calvin only sat and stared, hands folded in his lap, looking like a man who was beyond believing in hope.

"You're probably not gonna like it," Richie said, "but it's all I've got."

To Richie's right, an older vagrant with bushy eyebrows, scraggly beard, and enough grime under his nails to plant flowers in, seemed to take more interest in Richie's plan that Calvin did, so Richie leaned closer to Calvin's ear and quietly explained what they needed to make it work. Old Dirty-Nails bent closer, as though about to ask Richie to speak up, when the door to the holding tank swung wide and he ducked away like a frightened dog. Three officers entered, batons at the ready. Richie and Calvin looked up as they approached.

"On your feet," one of them ordered.

"What's going on?" Richie asked.

But there were no answers coming as the officers yanked them up and hustled them out.

It was early, a few ticks after seven. The sun hadn't built up the energy to break through the ghostly grey atmosphere the locals call "June Gloom." The dog days of summer might be barking at the door, but along the Southern California coast, the ocean was still cold and the air humid. The Mercedes was parked alongside the Pacific Coast Highway, enveloped in a bank of fog, much the same as its hungover occupant. Chad Richards was jarred awake by his phone, but he was not clear-minded enough to locate it before it fell silent.

Probably the wife, he figured. He had vague memories of talking to her sometime the night before, when it became apparent he was too drunk to find his way home. She, of course, believed he was sleeping it off in his office, having had too many drinks with a new client. She'd been understanding, as usual, appreciative even, that he was taking responsibility by not risking the drive, having no idea that he'd already driven under the influence all the way to Malibu. *Taking responsibility*. Ha. Taking responsibility was what had led him to drink in the first place— first to numb the emotional effects of signing death warrants for two young men who he'd betrayed, and then to stop thinking about the client who would kill him if he ever found out he'd been betrayed. Chad sighed deeply through his open mouth. Responsibility was for suckers and he was the biggest sucker of them all.

With an aggressive cough, he broke apart the drywall plastered in his lungs and ran his swollen tongue over his dry lips. "Son of a bitch," he moaned, readjusting his fat ass and stretching out his legs. He'd been in college the last time he'd spent the night passed out drunk in his car, and his older body was not responding well to the nostalgia. His limbs were cold and his mouth was hot. All at once it was an effort to keep his bladder in check. As he opened the door to a rush of cold air, the phone dinged with whatever message his wife had left him and he followed the sound to the floor of the car, somewhere between the brake and the accelerator. He tried to dig the phone out with his foot, but the effort only made his bladder scream louder. Climbing from the car, he set down one knee on the damp ground and reached back inside. By the time he got his hand on the dropped phone, it had dinged for a second time and he was in great danger of peeing in his pants for the first time since he was seven. One trip down memory lane was enough, so before checking the phone, he slammed the door closed and waddled down a steep four-foot incline to the sand.

Obscured from the few cars on PCH at that hour, he relieved himself. It took an extra effort to push the pee through his enlarged prostate but then he tucked himself away and zipped up his pants. Once squared away, he started back up the incline as he glanced at the phone's screen. It was a number he didn't recognize, but he sure as hell knew the 702 area code from which it originated. Vegas. Shit. As he reached the top, beads of perspiration seeped from his pasty forehead and his pulse hammered as though a woodpecker was feverishly pecking its way through the side of his neck. For a moment he considered the possibility he was having a heart attack, but there was no tingling down his arm, no labored effort to catch his breath, only the sensation of teetering on the edge of a cliff.

He slid his thumb across the screen to retrieve the voicemail, having no doubt it was a message from one of Winslow's pack of psychotic Lost-boys, informing him that he was a walking corpse. Somehow they'd figured out he'd called in the cavalry the night before, and it was time to pay the piper. What a fucking idiot he was to pay any attention to his goddamn conscience—even in the form of his dead son.

Standing there by the road, shivering in the gray morning cold, he half wished he was indeed having a heart attack, so he could just go ahead and get it over with. He pressed the phone to his cheek and held his breath. His mind was so wasted as he listened to the message, it took two or three sentences to realize it was not, in fact, one of the bikers of death, and he was not, in fact, in immediate danger. His relief was so sharp, he nearly dropped the phone. He paused the message and used his trembling finger on the screen to drag it back to the beginning. The voice that filled his fleshy ear was shaky, like a call in the dark from a frightened child convinced there was a monster under the bed.

"Mr. Richards, this is Richie Glass. I, ah, I get this is weird, me calling you and everything, after everything that happened, but I had nobody else to call and we need some serious help. We've been arrested in Vegas and we're being held at the Clark County Detention Center." Two deep breaths whistled in Chad's ear and Richie's voice returned, slightly more confident and moving twice as fast. "Look, I don't know what to say here. Winslow's dead and they think we killed him, but I swear to God we didn't. It was his fucking girlfriend, this psycho chick named Heather. She had some biker dude slit his throat and then she shot *him* and we left her tied up in Winslow's house, which sounds really bad, but we didn't have a choice. Shit, look, I don't know how to explain this. But you need to come here and talk to the cops because they don't believe a goddamn word we're saying.

"I told them you were my father's lawyer, that's all I said about you, I swear. I promise you're not involved beyond that, but Calvin and I are way beyond fucked because we also told them we were involved in the bank robbery in LA. We had to tell them because this other biker named S.D. took the coins after he and his brothers chased us when we stole Winslow's car, I forgot to mention that part. We stole Winslow's car and crashed it and lost the coins and that's why we need the cops to find this S.D. asshole and get the coins back. I told you it was a fucking mess. Anyway, you're our lawyer, right? You can help us? I hope this makes sense, because we have to get this all straightened out by two o'clock, so we can make the call to the guys who have Calvin's wife and kid, or they're gonna kill them. I mean, they probably won't kill both of them at the same time, because that would be fucking stupid before they get the coins back, but the point is we don't even have the coins anymore and we need to make that call at two, so you need to get here as fast as possible. Seriously, Chad, you need to do this for us or I swear to God I'll drag you down into the gutter along with us. Sorry, that's sounds like a dick move now that I'm saying it out loud, but anyway, yeah—the Clark County Detention Facility. Southwest has flights like every half-hour or something. What? Oh, all right, they're saying I have to get off the phone now, so, if you can—"

The line went dead and Chad dropped the phone onto the roof of his Mercedes, burying his face in his hands. Somewhere in the middle of the rambling message, he had leaned his sagging body against the car for support, his initial fear of Winslow's wrath replaced with a swirling nausea in his empty stomach. He lowered his hands and stared at the cars whipping past him through the fog, wondering if that heart attack was showing up after all.

CHAPTER TWENTY-FOUR

"YOU SURE YOU don't want to wait for your lawyer?"

Calvin shook his head at the detective sitting across the table taking up most of the space in the tiny interview room. "I don't have any idea if he's coming or not, and I don't have time to wait to and find out, so let's do this."

"To be clear, you're waiving your Miranda rights?" the detective asked.

Calvin glanced at the video camera tucked into the upper ceiling corner, his heel bouncing up and down beneath his chair. "Yes."

"Okay." Detective Kendrick leaned forward in his chair and rested his forearms on the table, hands folded together. He wore a blue polo shirt with the Las Vegas Metropolitan Police Department logo over the left breast pocket, his sandy blonde hair cut short, but still long enough to require some gel to keep it off his tanned forehead. He stared at Calvin like a Little League coach consoling a player after a hard-fought loss, the corners of his mouth slightly downturned and his eyes wide. But there was nothing little league about the conversation they were about to have. "I can help you here, Calvin," he said. "But first you're gonna have to help me understand what exactly happened this evening."

"Man, I've told you guys everything," Calvin snapped. "Have you even called the FBI in LA yet?"

"We'll get to that, but I have a more pressing issue right here. Because if what you've been saying is true, we have a couple of bikers out there we need to identify before they hurt anyone else. The problem is, we've been running the initials S.D. through our data base, but nothing's coming up, not even among any of the bikers at the house tonight following the bogus SWAT call. If this guy is as badass as you're describing, I'd assume he's been arrested before, so it makes me wonder why we can't find anyone with those initials fitting your description."

"What about Heather?" Calvin said. "You got her phone and the gun she used to shoot that dude who killed Winslow, so find her first."

Kendrick nodded. "I'd like to do that, but we can't open her phone. Other than a first name, we don't have much to go on."

"Her damn prints are on the gun. Run them through AFIS and arrest her ass along with her boy, S.D."

Kendrick smiled. "You're familiar with AFIS?"

"I've been in the system, man."

"Yes, you have. And if this Heather person you've described is also in the system, we'll find her fingerprints too. But that'll take several weeks, at minimum."

"Several weeks! They gonna be in Mexico by tonight."

"Well, life isn't like on TV with all that C.S.I. bullshit. We can't just enter the prints into a computer and wait for her picture to pop up with a last known address and her favorite flavor of ice cream. AFIS has over fifty million prints to compare hers to, and they'll all have to be overlaid and examined. And that's only if we're lucky enough to get anything clean enough off the gun. Truth of the matter is, only about a quarter or so of the cases the lab reviews come up with identifiable prints, which means we're already dealing with a long shot."

"Yeah, well, that's the only shot I got."

Kendrick sucked on his lower lip, looking confused. "It might seem that way, Calvin. But there are other options for you."

"Like what?"

"Like telling the truth."

"What the fuck you think I've been doing?"

"I think you've been trying to spin this thing any way you can to get out from under it."

Calvin bore his eyes into Kendrick's. "I ain't trying to spin nothing."

Kendrick sat back and folded his arms, waited a good thirty seconds before he continued. When he did, he began by holding out his right thumb. "We placed you in the house along with both victims at the time of their murders." He added his forefinger. "You already lied to the SWAT team about the true nature of your relationship after they responded to a suspicious call." His middle finger popped up. "You admitted that you robbed a bank and had gone to the victim's home to retrieve the stolen property." Now his ring finger joined the party. "You had the murder weapon in your possession, along with the phone of the person you're attempting to frame." And finally his pinky extended out to complete the picture. "You stole the victim's car in order to flee the scene." He help his open palm up, showed it to him. "I'm running out of fingers here, Calvin, and I'm only getting started."

Calvin's foot tapped faster under his chair. "What about the knife that dude with the scorpion tattoo used to cut Winslow's throat? You can run his prints, too."

Detective Kendrick shook his head. "You're hung up on prints, Calvin. But there was no knife found at the scene."

"Shit, that only means they took it."

"Again, you're asking us to trust your description of a pretty wild set of circumstances."

"Ain't you ever heard that truth is stranger than fiction?"

"Fair enough." Detective Kendrick again leaned back in his chair and took a deep breath. "And have you ever heard of Occam's Razor?"

Calvin sighed, shaking his head. "No."

"It's a problem-solving principle that suggests the simplest answer is usually the correct one. So let me lay this out for you. The simplest explanation for what went down here is that you and Richie got in deep with Winslow and some of his biker friends during your admitted involvement in the bank robbery in Los Angeles, which is why you lied to the SWAT team about him being an old family friend when they were called to his house under suspicious circumstances—something that I'm gonna guess had to do with a double-cross that led to you killing both men, and being chased and shot after you stole Winslow's car to return to LA." He leveled his eyes. "How close am I, Calvin? Razor thin, I'd say."

Richie's head felt as though it was filled with sand. He'd fallen asleep in his holding cell, waiting for his interview with Detective Kendrick to begin, and a half-hour or so of deep slumber had only made him feel worse. The dark bags under his eyes were swollen and heavy. His ears rang and his teeth tasted metallic.

Detective Kendrick leaned back in the chair opposite him and took a deep breath. Richie was sure they had gone over the same ground already covered with Calvin, but it was clear the detective had not gotten any further along and was losing the enthusiasm he'd demonstrated at the outset.

"You look like you could use a drink," Richie said.

"It's ten-thirty in the morning."

Richie shrugged. Beyond the two o'clock deadline, time meant nothing to him anymore.

Kendrick squinted at him. "Come on, Richie."

"We going somewhere?"

"So far, only in circles. I still can't understand why you're going to the mat for some guy you've known for less than a week."

"I'm not going to the mat for anyone, I'm telling the truth."

Kendrick nodded, holding the condescending gaze Richie was now used to. It didn't faze him because other than altering the bit about Chad's involvement in introducing them to Winslow, he had indeed been telling the honest-to-God truth. Scout's honor and all that shit. Though it was clear by now that the truth was not going to set them free.

"Whose idea was it to steal the Range Rover?" Kendrick asked, glancing down at the notes he'd taken over the past hour. "With his history, I'm guessing it was Calvin's."

"That doesn't—"

"And it was Calvin who hunted you down at your house, forcing you to go with him to this Connor Weeks' residence after the bank job, correct?"

"I didn't say he *hunted* me down. I said he came to my house to ask a few questions. And I don't blame him, I had plenty of questions, too."

"No, no, you're not seeing the big picture, Richie." Kendrick raised an eyebrow. "He had a gun when he arrived at your house, didn't he?"

Richie shifted in his seat. "Yeah, but he didn't use it. You wouldn't guess it by looking at him, but he's not—"

Kendrick's voice grew sharper. "He's not what?" He held out his thumb. "An ex-con?" He added his forefinger. "Who forced you at gunpoint to do what he wanted?" His middle finger rose up. "The one who *knew* ahead of time, unlike you, that the bank job was arranged by Connor Weeks?" His ring finger fully extended. "The one who was, unlike you, *in the house* tonight when the two men were killed?" His pinky popped out, and he showed Richie the back of his hand. He paused like that and leaned a few inches closer. "The one who's been playing you since the beginning and will *turn* on you the minute he realizes there's no other way out of this."

Richie's gaze wavered. "It's not like that."

"It's *exactly* like that. You're a chump. He's leading you around like a dog on a leash. How do you know he didn't kill those two men tonight? Because he told you? How do you know he wasn't in on the double-cross at the bank from the very beginning? Because he told you that too? Pay attention here, Richie, because I'm offering you a way out of this. You've already admitted you were forced into driving for the bank robbery against your will and that Calvin also took you to Connor Weeks' house against your will."

"Save your breath," Richie said.

Kendrick gave him an incredulous stare, his mouth slightly open as if Richie's apparent naiveté was difficult to take. "Whatever trouble you're in for that bank job, you're only making it worse by aiding and abetting a double homicide, when you weren't even in the house when it was committed. It's time to wake up, Richie."

Richie swallowed the saliva pooling at the back of his throat. "Actually," he said. "It's time for me to shut up."

Detective Kendrick shook his head. "That would be another mistake to add to the list. Think clearly about what I'm saying, because this is your last chance, son."

Richie clenched his teeth. "Thanks for the advice, *dad*. But I'm gonna wait for my lawyer."

The door behind Detective Kendrick opened and a blonde woman in dark slacks and a dark blue blazer stepped inside. Richie looked up at her. "If I'd known we had an audience I would've brushed my hair. You his partner? Here to play good cop, bad cop? Let me guess, you're about to say that Calvin's turned on me, right? That I have one last shot at playing ball before it's too late."

The woman's half-smile disappeared, but her eyes remained wide as she held up her I.D. "My name's Special Agent Grace Luelle with the F.B.I. You're right, Mr. Glass, the ball is definitely in your court. And I'm here to figure out exactly what sort of game you and Calvin Russel are playing with it."

Richie was brought out to a large office behind the jail processing counter and reunited with Calvin, who sat on one side of a desk, sandwiched between Detective Kendrick and Agent Frank Daniels, the newest and youngest on Luelle's team. Agent Luelle indicated one of two empty seats to Richie and then sat down beside him.

"Snake Plissken," she said.

"Excuse me?" asked Detective Kendrick.

"Snake Plissken," she repeated. "He's a character played by Kurt Russell in the movie, *Escape from New York*."

Kendrick shrugged. "So?"

"So before Snake Plissken tattooed his stomach with a snake

and turned outlaw biker, he was a special forces officer by the name S.D. Bob Plissken.

"S.D. Bob?" Kendrick said. "Are you being serious?"

Her stare didn't waver. "I'm with the FBI, we're always serious."

"How the hell d'you figure that out?"

"My ex was a connoisseur of eighties movies," she said. "Can't tell you how many times I had to sit through *Beetlejuice*."

Detective Kendrick chuckled. "And *Escape From New York*, evidently."

"I didn't mind that one," she shrugged. "I've always had a thing for Kurt Russell. Anyway, once we realized the connection, we ran the first name against known biker gangs in the Las Vegas area, got a hit right away. Our S.D.'s name is Bob Matthews."

"Once 'we' made the connection," Agent Daniels said. "That's very big of you, but clearly it was all you."

"We're on the same team," Agent Luelle said, her half-smile returning.

"Hold up," Richie said. "Are you saying that dude who chased us down and took the coins is named *Bob*?"

Agent Luelle shrugged. "Worked for Kurt Russell."

"I guess Heather was a fan of nicknames after all," Calvin said.

"Can't say I blame her on that one."

Richie placed both elbows on the desk and spread his hands wide. "So we were almost murdered by psychotic bikers named *Bob* and *Heather*?"

"You know where they are?" Calvin asked.

Luelle looked to Agent Daniels, who said, "Mr. Matthews last used a credit card at a Jack-In-The-Box in Riverside, California."

"When?" Calvin asked.

"Thirty-minutes ago."

Calvin snapped at Detective Kendrick. "Man, I *told* you they were going to Mexico."

Kendrick lowered his chin to a condescending angle. "You're a genius," he said.

"Hey, fuck you, Chief Wiggum."

Daniels laughed, said to Agent Luelle, "Incompetent cop on the Simpsons."

"Yes, I got that." She dropped a manila folder on the table. "Moving on. We have a BOLO out on all three of the Matthews brothers as well as the Dodge Charger, though we assume they've most likely dumped it. Border Patrol has also been notified, so let's not worry about Bob and Heather getting into Mexico at the moment. Right now I'd like to hear about the bank robbery in Reseda and the murder of Connor Weeks and his men."

Calvin waved dismissively at Kendrick. "We already told this guy everything, what the hell more you need?"

Agent Luelle rested her hands on the table. "Start at the beginning and I'll stop you when I've heard enough."

Calvin pointed at her. "You gotta guarantee me you'll let me make that call at two."

"I'm not guaranteeing anything, Calvin," she said, her voice remaining even despite the belligerent demand thrown her way. "You have no idea how much trouble you're in here, do you?"

"I do," Richie said, raising his hand.

Agent Luelle kept her eyes on Calvin. "You lied to me when I talked to you in your home. You looked me right in the eye and lied. So did your wife. Now you're telling me that she and your son have disappeared because they've been kidnapped by some mysterious men of unknown origin—could be Italian, could be Russian, who knows? Maybe they exist, maybe they don't. Maybe I let you make that call you're so desperate about and you're really calling your wife or some other partner, tipping them off that you're in custody and they should stay in hiding or leave town." Her voice grew harder, more accusatory. "Maybe you were working with Bob and Heather and Connor Weeks this whole time, as Detective Kendrick suspects. Maybe this is all about a double-cross between you and them. Maybe you're sitting here about to lie to my face again, trying to figure out the best way to play me like you did last time. It's all such a goddamn mess because you made the choice to not tell the truth. So, forget about your phone call and forget about me guaranteeing you anything."

Richie stared with wide eyes across the table at Calvin, who sat there looking as though he were stuck in a glass box, unable to break free. He glanced at the clock on the wall. It was now ten minutes to noon. "I'm not lying to you now," he said.

Agent Luelle's expression remained unyielding. "Start from the beginning," she said.

But still Calvin didn't speak. His eyes drifted back to the clock and then focused on something no one else could see, something that wasn't in the room.

"We were both outside the bank when the shooting started," Richie said, filling the uncomfortable silence. "Neither of us had any idea what was going on. Connor Weeks was behind this whole damn—"

Agent Luelle held up her hand, stopping him. Her stare finally came off Calvin and landed on Richie. She was silent for a moment, letting him squirm in discomfort, before saying, "And maybe Detective Kendrick was right about you, too. Maybe you're the idiot patsy in all of this. Or maybe you're the mastermind behind the whole damn thing. So difficult to tell when everyone's been lying for so long. Detective Kendrick, will you please escort Mr. Glass back to a holding cell? I'll talk to him as soon as I'm finished with Mr. Russell."

Richie quickly lost track of time. It had been noon when he was brought to the holding cell, so he guessed it had to be after one by now. Hell, maybe even close to two. He laid back on the bench and closed his eyes, trying not to envision Tracey and Martin being cut into, chunks of their flesh being packaged up and delivered to his empty house as an incentive to be taken seriously. If only those assholes realized how seriously they were being taken. Of course, if they found out the call hadn't been made because Richie and Calvin had been too busy talking to the fucking FBI, more than pieces of flesh would be taken—Tracey and Martin would disappear completely.

The door to Richie's cell rattled open and an officer motioned for him. "Let's go,"he said. "They're ready for you."

Richie stood up, his back sore, his knees stiff. Jesus, he felt like a ninety-year-old. The combined effect of the beatings were really taking their toll. "What time is it?" he asked as he stepped into the hallway.

"One-thirty-five," the officer told him. "That way, down there."

Richie started the slow walk past a line of other cells, aware that it no longer mattered how long it took to get where he was going. If Special Agent Luelle took close to two hours to inter-rogate Calvin, by the time she finished with him, the two o'clock deadline would be well in the rearview mirror and any phone call would only be made to confirm their worst nightmares. "Hold it," the officer following Richie said. Richie stared at his shoes as the officer opened up the last cell on the right. "Let's go," he said to someone inside.

Calvin stepped from the cell, saying, "'Bout damn time, Richie. I hope they believed you more than they believed me."

Richie's face pinched in confusion. "What're you talking about? They never came for me. I thought you were still being interviewed this whole time."

Calvin's expression was a mirror image of Richie's. "No, man, they brought me back an hour ago."

"Well, if they're not talking to me and they're not talking to you, who the hell are they talking to?"

The officer led them to the open bullpen behind the intake processing counter where Agent Luelle was sipping a cup of coffee with Chad Richards.

CHAPTER TWENTY-FIVE

"THE MEN WHO took your wife and son work for a man named Mikos Sotereanos. And based on your description, there is a strong likelihood that one of them is his son, Stavos."

Calvin and Richie looked at each other, then back at Carol Lee, the Assistant District Attorney standing at the head of a table in the back office of the Clark County Detention Facility. She was short, five-three in heels, with short black hair, and—they would soon discover—a short temper.

"How the hell did you figure that out?" Calvin asked.

Agent Luelle picked up where Carol Lee left off. "As soon as we learned ancient coins were taken from the security deposit box during the robbery of American Federal, we started looking for anything that might lead us to the owner of the box. One of our agents found a report from last year detailing the theft of ancient Greek and Roman coins from a private collector in Chicago, as they were being transferred to the Metropolitan Museum of Art in New York City for a temporary exhibition. Nobody was ever apprehended in the theft; however, David Perlstein, the manager of American Federal, who turned out to be the brother of Connor Weeks—"

"Wait, really?" Richie said. "No shit? His brother?"

"Keep your mouth shut," Carol Lee snapped.

"As I was saying," Agent Luelle continued. "David Perlstein, whose real name was David Weeks, previously worked for an import company in Boston named United Marketing which was owned by—"

"Mikos, fucking, Sort-e-al-a-nostros," Richie said. "I'm sorry, what was that name again?"

Carol Lee leaned on the table. "Mr. Glass, use whatever brain cells that haven't died from neglect to understand the situation you find yourself in, because if you interrupt one more time, your ass is going back in that cell, where it will stay until a judge sentences it to be moved to the darkest hole we can find in our Federal Penitentiary system."

Richie glanced at Chad, but Chad only raised a warning eyebrow of agreement. Beyond nodding hello when Richie and Calvin had walked in and were told to sit down, it was the only time he'd even looked in Richie's direction. His irritation was as palpable as the ADA's.

Agent Luelle kept her eyes on Calvin and picked up as though there'd been no interruption. "When Mikos Sotereanos fled Greece eighteen years ago, the Inspector General of the Hellenic Police Force was working on a joint task investigation with Interpol to bring him down. Evidently Mr. Sotereanos has quite the reputation in London as well. Though no formal charges were ever brought, he'd been suspected of murder, extortion, money laundering and dealing in stolen goods. We are now working under the assumption that David Perlstein-Weeks was cooking their books for them while he worked at the import company and, currently, Mr. Sotereanos was using him to store stolen property at the bank. That is until David decided to dip his hands into their gold coins, which we believe was his broth-er's idea."

"So where does that leave us?" Calvin asked.

"In a world of trouble," answered Carol Lee. "The list of charges against the two of you is truly impressive."

"But," Chad said, finally breaking his silence, "not as impres-sive as the ones against Mikos Sotereanos."

Carol Lee's eyes darted sideways, landed on the lawyer. "Eye of the beholder."

Chad turned his bloated frame toward Agent Luelle. "And how do you suppose your counterparts at Interpol will *behold* the opportunity to bring down two American idiots, versus the international criminal who continues to mock their efforts at justice by living the high-life in the land of milk and honey?"

Calvin and Agent Luelle met each other's stare across the table. In the time they'd spent together, he had worked hard to convince her that Chad's assessment was the correct one. That Calvin and Richie were merely two fuckups who had not person-ally harmed anyone, but had only made bad choices and wound up in a situation beyond anything they could have expected. The problem was she'd heard it all before, countless times.

"We are all the result of the choices we make," she had said to Calvin, before sending him back to his cell. "None of us are passive recipients of life. We choose to act, it affects where we end up. We choose not to act, it affects the outcome much the same. You *chose* to get behind the wheel of that car last Saturday in Reseda, Calvin. You chose to go to Connor Weeks' home. You chose to take the coins. You chose to put your family in harm's way to make a fast buck. And when I came to your house, you chose to lie to me. I believe you when you say you're not lying to me anymore, but there's no doubt in my mind that you're only telling the truth because it's the only choice you have left."

And now she was the one with the final choice to make.

"We have agents staking out the Sotereanos home in Bel Air," Agent Luelle said to Calvin. "But we can't be sure your wife and son are there, so we can't risk moving on them now. We have a plan of action, but we can't put it in motion until we have your cooperation." She glanced at her watch. Five minutes past two.

She turned to ADA Lee and nodded. "Tell them."

Carol Lee straightened and spoke in a flat tone. "Pending the arrests of Heather Patterson and Bob Matthews, along with the retrieval of evidence proving they are indeed the parties responsible for the deaths of Mr. Winslow and the as-yet-unidentified biker last night in the Winslow home—we are prepared, in exchange for your full cooperation, to offer Mr. Glass six months in a minimum security federal prison for his involvement in the bank robbery, with an additional twelve months suspended, along with five years probation, and one hundred hours of community service."

Richie's face flushed. "Six months?"

"With good behavior you'll be out in four," Chad said.

Carol Lee then continued. "Mr. Russell," she said, turning to Calvin. "In light of the fact that, unlike Mr. Glass, you were fully complicit in the armed robbery of American Federal without being coerced, as well as having a prior record, and having lied to a Federal Officer during the course of an investigation, you will agree to serve eighteen months in a Federal Penitentiary, with the remaining one hundred and four months of your sentence suspended, along with the same five-year term of probation and one hundred hours of community service."

"Wait a minute," Richie said. "You mean he goes to prison for a year and a half, but I get four months?"

Calvin stared at Agent Luelle. She didn't blink.

"With good behavior, Mr. Russell will be eligible for release after serving fifteen months," Carol Lee said.

"Explain to them what 'full cooperation' entails," said Chad.

Agent Luelle turned to Agent Daniels standing by the door, holding a stack of manila folders, presumedly all the police reports they'd compiled during their time in Vegas. "Frank?" she said, inviting him to step forward.

He said, "In addition to testifying in open court against Heather Patterson, Bob Matthews and his brothers, you'll wear a wire in an undercover sting on Mikos Sotereanos. We get Sotereanos on tape exchanging Tracey and Martin and admitting to the ownership of the stolen coins, the murders of Conner Weeks, his brother, and their men."

"But we don't have the coins," Calvin said.

"That is a problem," Agent Daniels agreed.

"Yeah, I'd say that's a big fucking problem," Calvin said.

Agent Luelle leaned in. "Mr. Russell, we can either sit here and worry about the things we can't control, or act upon the things we can. The clock is ticking."

"Do we have a deal?" Carol Lee asked.

"I advise you to take the offer," Chad said. "But before you do, it's important you both understand: these guys won't hesitate to kill any of you, including Tracey and Martin, if everything doesn't go their way. And things are definitely not going to go their way."

Calvin listened to his lawyer, then tapped the desk with his knuckles and stood. "I gotta make that phone call."

When Agent Luelle handed Calvin the cell phone, it was a quarter past two. "Stay calm and agree to whatever they say. If they ask if you have the coins, tell them you do."

Richie hovered close, saying, "You want to rehearse? Maybe you should run lines first, I can—" Calvin shot him a look and Richie relented. "You'll be fine, you're good."

Calvin looked at the business card Stavos had given him and dialed. Everyone noticed his fingers shaking, but nobody said anything.

"Fifteen minutes late," Stavos's voice sounded on the other end of the line.

"Couldn't be helped," Calvin said. "We had no phone service and had to drive to get a connection."

"Cellphones, so unreliable, no? And now it will cost you two fingers."

"What the hell you talking about?"

Agent Luelle placed her hand on Calvin's back, but he shook it free.

"Tell me whose I should cut?" Stavos said. "Your wife's or your son's. It's fine if you can't decide, I can take one from each."

Calvin's stomach knotted, squeezing his diaphragm, cutting off his air. The exhaustion he had been living with over the past twenty-four hours deepened, seeping further into his bones. "Goddamn, motherfucker," he seethed.

"Yes, okay," Stavos said. "One of each."

"No!" Calvin screamed.

Agent Luelle moved to stand in front of Calvin, her hands up, imploring him to calm down.

"We have your coins," Calvin said, working hard to stay in

control. "We have them right here. You're gonna get everything you want. Just let me talk to my wife."

Stavos laughed. "You are in no position to be making demands."

"I want to hear her voice."

"Fine," Stavos said with the taunting joy of a true sociopath. "Then I'll make her scream for you."

Calvin's nerves exploded, splintering off like fireworks throughout his body. "I'll fucking kill you!" he yelled into the phone.

Agent Luelle and Richie were twin dancers, pirouetting away in disbelief that Calvin could lose control as he had. Stavos's laughter grew louder and Calvin's body shook. After a muffled exchange on Stavos's end of the line, a new voice darted into Calvin's ear. The new voice was deeper, the Greek accent more pronounced. "Listen to me," the new voice said, each word like a nail being driven into a block of wood. "You are finished talking now. I do not like these games. If you do not do exactly as I say, you will never see this woman and boy again, it is as simple as that. Am I understood?"

I was clear that Calvin was speaking to the man behind the curtain. His chest expanded to capacity before he let the air out silently, as if it was in danger of exploding. "Yes," he said.

"Your wife told me of a park on Florence Avenue," Mikos said. "There are tennis courts there, do you know them?"

"Yes."

"You and your companion will be there at four o'clock."

Calvin looked desperately at Agent Luelle. "That's less than two hours. We can't—"

"We are done talking," Mikos said.

The line went dead.

"Shit," Calvin said. "We're screwed."

"When and where?" Agent Luelle asked.

"Vincent Park in Inglewood. Four."

"You gotta be kidding," Richie said. "It's after two now. We're never gonna make it."

"Check the flight schedule at McCarran," she said to Agent Daniels.

"I'm on it."

"Flight schedule?" Richie said. "You're the goddamned FBI. Don't you have a company jet?"

"Only on T.V.," Agent Daniels said, typing furiously on his phone.

"Yeah, that seems to be a theme with you guys," Richie said.

"We'll have undercover police there on time, even if we aren't," Agent Luelle said, pulling out her own phone, dialing Agent Hicks in LA to put things in motion.

Calvin collapsed into the chair. The stress poured from him like water as he buried his face in his hands.

Agent Luelle said, "Don't worry. We'll move in if there's any sign your wife and son are in danger."

"Excuse me," Chad said, hauling himself up from his chair. Throughout his time at the Clark County Detention Center, his attitude toward Richie and Calvin had remained aloof, disinterested in anything beyond the necessary formalities of the moment. But now, as he ran his hand down his tie and buttoned his sport coat, he looked at them with compassion, as if he finally understood the grinding machinery of chaos they'd been enmeshed in since that fateful meeting in his office. "I might be able to help," he said.

CHAPTER TWENTY-SIX

STAVOS WALKED DOWN the hallway with his father, making sure to keep a few respectful paces behind. Mikos said nothing, content to let his son trail in his wake like a puppy who'd just been corrected. "There is no need for you to go with us," Stavos said. If he didn't speak now, his father would disappear into his room and slam the door in Stavos's face—a final embarrassment in front of the men who watched and judged. Just as they had when Mikos yanked the phone from him and called him, "adýnamos," weak.

"You have failed too many times." Mikos said with a dismissive wave over his shoulder. "This has become an embarrassment."

"I'm handling it," Stavos insisted.

Mikos spun around. "You are handling nothing," he said. "It should never have come this far!"

"But it has, hasn't it?"

Mikos slapped him. "Show respect," he growled. "You have not earned the right to be so cavalier with my business."

Stavos's mouth opened and closed as he worked to find a way to respond that wouldn't result in another lashing. "And what of respect for me?" he asked. "Doing our business in that pathetic man's bank was not my idea. But I have made it my job to clean up the mess he left."

"All you have done is make a bigger mess!"

Stavos shook his head. "No, I have done everything you've asked of me. I've killed for you, Papa. What more do I need to show you?"

Mikos rocked back on his heels as though he needed extra distance to see his son clearly. "You have not killed for me, Stavos. You have only killed for what I give you."

Stavos lowered his chin, not allowing his father to see the pain in his eyes. Mikos reached out and used the tips of his fingers to raise his face back up. "It is not easy for me to see the way things have become between us," he said, his tone patient, though without any hint of apology. "You are my son. It should not be this way. Do you agree?"

His hand came off Stavos's chin and Stavos nodded.

"I see you are doing the best you can," Mikos went on. "But you have made many mistakes, no?"

It took a moment, but Stavos again nodded.

"Good. Good. Tell me," Mikos said. "So I know you understand."

Stavos bit hard on his molars. "I could have sold the coins to someone else. I should have not pursued that idiot Luke Stanton to begin with."

"Hmm, yes. What else?"

"I should have kept a closer eye on David Perlstein once we left the coins in his bank."

Mikos was quiet a long moment. The men standing at the end of the hallway might have thought the confrontation was over, but Mikos remained intent on humiliating his son. "What else?" he asked.

Stavos shifted his weight from one leg to the other. The abasement was not going to end until he was reduced to ash. "I should not have brought this into our home," he said, his voice thin, defeated.

Mikos did not reach out for him, offering only a grunt of air through this nostrils. "Where we find ourselves is your fault, yes. But I have made mistakes as well, Stavos. It is my fault you are so undisciplined. I should not have put you in this position. Your life has been too sheltered, too much of it spent in clubs chasing women, instead of learning the way to conduct business. You have no sense of the world. That is why you would bring these people into our home." He sniffed the air. "Their stench lingers. They are like animals. Do you see that?"

"Yes, Papa."

"We will use your mistakes to our advantage. Animals such as these kill each other all the time. In their neighborhoods, nobody notices. That is why we will go there to end this. And you will see the proper way to conduct business with thieves."

Chad Richards stood outside the Sheriff's van, looking in on the two uniformed police escorts, Agents Luelle and Daniels, and Calvin and Richie—both with hands tucked in their laps, held together in matching handcuffs.

"You sure you don't want to go back with us?" Agent Daniels asked.

"I'm sure. I'm gonna check in at the Bellagio. Take a hot shower and get a massage."

"Maybe hit the clubs?" Richie said.

Chad grimaced. "I'm a married man, remember?"

Richie smiled at him, but Chad only shrugged, his wrinkled

suit bunching up around his shoulders. "Good luck, gentlemen. I hope you make it on time."

If they did make it, it would be because of him. He had several clients with private jets and a jones for Vegas, and, as it turned out, one of them was in town getting his weekly fix. Once the situation was explained, the jet was theirs to borrow and Chad's client had a hell of a cocktail party story.

"We appreciate the help," Richie said. "With everything."

"Sometimes it all works out," Chad said, half grinning.

"That would be a nice change of pace," Calvin said, leaning forward and holding out his handcuffed hands. "Thank you for… thank you."

"Glad I could be of service," he said shaking Calvin's hand. "You be sure to take care of that little boy of yours."

"No doubt."

"I'll call you when this is all over," Richie said.

Chad shook his head. "Please don't."

Agent Daniels rattled the door closed and the van sped off. Normally, the drive from the county jail to to McCarran International Airport took fifteen minutes. With a motorcycle cop's siren leading the way, they made it in six. The Gulfstream G650 belonging to the vice-president of a private equity firm in San Diego was in the air eleven minutes later.

"These stings usually go pretty well?" Richie asked Agent Daniels once they were at cruising altitude.

Daniels looked up from the field notes in his lap. "I assume so, but this is my first one."

"That's great," Richie said. "Listen, don't take this the wrong way, but you don't still have your training wheels on that gun, do you?"

Daniels glanced over his shoulder at Agent Luelle, who was

busy working the phone, arranging things with Hicks and a scrambling task force of LAPD officers. "I'm perfectly qualified to handle my firearm in any situation that may arise," he said, settling his stare back on Richie. "However, for your edification, there will be a highly trained team of federal agents working in conjunction with local authorities, should they become necessary to ensure your safety."

Richie repositioned himself in the most comfortable seat he'd been in for a week, and nodded at Calvin. "You hear that? I'm sure that was for your *edification* as well."

But Calvin only turned and looked out the window as clouds brushed past like smoke from a distant fire.

Turned out that Chad Richards was right—sometimes things do work out. Of course, things "working out" is entirely perspective-dependent. From Eric Matthews' perspective, it was a pain in his ass that he had to accompany his brother and his brother's bitch of a girlfriend to Mexico, all because of a couple of fuck-heads from LA who got boned by Winslow. Their other brother, Patrick, the baby of the family, had insisted he ride back to Idaho on his own to pick up his fiancé. If he went to Mexico without her, she'd break off the engagement for sure. She was already unhappy enough with him spending so much time in Vegas.

With no fiancé to worry about, Eric had eyes only for his share of the money they'd get once they found a way to sell the coins. But first he had a paycheck waiting for him, and eighteen hundred bucks was eighteen hundred bucks. So the plan was for them to zip down the 91 freeway on their Harleys (the Dodge Charger safely tucked into storage), swing by the Oil Products warehouse in Corona where Eric had worked the past two years, pick up the check, and then hightail it to the border with a little extra spending cash until they were sure the heat was off.

Once they arrived at the warehouse, Heather and Bob waited on their bikes in the parking lot as Eric argued with his boss about the amount of time he could have off and still expect his job to be there when he got back.

Bob looked at his watch and mumbled, "This fucking guy."

"He takes much longer," Heather said, squinting into the sun. "I'm gonna go in there and shoot his fucking boss on principle."

Bob wiped the sweat from the bristly three-day growth under his jaw. "Shit-for-brains is so fat, you'd have to shoot him twice for him to notice."

"Why's E so intent on keeping his job anyway? He's gonna make more on these fucking coins than he would in five years working the line down here."

Bob looked at the warehouse door through his Ray-Bans. "Gainful employment," he said. "Terms of parole. Hell a lot easier keeping a job than finding one, and his P.O. is a bigger prick than his boss."

Heather stepped close and took the pack of Camels from the pocket of his leather jacket, lit one, and put the pack back. "He should have shot those assholes when he had the chance."

Bob spit on the ground, barely missing her black cowboy boot. "He got the fucking coins from the car, didn't he? I swear, the two of you better not be barking at each other the whole goddamn time."

"Relax," she said.

"Don't fucking tell me to relax, either. I'll fucking relax once those coins are sold."

Heather took a deep pull on the cigarette. "All I'm saying is, it would have saved us a lot of trouble."

He looked at her over the top of his sunglasses. "You had a gun pointed at the nigger, too, so stop playing it like E's the only fuck-up here."

Heather looked away, was quiet for a minute. "I'm gonna be okay," she said eventually. "If it comes to it, it's their word against mine and they're the ones had the grudge with Winslow."

"Winslow was an asshole."

She blew more smoke into the air. "Ain't that the truth."

"Besides," Bob said. "I've already talked to Bones and Rusty about taking them out eventually. They ain't never gonna get to trial to say shit about you."

Heather crushed the cigarette under her boot and gave him a deep kiss.

And then, their entire perspective changed.

The CHP sedans arrived without the benefit of sirens. Before Heather or Bob even noticed them, there were four pulling into the parking lot, with three more right behind. The screeched to a stop and, suddenly, seven officers with guns drawn were yelling at them to get on the ground. They obliged, with Heather's face ending up right next to the cigarette she'd dropped. Turned out that Eric's fat-fuck of a boss, a badly-sweating redhead named Emmett Gilroy, was stalling the whole time. FBI Agent Hicks had spoken to him an hour before Eric's arrival, requesting him to make a very specific phone call if he heard from him.

Emmett and about twenty other curious employees stood in front of the open warehouse doors as Eric was led off in handcuffs to join his brother and some mystery woman in the back of the waiting CHP sedans.

"What he do?" one of the employees asked.

"Probably dealing drugs," Emmett said, reframing his cell phone to get a better shot. He zoomed in as a CHP officer pulled a wooden box from the satchel attached to one of the Harleys. "What do you suppose is in there?" he asked nobody in particular.

By the time the Gulfstream landed at the Hawthorne Municipal Airport at three-thirty, news of the arrest in Corona had arrived, along with the information that the coins were already being driven up to Los Angeles.

"It's all working out," Agent Daniels said with the confidence you'd expect from a freshly-minted FBI Agent on his first sting.

"Yeah, well, you haven't been hanging out with us very long," Richie told him. "Don't get too comfortable."

The Hawthorne airport was only a twenty-minute drive from Edward Vincent, Jr. Park in Inglewood, leaving little time for the agents to brief Richie and Calvin and get everyone in position. Agent Luelle led them quickly across the tarmac toward yet another van, this one emblazoned not with a County Sheriff's star and insignia, but with an aqua-blue "Pool Brothers" logo.

"No planes," Richie said. "But you're lousy with vans."

Agent Luelle's cell rang. "Go," she said, answering.

Agent Hicks' gravelly voice came through. He'd taken position inside the pool house at the park, he said. The box of coins would be arriving within ten minutes at the incident command center center set up behind the Good Shepherd Community Church on Redondo, two blocks from the park. "Once you have the coins," he said, "send Richie and Calvin down East Redondo. Have them enter the park at the corner and cut directly across to the tennis courts. We'll have eyes on them the entire way."

"Copy that," acknowledged Agent Luelle. "Once they're on foot and heading in, we'll repo the van to the corner of Warren and Stepney and remain in radio contact."

"Like clockwork," Agent Daniels said to Calvin and Richie as they all climbed inside the van. "You're gonna be fine."

"You really need to stop doing that," Richie told him. "It's only gonna be embarrassing later."

"All right, let's go," Agent Luelle said to the driver as she rattled the side door closed.

During the short drive to the incident command center, Agent Luelle continued briefing them as an FBI Tech attached recording devices smaller than a button to the insides of their shirts. "This was put together quickly, so there's no way to cover the entire park," she said. "But we will be watching and listening to you the entire time. We don't know how many cars they'll have, but we're working under the assumption that they'll have unseen support in the area. LAPD won't enter the area until we give the all clear. We don't want any units coming around to spook these guys. Calvin, they're assholes, understand? As they did on the phone, they're gonna say things to antagonize you, but don't let them. Engage them in conversation to get as much as you can on record, but don't lose your cool. There's a reason Mikos requested you both to be there."

"What's that?" Richie asked.

"I'm sure he's planning on killing you once the exchange is made. If you antagonize him, it's only going to make things more difficult on our end."

"Maybe I should do the talking," Richie said.

Calvin waived him off. "I'll be fine."

"But you do have a short fuse and—"

"Shut the fuck up," Calvin snapped at him. "I said I'll be fine."

Richie sat back and rubbed his forehead. "That's very reassuring."

"Don't worry," Agent Luelle said. "We'll move in quickly once the exchange is made. Remember, we'll be listening the whole time. Any questions?"

Richie lowered his chin towards his chest. "Not at the moment."

"You don't have to do that," the Tech said. "Just talk normally."

Calvin shook his head at Richie and Richie gave him a reassuring thumbs up.

The van pulled into the incident command behind the Good Shepherd Church and they were met with a handful of additional agents in blue windbreakers emblazoned with bright yellow FBI letters. The agents were monitoring live images of the park being beamed to four laptops set up on a metal folding table.

"How's it look?" Agent Luelle asked.

"Everyone's in place," a SWAT Captain with a buzz-cut and tight brown mustache answered as she stepped up. He pointed at a park map laid out on a second table. "We have clean LOS on the tennis courts from here, here, here, and here."

Luelle turned to Detective Sutherland, who was on a walkie-talkie, coordinating his men in the field. "Where are our guys?" she asked.

Sutherland used the antenna of his walkie to point at the laptop screens. "The homeless man there is ours," he said. "The couple at the picnic table and the woman reading on the blanket, there."

"How many civilians?"

"Weekday, so not as crowded as it could be. As of now, only one of the tennis courts is in use, but there are a five young kids on the hill, here, with three adults. We also have a couple of bike riders making a loop on the path and this one guy and his dog."

Agent Luelle squinted at the grainy live feed on the screen. "So much for leash laws."

"My team's aware of everyone in the park," the SWAT Captain said. "They won't be an issue."

A CHP sedan pulled into the parking lot and stopped directly behind them. An officer climbed out from behind the wheel and handed Agent Luelle the familiar wooden box. "Sorry for the delay, ma'am," he said.

"Not at all, officer," she assured him. "The timing is perfect."

Agent Daniels smiled smugly at Richie.

Richie sighed. "Just keep watching."

CHAPTER TWENTY-SEVEN

EDWARD VINCENT, JR. Park covered fifty-five rolling acres, replete with red brick buildings, picnic areas, a soccer field, two softball fields, two basketball courts, an Olympic size pool and a thousand-seat amphitheater. The park was one of the city's crown jewels, though, like every other urban attraction, it collected its share of crime, graffiti, homelessness, and trash. In that way, it was a perfect manifestation of humanity's twin impulses—hope and despair.

On the opposite side of the street, running south along Florence, lay an even bigger park—the Inglewood Park Cemetery, the final resting spot of an impressive number of luminaries, from Ray Charles to Betty Grable to Billie "Buckwheat" Thomas of The Little Rascals. It stretched for over two hundred acres, covering sixteen city blocks all the way down to Manchester Boulevard. As Calvin and Richie walked alone past its northern edge, the sun beating down as if to remind them not to get too comfortable, Richie jabbed a thumb toward the cemetery, saying, "I hope that's not an omen."

"That place don't bother me," Calvin said. "When we was kids we used to go in there and look for ghosts."

"Ever see any?"

"Never did." He glanced sideways at the cemetery as they continued on. "What do you say, Garrison?" he said under his breath.

Another fifty feet or so down Florence Avenue, they turned off the sidewalk as instructed, away from the cars whizzing past with their exhaust and honking horns, and entered the park. Leaving the cement and asphalt of the city behind, they walked across the green grass on the prescribed diagonal toward the tennis courts. The day was summertime bright, with no breeze to whisk away their stress sweat, the sun on them like a spotlight on a stage.

"Damn," Richie said.

"What?"

"I gotta pee."

"You're just nervous."

"Yeah, nervous I'm gonna pee."

They reached the top of a sloping hill overlooking the tennis courts and stood there like mannequins advertising utter discomfort, the box of coins tucked under Calvin's arm like a football, Richie with his hands shoved into his pant pockets. Distant horns honked and city voices occasionally wafted into earshot. It was, all in all, surreal. They were totally alone amid the bustling city, yet every movement was monitored by an untold number of invisible eyes, every breath heard and recorded.

"Where the fuck are they?" Calvin said, looking around, trying to act like breathing wasn't a chore.

"So much for rushing to get here on time, looks like I had a minute to take a piss."

"Seriously, stop talking about peeing."

"You gotta go too, huh?"

"Man, you do remember this is all being recorded, right?"

"Pee. Piss. Poop. Caca," Richie said. "How's everyone out there enjoying this?" He nodded toward the homeless man in the distance, laying on a piece of dirty cardboard inside a ratty sleeping bag. "That one the cop?"

"Man, I don't know. Stop being so obvious though."

Richie turned in the opposite direction, pretended to scratch his cheek for some reason. "I'm not being obvious. I only asked because of that other dude over there."

Calvin casually glanced over at a second homeless man arriving on the scene, pushing a shopping cart over-filled with soiled blankets and shopping bags stuffed with trash. "What difference does it make?"

"I didn't say it made a difference," Richie pointed out. "I was only making conversation."

"Well, shut up, you're making me nervous."

"That's why you gotta pee."

"For the record, I never said I had to pee."

Richie noticed at a young black guy and woman at a picnic table. They were sitting side by side, looking at their phones and ignoring each other. She glanced up from her phone and stared at Richie, and he quickly averted his eyes. "I'm beginning to feel like I'm the only one sticking out around here," he said.

"We got plenty white people in Inglewood," Calvin said.

Richie nodded. "They must all be shopping at the GAP today."

"Hold up," Calvin said, his voice coming out of his chest with a burst of adrenaline. "We got company."

As soon as he said it, Richie turned back and saw the homeless man in the sleeping bag roll over, his sleepy eyes barely peeking out of the cozy darkness. He then spotted the approaching man. He was still about a hundred yards away, but Richie immediately recognized him. "That guy was at my house when they took Tracey and Martin," he said. "He choked me with a leather strap. He works for Soto-ra-meos. Shit, I still can't say that dude's name."

"We're not supposed to *know* his name," Calvin said under his breath. "So stop with the fucking play-by-play."

"Okay, yeah," Richie said. He lowered his chin half an inch. "But that's who it is."

Christos walked up the sloping hill of grass as if he hadn't a care in the world. He was dressed as he'd been the last time they'd met—dark slacks with a dark belt, dark shirt and dark shoes. Only this time, his eyes were hidden behind dark sunglasses. He came up and stood before them without saying a thing, hovering there like a black hole in designer clothes, waiting to suck them into the darkness.

"What's the deal?" Calvin said, after half a minute of staring.

"I'm trying to decide if you did as instructed," Christos asked. "It would be unfortunate if you chose to involve anyone else."

"You see anyone else here?" Calvin asked.

Christos made an exaggerated display of looking around the park. "I see lots of people."

"We're alone," Richie said.

Christos mimed drawing a gun, used his fingers to fire an invisible bullet at him. "Okay."

"How 'bout you?" Calvin asked.

"Oh, no," Christos said. "I'm not alone."

They stood there for another round of silence.

Calvin asked, "So how we gonna do this?"

"You're going to give me the coins."

The coins stayed where they were, tucked under Calvin's arm.

Christos extended his arm. "The box."

"Where's my wife and son?"

"The coins first."

Calvin shook his head. "Ain't gonna happen, pimp."

Christos kept his arm extended a moment, before lowering it with a shrug. "Worth a shot, right?"

Calvin stared, giving no indication if he agreed.

"Okay, come with me," Christos said.

"We're not going anywhere until my wife and kid are here too."

A flash of irritation rearranged Christos's face, before it settled back into place. "I believe you, you believe me, okay? I'll take you to them."

"Where?"

The irritation returned to Christos's expression and stuck. "A short walk."

"My throat's much better, by the way," Richie said. "So don't feel bad about nearly choking me to death the other day."

"I don't," Christos said, and then turned to walk away.

"But that was you, right?" Richie called after him.

Calvin gave him a side-eye warning as they followed Christos back down the slope.

Inside the Pool Brothers van, Agents Luelle and Daniels listened to the feed.

"Jesus," Agent Daniels said. "Maybe Richie can ask him to sign an affidavit while he's at it."

Agent Luelle keyed the walkie. "You got them?"

"That's affirmative," a voice squawked back. "Alpha three, they're coming your way."

"Alpha three, copy," another voice answered. "We have them. I see no other targets in the area. Looks like they could be headed for the north-side parking lot."

Agent Daniels looked up from the monitor. "Do we have anybody that far, on that side of the park?"

"No." She spoke again into the walkie. "All Alpha teams, keep your distance and repo to follow only when you're sure you are clear. If they get to the parking lot, do not engage until we have Sotereanos. I repeat, do not engage, we need Sotereanos first." She raised her thumb off the walkie. "Get us back up to 67th street and we'll swing around the other side," she said to the driver, who already had the van moving.

As Christos led Calvin and Richie in silence across the park, away from the tennis courts and the Pool Brothers van, their nervous perspiration had time to turn into actual sweat. Both men kept their eyes on the back of the Greek's head, only occasionally allowing their stares to wander to various homeless people aimlessly dragging everything they owned in the word, or joggers huffing up the winding paths or old men playing dominoes at picnic tables, wondering if any of them could be undercover. But it was a fool's game; even if they'd had days to plan the operation—instead of two hours—the Feds wouldn't have enough agents to cover fifty-five acres.

"You said a short walk," Richie called up to Christos.

But Christos kept walking as if he hadn't heard him.

They walked all the way to the opposite side of the park, cutting across one of two basketball courts to get to a circular parking lot rimmed by several large birch trees. The court they cut across was empty, but the other was occupied by four loud young men in full sweat, jacking up wild shots and yelling "foul" whenever a layup was missed. On the opposite side of the basketball courts was a playground of blue swings, yellow slides, and green monkey-bars, all set inside a massive sandbox. Unless the FBI had recently recruited a team of crappy street-ballers with egos that outpaced their talent, or a bunch of Latino four-year-olds and their young mothers, there was no police support anywhere near them as far as they could tell.

A black SUV with dark tinted windows rounded the corner into the parking lot and stopped sideways, less than ten feet in front of them. Christos obediently opened the rear passenger door and stood back, hands at his sides.

"You're not seriously expecting us to get in, are you?" Richie asked.

Christos remained as silent as he had been since they left the tennis court, and it became clear that any questions would no longer by answered by him. Not that it really mattered, he'd been about as chatty as a bag of rocks.

"Tracey?" Calvin called out. "You in there?"

No answer.

"What the hell are we supposed to do here?" Richie asked quietly, as much to Calvin as to the people listening through the tiny mic attached to his shirt.

"Hold this," Calvin said, pushing the box of coins into Richie's gut.

"Why do you want me to hold it?"

"Walk back up there, toward the courts."

"Why?"

"So if you have to run, you'll have a head start."

Richie gripped the box tight to his stomach. "Why would I have to run?"

Calvin flicked his head toward the SUV as Stavos stepped out, opening his jacket up wide enough to reveal the pistol tucked into his waist.

"Yeah, okay," Richie said, taking a few steps backward.

"Let's go," Stavos said.

"My wife and kid, now," Calvin said.

Stavos put his hand on his gun.

"What's the gun for?" Richie called out to him. "So you can shoot us the way you killed Connor and all his men? Not to mention my buddy, Sam. 'Cause now that I'm thinking about it, you probably killed him too, didn't you?"

Stavos gave him an oily grin that only darkened his eyes. "I wouldn't do that, no," he said. "You, I would kill much slower."

Richie took another few steps backward. "Well, I guess that clears that up."

"Enough of these games," Mikos said as he stepped from inside the SUV. "So goddamned undisciplined." He yanked Stavos back as he walked up to stand directly in front of Calvin. He looked him up and down, then shook his head in disappointment. "You are nothing."

"Fuck you, Zorba. Get my wife and son here, right now."

Mikos leaned in, his face so close that Calvin could smell the faint hint of booze under his cologne. "You should show more respect."

"I think you dress real nice," Calvin said.

A small twitch of controlled rage spread across Mikos' face. He stepped back and said something in Greek. Stavos, in turn, nodded to Christos, who made a phone call.

"Your father must have been a weak man," Mikos said to Calvin as they waited.

Calvin didn't debate the point as he looked off toward a second SUV pulling into the parking lot. Even if he had something to say in his father's defense, his heart was now beating so fast that speaking at all would have been difficult. He realized he'd been holding his breath and let it out slowly, trying to stay calm. All he cared about was seeing Tracey and Martin step out of that SUV without any scars or missing digits that would forever remind him of his selfishness. But what of the scars he couldn't see? How would Martin survive those? Calvin had seen it in so many kids growing up, had seen it in Garrison, but had never recognized it. The most dangerous scars are not noticed until it's too late. Despite what Martin looked like when he climbed from that SUV, part of him would be broken, there would be cracks on the inside of his fragile body. If left untended, those cracks would splinter, until one day his soul would shatter. He'd look the same, but he'd be a different person, a broken man who'd end up like Sollo, or Garrison, or Uncle Bucky, or Stitch or Andre, or his own father, and people would say they remembered when he was a sweet little boy, instead of another dead nigger nobody gave a shit about.

Calvin's throat constricted and he coughed, wiping the tears from his eyes before they were noticed. The second SUV pulled up beside the first and Christos opened the rear door. Tracey stepped out first, immediately shielding her eyes from the sun as though she'd had a blindfold removed and her pupils needed to acclimate. She squinted and turned back to the SUV as Martin jumped into her arms, burying his face into her shoulder.

"I'm right here," Calvin called, the words out of his mouth before he even knew he was speaking them.

Martin peeled away from Tracey, his bright eyes searching desperately for his father as his feet hit the pavement. When he spotted Calvin, he ran to him, but was stopped by Stavos, who yanked him back by the collar of his shirt. Martin did not struggle to get away, he only made himself even smaller, too scared to resist. He'd obviously learned not to cause problems.

"You okay, little man?" Calvin asked.

"I wanna go home," Martin said, his voice weak.

"You are, right now." Calvin looked to Tracey, who had tentatively inched her way to stand beside Stavos, her reassuring hand on Martin's head. "How 'bout you, baby? You ready to come home, too?"

Tracey's eyes glistened in the sun as she nodded. "Yeah, baby. I'm ready."

Mikos looked at Richie, still standing off in the distance. "The coins," he said.

From his vantage point, Richie noticed that both Stavos and Christos had their right hands tucked inside their jackets, ready to shoot him dead, but he had no choice.

He took two steps toward the parking lot and then everything went to shit.

CHAPTER TWENTY-EIGHT

THE VOICES CAME across like flies buzzing in her receiver. Agent Hicks was the first to call it in. He had moved from his original location inside the pool house and had taken up position four hundred yards away from the parking lot, behind a red-bricked bathroom, along with the SWAT officer designated as Alpha 2.

"Who the hell are these guys?" he yelled into his walkie.

Alpha 1, Alpha 3, and Alpha 4 were next, their barked assessments coming in almost at once. Nobody had any idea what was happening, but they were ready to move if the order was given. From their vantage point near the playground, hidden by the slope of a hill, Detective Kevin Sutherland and his partner squawked at the handful of LAPD officers in and around the park, trying to determine the correct course of action.

"Weapons tight," Agent Luelle ordered into her walkie. "Stay eyes on until we know what we're dealing with."

Calvin and Richie knew exactly what they were dealing with. The Greeks, however, were as confused as the cops. Turned out that one of the four sweating young men on the basketball court was a drug dealer with connections, and when he saw Calvin walking past with a couple white dudes, he had made a call to the one guy he was most tightly connected with.

The Thunderbird chirp-turned into the parking lot and skidded to a stop behind the SUVs.

"What up, punks?" Randall asked as he jumped from the car, his unbuttoned shirt flapping open.

Calvin stepped forward, startling Stavos, whose hand twitched on the gun in his waist. Calvin froze, raising his hands. "It's cool, we're cool," he said. "Yo, Randall, you don't want any part of this, man."

Randall sized up the situation as Big Mike stepped out from behind the wheel of the idling Thunderbird and Ghosty climbed from the back seat, his tightly-coiled body ready to explode.

"Damn," Randall seethed. "I knew you was holding out on me, motherfucker."

"You have no idea what's happening here," Calvin warned, his fevered eyes leaping back and forth between Randall, Tracey, and Martin.

"Who are you?" Stavos asked.

"I'm the head nigger in charge now," Randall said. "So why don't you back the fuck up?"

Stavos pulled the gun from his waist and Christos followed suit. In a flash, Ghosty had his Tech-9 out. Even Big Mike, who never carried, suddenly had a .38 in his t-bone-sized hand. Two more Greeks climbed from behind the wheel of each SUV, guns already drawn.

"No!" Calvin yelled. "Nobody shoot!"

For a moment, nobody did. They all faced each other, wide-eyed.

But then the drug-dealing basketball player stuck his own

.38 into the back of Richie's head. "What you got in the box?" he asked.

"Shit. What am I supposed to do here?" Richie said into his mic.

"Yo, Randall?" the basketball player called out. "How we gonna play this?"

"Shoot that white bitch," Randall ordered.

Half a second later, a SWAT bullet entered the left temple of the basketball player, then exited through his right, a chunk of his skull landing in the dry grass a few feet away. The wooden box fell from Richie's hand upon the sickening impact of bullet and brain, coins spilling out.

A crystallized moment of white-hot confusion followed. Nobody was sure who fired that first shot, but Mikos made sure who would fire the second. He ducked to the ground, yelling in Greek for his son to kill them all.

Stavos shot Ghosty in the stomach before the young man who used to be known as Leonard could decide where to aim. Ghosty shuddered backward, the Tech-9 strafing one of the SUVs as he fell, the bullets popping the metal like exploding popcorn. The Tech-9 hit the pavement and fired off a few more rounds into the air before falling as silent as Ghosty, who would make only a few gasping attempts at breath before dying, staring up at the blue, summer sky.

Tracey screamed as one of the SUV drivers grabbed her, but a SWAT bullet split his chest right down the middle and he fell away. Tracey leapt on top of Martin, shielding him as they both collapsed to the pavement and the surrounding park erupted in panic.

Big Mike turned out to be a lousy shot and he managed only to hit Christos in the arm. Christos, who was much better with a gun, even with one arm now useless, put one in Big Mike's leg, one in his stomach, and one in his chest before Randall managed to end Christos's target practice by lodging a lead bullet in his forehead.

As Randall was putting an end to Christos, the remaining SUV driver spun around firing indiscriminately, accomplishing nothing more than depositing several more bullets in the already dinged-up SUV, before his shoulder was shattered by a distant SWAT sniper and his gun fell from his hand. With little recourse, he dropped to the ground and covered his head.

Randall had no time to enjoy his kill before Stavos knocked him on his ass with a bullet to his right knee. He screamed in pain, gripping his bloodied leg, the kneecap blown clean off. "Motherfucker!" he yelled for the last time in his miserable waste of a life, before Stavos was standing over him. A second later Randall Washington no longer had a face from which to say anything.

In all the chaos, Calvin raced toward Tracey and Martin cowering on the ground, but he never made it. The first bullet from the gun Mikos had picked up from the pavement entered his left hip and the second found his calf, spinning him like a top. He collapsed as the third bullet found his shoulder.

"No!" Tracey wailed, her hand pressing her son's head down, making sure it was turned away as her own tears blurred the images of destruction surrounding them. "No! No! No! No!"

Leaving Randall's corpse, Stavos ran for the coins, but tripped forward like a snared animal when he reached the grass, the SWAT bullet having entered the meaty part of his thigh, doing little damage other than to his effort to retrieve the scattered coins.

The entire shootout lasted no more than thirty seconds. Agent Luelle was out of breath as she and Daniels arrived on the scene alongside Agent Hicks. LAPD cruisers screeched into the lot and officers hustled away any eyewitnesses, while Detective Sutherland wildly waved his hands to get everyone back. SWAT snipers ran up from all angles, rifles at the ready to finish off the only remaining Greeks with a pulse—Stavos, Mikos, and one driver.

"Hold your fire!" Agent Luelle yelled. "Hold your fire!"

The reason for the directive was clear. Mikos had pulled Martin free from Tracey's panicked grasp and had him tucked close to his chest, the gun he'd used to strike down Calvin now pointed at Martin's head. "Don't come any closer!" he ordered the surrounding cops, his back pressed to the pockmarked SUV.

"Let the boy go," Agent Luelle ordered, taking three small steps toward him.

"Stay back!" he yelled.

She stopped. "It's over, Mikos."

"You're not in control here," he said, despite all evidence to the contrary.

"That's right." She held up her empty hands. "What happens next is entirely up to you. So why don't you make the right decision. Let the boy go and we'll continue to talk."

Mikos chuckled at the absurdity of the suggestion. "What is there to talk about?"

"You tell me," said Agent Luelle. "Whatever it is, we can work something out. There's no reason for any more people to die here today."

"I agree. That is why the boy is coming with me."

Tracey let loose a primal scream as she charged forward. Agent Luelle stepped in front of her to keep her from attacking Mikos in an effort to free her son. If she got any closer, there was no doubt Mikos would shoot her before she got within arm's reach. An LAPD officer ran close and pulled Tracey back, her arms and legs flailing, unable to stem the emotions that lit her insides like fire.

Calvin gasped at the sound of his wife's screams, his pain so intense that he struggled to stay conscious. On his stomach, legs stretched immobile behind him, he reached for his son, but he might as well have been reaching for the moon.

Agent Luelle inched closer to Mikos. "You know we can't let you take that child."

"Geno!" Mikos called to his driver, who was presently hiding beneath the SUV. "Get your ass out here," he ordered, spit flying from his mouth.

Geno grunted something in Greek, then shimmied out from underneath the SUV on the opposite side of Mikos and Martin, his left hand pressed to his shattered right shoulder, and quickly ducked back into the car, slamming the door and turning over the engine.

"You have nowhere to run, Mikos," Agent Luelle said.

Mikos's wild eyes focused and his voice was eerily calm in its absolute certainty. "Of course I do. And if you try to stop me, the child dies."

"Daddy," Martin cried, reaching for his father. "Daddy, Daddy, Daddy."

Calvin grunted and heaved, making a final effort to crawl forward, his arm still impotently outstretched, grasping at the air. But every movement felt as if his spine was being ripped through his skin, immobilizing him. Their hands stayed extended toward each other, unable to bridge the gap.

"Papa!" Stavos screamed from the grass behind Agent Luelle, trying to stand, but falling under the useless weight of his leg. He panted like a dog and tried to push himself back to his feet. "Don't leave me like this!"

"You have done this to yourself," Mikos answered his son as he inched his way sideways, to the open rear passenger door. His eyes darted between the guns pointed toward them and leaned back, his head and shoulders disappearing inside the backseat of the SUV. With Martin in front of him like a shield, the gun briefly slipped clear of his head. If the surrounding SWAT officers were ever going to have a shot, it would have been then, but the risk of hitting Martin was still too great.

But as Mikos rose up on his toes to fully retreat into the SUV, he was pushed from behind. His body crested forward, back into the light of day, his head violently snapping as though his neck had been replaced with a spring. A high-pitched yelp escaped his mouth as his grip loosened and Martin tumbled from his arms, landing outside the SUV, beside the gun that fell along with him. Mikos was barely able to maintain his shaky balance, his knees buckling as his feet again found themselves on the pavement.

In that desperate moment of suddenly-exposed shock, Mikos Sotereanos could not have known that, during the chaos that began when the drug-dealing basketball player was separated from his brain stem, Richie had picked up his fallen gun and run for Calvin, seeing that his friend had no way to protect himself. Geno the driver wasn't shooting indiscriminately after all when he sent those bullets into the SUV; he was trying to put an end to the annoying white boy who had ducked behind the car when he got caught in the crossfire between Big Mike and Christos. Having dropped his gun as Geno's bullets chased him down, Richie had climbed inside the backseat for safety, unaware how fortuitous the choice would end up being.

And now, as Agent Luelle stepped toward Mikos, a gun once again in her hands, he displayed his misplaced ego by smoothing out his crushed satin shirt and raising his hands. "Looks like we'll be doing it your way," he said with an indifferent shrug.

Agent Luelle said, "Put your hands behind your head and—"

A hole opened up in Mikos's chest as a gunshot echoed across the park.

The proud Greek looked momentarily confused. As did Agent Luelle.

(Whether or not Mikos put together who it was that fired the fateful shot before he collapsed dead to the ground would be endlessly debated amongst the SWAT officers, detectives, and FBI Agents who bore witness. But, as he was sentenced to life in prison, Stavos would say he had no regrets for killing him. "I blame my father for all of this," was all he had to say on the matter.)

Inside the SUV, Richie sat up after having used his two feet like a battering ram to send Mikos out to meet his son's bullet, and he stared down Geno, who looked at him over his one good shoulder with a mixture of surprise and anger.

"It's a goddamn Greek tragedy, isn't it?" Richie said.

Geno raised his gun and pointed it at Richie. And while the side windows of the SUV were heavily tinted and shielded the men from view, the windshield was clear as day. And that was how Agent Frank Daniels, whom Richie had been worried still had training wheels on his weapon, saw Geno lift his gun before sending a bullet into the back of his head.

With a fine mist of Geno's blood on his face, Richie climbed from the backseat of the SUV with his hands raised and stepped over Mikos's lifeless body. He stood there a moment, making sure any other guns pointed in his direction were friendly. With distant sirens approaching and a parade of LAPD cruisers arriving on the scene, much of the attention was on Stavos, still lying on the grass, now with his hands cuffed behind his back, the scattered gold and silver coins around him forever out of his reach.

But Richie's eyes zeroed in on Tracey and Martin, huddled over Calvin, a family united at last. Calvin, his body twisted and bloodied, reached up and cupped his palm to Tracey's face as Martin buried his face in his father's chest and cried.

The impulse to go to them, to push his way through the swirl of cops who seemed to be moving in slow motion as they took stock of what had gone down, rose up and twitched Richie's legs, but then the impulse dissipated and he remained where he was.

It came to him all at once that it was finally over.

Whatever was next, he'd have to face it alone.

"Are you hit?" Agent Luelle asked him.

"What?"

"Have you been shot?"

"No, ma'am. None of this blood is mine. Is Calvin gonna be okay?"

"Paramedics are arriving now," she said, distracted by an agent calling her name. "They'll take care of him." She squeezed his arm as she turned away. "Hell of a thing getting in that car."

Richie shrugged. "Planned it the entire time."

Alone once again, the blaring sirens and agitated voices battered his ears and his body shook from the rush of adrenaline, all of it giving him a bit of vertigo. His eyes fluttered as he tried to steady himself.

"You're not gonna faint on me, are you?" Tracey's voice cut through the haze, her strong arms suddenly around him.

"No," he said.

She held his face in her hands and kissed him, right on the mouth.

"Maybe now I will," he said.

She leaned back and shook her head. "You're a fool, you know that?"

"Actually, yeah, I do."

Her expression softened and Richie saw the exhaustion, the

tension and fear, seeping out of every pore. What that must do to a person, having a gun pressed to your head for so long, waiting for it to go off.

"I'm so sorry for all the—for everything, Tracey," he said.

She hugged him again as tightly as before. "Thank you for being in that car," she whispered in his ear.

Richie looked over her shoulder as a team of paramedics strapped Calvin onto a gurney, wrapped his wounds and pricked his arm with an IV. "He gonna be okay?"

Tracey looked back at her husband. "They said he'll live."

"Hell, I could've told them that. At this point, I think he and I might be immortal."

Tracey let out a weary chuckle. "You really are a damn fool."

Another paramedic kneeled in front of Martin, shinning a light into his eyes.

"What about little man?" Richie asked.

Tracey smiled. "Little man's gonna be okay too. He's gonna need some help, but we'll make sure he gets whatever it is he needs."

"What about you? You don't need any help?"

The afternoon sun bounced into her hazel eyes, glinting off the tears welling up in them. She considered her answer for a long time. "All of us need a little help, Richie," she said at last. "That's the damn truth of it."

CHAPTER TWENTY-NINE

TRACEY WAS MORE right than she realized. She was going to need all the help she could get.

In the confusion of the Sotereanos sting, she'd not been told of the deal Calvin and Richie had struck with the FBI. During Calvin's three-hour surgery at the Centinela Hospital Medical Center, as two surgeons painstakingly repaired the hip Mikos's bullet had shattered, Agent Luelle sat and explained that once Calvin was released from the hospital, he'd be remanded into custody, pending the determination of where he would serve out his eighteen-month sentence.

Tracey took in the news without so much as a question. She only sat and stared, her hands in her lap, her shoulders slumped, as the words fell out of Agent Luelle's mouth and piled up at her feet. But when Martin rounded the corner and started that long walk down the hospital corridor, she began to cry. His hands were held up over his shoulders by his grandmother Vanessa and G-Dad Singletary as they lifted him into the air on every third step, his little body flying forward as if he were on a swing. Seeing his mother, Martin pulled his hands free and ran into her arms and she buried her tears in his scalp so he couldn't see them.

Two weeks later, Calvin limped into Lompoc Federal Prison.

He was given some forms to fill out and an orange jumpsuit to change into. He had brought only a few items with him—pictures of Martin and Tracey, two pairs of shoes, two ball-point pens and a ream of paper, three paperback spy novels from Singletary and a Bible Vanessa had insisted upon. Having been in prison before, the atmosphere didn't shock him. Even though the intake at Lompoc was done inside the maximum security prison, where giving someone the wrong look could result in a shiv getting shoved into your kidney as you stood at a urinal, Calvin was to serve his time in the adjacent facility, a low-security prison for non-violent offenders—*Camp Cupcake*, it was often referred to. Calvin learned from the Prison Board that Agent Luelle had pushed for the designation. The first letter he planned on writing with that pen and paper would be to her.

The city of Lompoc was only one hundred and seventy-five miles northwest of Los Angeles, adjacent to Vandenberg Air Force Base in Santa Barbara County, but that wasn't the distance Calvin felt as he was processed into the life he'd inhabit for the next year and a half. No, that was something he could comprehend, could measure by running a mental string all the way down the coast, right into the small house in Inglewood where Tracey and Martin waited for him. What he couldn't comprehend, what he couldn't measure, was the distance between his true self and the man he'd presented to the world for so long.

The day before, he'd sat with Martin on the porch, watching the sun dip behind the houses to the west, the sky above them streaked orange and red before the bright colors dimmed and slowly evaporated into darkness.

"I'm gonna miss you every day," he said.

Martin leaned against his father and sniffed back a few tears. "I don't want you to go," he softly cried.

Calvin put his arm around his son's shoulder, pulled him closer. But he couldn't quite get him close enough.

"Look forward," the prison photographer said.

Calvin stood on the line, looked into the lens and wondered about the image the camera would capture. It would be frozen in time, stamped and filed, added to the list of the other men that came before it and the ones who would come after. All those dead-eyed stares. The flash popped and Calvin turned to one side and then the other. Got to get those profiles. But how many of the men in that chain fit the profile? How many of them saw themselves as he did—good men who had lost their way because of their own laziness, greed, anger, addiction, or insanity? How many saw themselves differently than how the camera saw them? Black men, white men, brown men, it didn't matter, they were all reduced to a one-dimensional image and an eight-digit number. Inmate 74926-098, that was Calvin.

"Walk down there," he was ordered.

He walked. Did as he was told without complaint.

He was put into a large cell with twenty other men, some of whom looked scared, others bored. There was some conversation, mostly about what had landed them there. One man, a white-haired accountant in his fifties with a golfer's tan, told Calvin he'd embezzled seven hundred thousand dollars from a private school up in Bakersfield. When he asked what Calvin had done, Calvin said, "I was an asshole like you." The man snidely asked if that meant he was an accountant, but Calvin ignored him. The tanned embezzler eventually struck up a friendship with another asshole who was in for tax evasion. Birds of a feather and all that shit, Calvin guessed.

Eventually a guard wheeled a gray cart to the front of the cell, the type flight attendants push down the aisle of a plane. The guard opened the cell door and started handing out plastic trays containing something that slightly resembled food. Turned out to be chicken casserole, or so they claimed. Whatever it was, most of it was still on the trays when the guard returned to collect them, and he pissed and moaned about them not being appreciative.

Another few hours passed and they were all led outside and filed into a bus to be transferred to the minimum-security camp. While the two main institutions at Lompoc—one low security, the other medium—are surrounded by chain-link fences topped with razor-wire, with guard towers holding officers equipped with binoculars and rifles, Camp Cupcake was rimmed only by a wooden fence.

The new arrivals were led to a gymnasium filled with row upon row of bunk beds, the bottom for the old-timers, the top for the fresh fish. Each set had a double-decker blue locker in front, top for top, bottom for bottom. A bed and a locker, the entirety of Calvin's kingdom for the next year and a half.

"Black dude, huh?" the wiry Latino guy said from the bottom bunk as Calvin stepped up with his duffle bag. "Let me guess, drug possession with intent to sell?"

Calvin deposited his duffle inside the locker. "No," he said. "I cut out some guy's tongue because he talked out of turn and then I lit him on fire when he wouldn't stop screaming."

The wiry Latino looked up from his Rolling Stone magazine, trying to figure out if his new bunkmate was for real. It took a while for him to decide, but then he smiled broadly, revealing three silver teeth, and laughed as though they were in a comedy club. "Fuck you, esé!"

Calvin smiled back and offered his hand. "Calvin Russel, nice to meet you."

"Miguel Lopez," his downstairs neighbor said as they shook.

"What you in for, Miguel?" Calvin asked.

"Drug possession with intent to sell."

Calvin chuckled. "I helped some people rob a bank."

"No shit?"

"No shit."

"That's bad ass," Miguel said.

"No, it's not. It was stupid." He looked him dead in the eye, choosing to keep the part about wearing a wire and cooperating with federal authorities to himself. "I'm here for eighteen months. So we need to have an understanding. We gonna be cool with each other?"

"Fuck yeah, esé. I got this place wired, so if you need anything let me know."

"You can start by stop calling me esé."

Miguel laughed and went back to his magazine.

Calvin struggled up the round metal rungs at the foot of the bunks to climb into his bed. It was a grueling effort, as the metal dug into the bottom of his foot and his hip still felt as if it was made of balsa wood and broken glass.

He lay in his narrow bunk, the mattress sagging just enough to be noticeable, and stared at the ceiling. A healthy mixture of Spanish and English mixed together with competing radios playing a wide spectrum of crappy music. Damn, he'd forgotten how loud prison could be and he made a mental note to pick up some earplugs at the commissary in the morning. Reaching into the pocket of his overalls, he pulled out the picture of Tracey and Martin, ran his thumb along the edge of their faces. It wasn't long before his chest contracted and his throat closed off. It would be a hell of a first impression to start crying, so he dropped the picture onto his stomach and closed his eyes.

He wasn't sure how long he'd been asleep when he stirred awake—could have been five minutes, could have been an hour. He reached down for the photo, but it was gone. His fingers searched down both sides of the bunk next to his thighs, hoping it had only slipped to the side as he slept, but it was nowhere to be found. He shot upright, ready to tear the room apart if he had to.

"Sight for sore eyes," a voice came from the bunk beside him.

Calvin's legs were already dangling halfway off the opposite side of his bunk, his grip on the side rail turning his knuckles white as he prepared to lower himself over the edge, his hip unable to handle another trip on the round metal rungs so soon after the first. He slowly twisted back around, his legs again landing with a dull thump on the sagging mattress. "We're gonna have to come to an understanding about personal space," he said.

Richie reached across the space between the two upper bunks and handed back the photo. "I'll ask next time, but I didn't want to wake you. You looked so peaceful lying there, like a princess waiting for a kiss from a prince."

"Look around, idiot. You sure that's the analogy you want to go with?"

Richie laughed. "Sorry I couldn't be here to greet you. I was working my shift in the kitchen. Made eighty-six cents."

"You back to being Richie Rich, huh?"

"Oh yeah, I'm swimming in it. By the time I get released, I'll be able to buy two packs of gum. If you'd like, I'll put in a word for you to get a good work assignment. The screws tend to listen to us old-timers."

"You've been here a week."

Richie smiled at his friend. "Time has no meaning on the inside."

It had been one final present from Agent Luelle. She was

the one who'd made sure they were placed in the same facility. "They've come to rely on each other," she'd written to the sentencing judge. "I firmly believe they will continue to lean on each other to take full advantage of the rehabilitation resources available to them. In light of their full cooperation in ensuring the Sotereanos crime family was fully dismantled, it is my request that you grant them the benefit of a joint stay within the Federal Penitentiary System."

That night they sat amid a sea of cheering men, all of them victims of the choices they'd made, watching the Lakers win game seven of the NBA finals, ninety-four to eighty-five.

"Son-of-a-bitch," Richie said.

"What?"

"Eighteen days ago I put five hundred bucks of that bank money on the Lakers."

Calvin looked at the players on the TV pouring champagne on each other. "Congratulations."

"Yeah, except my bookie is dead so there's nobody to collect from."

"There's always football season," Calvin said, standing up.

Richie followed him back to their bunks for lights out. "I think I'll let it go," he said. "End my gambling career on a winning streak."

Two weeks later a guard called Calvin over as he entered the classroom for his vocational training. He'd enrolled in the barbering program, a skill he'd never considered, but one imbued with the few happy memories he had of his father. The memories were all glimpses, snapshots from a movie without sound that he could no longer run at any length, but they were there. Most of the glimpses were of happy men, sitting around a barbershop, laughing. What they were laughing at was lost, but the image of his father's smile as he winked at his seven-year-old boy remained in bright color. It would take fifteen hundred hours before he could call himself a barber, but time he had.

"Got some news for you," the guard said.

"Oh yeah, what's that?"

"Your old buddy Bob Matthews and his brothers aren't gonna go to trial for Winslow's murder after all."

Calvin's heart skipped a beat. The guards were all big talkers; no secrets were safe with them, and the story of Richie and Calvin's exploits with the biker gang had gone viral inside Camp Cupcake. And now the legend was evidently going to grow.

"That right?" he cautiously asked.

The guard smiled. "Word is Bob and Eric were knifed to death yesterday inside a Riverside jail. Seventeen stab wounds each. Turns out the brotherhood doesn't like it when you murder their benefactor. The third brother disappeared with some chick he was engaged to. There's rumors they're already in Mexico."

Calvin's smile now matched the guard's. Up until that moment, every time someone asked about their confrontation with the gang, about rumors of being nearly drowned in a pool, saved by a SWAT raid, and being chased down the Vegas Strip, Calvin wondered if it was all going to catch up to him. Someday, he feared, some inmate would come up to talk about it and stick a sharpened toothbrush into his neck. But now, all of a sudden, as he was about to sit for a lesson on hair follicle damage, the threat evaporated as though it had been a mirage all along. Whatever good old Bob had said to convince the brotherhood that he and his brothers were being framed by that nigger from LA, didn't fly.

"What about Heather Patterson?" he asked.

The guard shrugged. "She requested to be placed into solitary for her own protection."

Calvin told Richie what he'd learned and they both had a good time picturing her in that dark hole, afraid to stick her head into the light, pissed off that two morons got the best of her.

"Hell," Calvin said. "Maybe we're both on a winning streak after all."

And so the months went. Richie chose not to participate in any vocational training, spending his hours instead working in the kitchen, playing ping pong, and occasionally taking part in group therapy sessions for recovering addicts. He didn't truly think he was a gambling addict, but he figured going would help his chances at early release. Whenever Tracey and Martin visited, which was often, he'd stop by and they'd make fun of his hair, ask if Calvin cut it. The joke got old real fast, but Martin enjoyed it so much that Richie went on pretending to be embarrassed, begging them to bring a hat next time.

"Daddy," Martin would say. "You need a lot more classes."

Four months after Richie arrived at Lompoc, he was granted the early release he'd been gunning for. "It feels strange leaving you behind," he said to Calvin as he cleaned out the blue locker at the foot of his bunk.

"Be happy to switch places with you if it makes you too uncomfortable," Calvin said.

"Let's not get carried away," Richie said. He offered up a deck of cards he'd traded a few magazines for. Calvin took the cards and tossed them onto his bunk. Richie stuffed the last of his shirts into his bag and slammed his locker closed. He stood there a moment.

"You forget something?" Calvin asked after a few beats of silence.

Richie shook his head. "I don't know what the hell I'm gonna do now."

Calvin nodded. He didn't know either.

They walked together through the maze of bunk beds, to the thick metal door at the front of the room, where a guard waited to take Richie and process him out.

"I'll be seeing you," Richie said.

Calvin half smiled. "No doubt."

The guard opened the door and waved Richie forward.

"You're gonna be all right," Calvin called after him. "Go have a drink with your boy, Chad, at the Isis Lounge."

"Chad ain't my boy," he said, hesitating, but not looking back. "You're my boy, Calvin."

He then stepped fully through the door for the last time as inmate 72753-098. When he finally turned, he saw that Calvin was grinning. "You my boy, too," Calvin said.

And then the guard swung the door closed.

That first night without Richie, the bunk next to Calvin was taken over by a nineteen-year-old black kid from Fresno named Jason. Jason was a first-timer, in for twelve months on a drug charge. Long after the lights had been shut off, a cacophony of sighs, coughs, and snores rattled up the walls, and the clang of distant metal doors slamming echoed off the ceiling.

"How do you stand it?" Jason asked. "It's so damn loud."

"You'll get used to it," Calvin told him.

"Uh-uh. I ain't ever gonna get used to this."

Calvin turned his head to the young man. He reminded him of Delvon's little brother, Reese. "That's good," he said. "That means you still have a shot, so don't fuck it up."

He reached into the pouch hanging off the side of his bunk and pulled out two foam earplugs, then tossed them onto Jason's lap.

Richie came up from LA once a month to visit, usually with tales of what life was like as a broke ex-con living in a studio apartment in the valley, his house in the Hollywood Hills now property of the bank. His days were filled by volunteering at various homeless shelters as part of his court-ordered community service and working as a production assistant for a small-time producer in Hollywood who made straight-to-streaming horror flicks. Turned out Richie had called Chad after all, and Chad had stepped up once again.

"He even got me a permanent spot on the VIP list at the Isis Lounge," he told Calvin.

"Watch yourself, Richie," was all Calvin had to say about that. "You sound like your wife."

Truth was that Richie and Tracey were getting along fine. She'd even had him over to the house in Inglewood for dinner a few times. And he had, on five separate occasions, sat for Martin when Vanessa and Singletary were tied up at church and Tracey was at school or working the register down at Target.

"It's like I'm the white you," Richie said.

Calvin was too proud to admit it, but he was happy Richie was there to help out.

"He's still a pain in the ass," Tracey confided to Calvin during one of her last visits before he became eligible for early release. "Momma said she gonna get Jesus in him though, so we'll see."

"Looks like we're stuck with him," Calvin said, holding his wife's hand.

And they were. That was why it came as no surprise that

when Tracey, Martin, Vanessa and Singletary drove up to Lompoc from Inglewood for the last time, fifteen months after Calvin first entered Camp-Cupcake, it was Richie who was behind the wheel.

He had insisted on it.

It was, he said, his last job as the getaway driver.

ABOUT THE AUTHOR

Clay Savage is a writer and voice-over actor. His voice has been heard on hundreds of television shows and movies, from a babysitter locked in a closet on *Malcom In The Middle*, a newscaster on *NCIS*, and a doomed pilot on *Scandal*, to a scientist studying E.T. in the 25th Anniversary special release of *E. T. The Extra Terrestrial*. Though his work almost always goes uncredited, his family enjoys playing, "I heard you!"

He lives in Santa Monica, where he enjoys time with his wife, three kids and his dog. Mostly in that order, though he refuses to get too specific.

52233792R00192

Made in the USA
San Bernardino, CA
06 September 2019